Introduction

Everlasting Light by Andrea Boeshaar
Hope is dim in the aftermath of the Civil War. Alaina McKenna's Carolina home and family have been torn apart, and her husband, Braeden, is presumed dead. Another Christmas without him seems unbearable, and her heart has shriveled under the weight of her bitterness. But her husband's best friend is offering her a new start, and Alaina is sure she would be loved. Can she face the possibility that Braeden may never return to her. . .or is there still an ember of hope?

Yuletide Treasure by Gail Gaymer Martin
Olivia Schuler has waited for her life to begin with marriage, and now, still single, she considers herself a spinster. She soon realizes her freedom is a blessing when she can help her brother and his sick wife by taking their son to Grand Rapids over the Christmas holiday. But her trip means leaving behind a potential suitor. Will Livy trust love to God's place and time?

Angels in the Snow by Colleen L. Reece
Life dramatically changed for Lass Talbot when her mother died. Christmas became a dreaded time of frozen memories, and he father wrapped himself in a blanket of bitterness and booze. The only man Lass ever loved was driven from town seven years ago. What will it take to bring joy back to Lass's bleak existence among the Teton Mountains?

Christmas Cake by Janet Spaeth
Elizabeth Evans wants her first Christmas with her husband to be perfect. She is used to a prairie Christmas, but her husband is from the East where traditions are established in wealth and finery. All Elizabeth has is a little egg money, so she sets out to recreate an Evans's family recipe. Do her Christmas dreams rely only on the outcome of a baking experiment?

Christmas Threads

*Four Romantic Novellas
about the Roots
of Family Traditions*

Andrea Boeshaar
Gail Gaymer Martin
Colleen L. Reece
Janet Spaeth

BARBOUR
PUBLISHING, INC.
Uhrichsville, Ohio

Everlasting Light ©2000 by Andrea Boeshaar.
Yuletide Treasure ©2000 by Gail Gaymer Martin.
Angels in the Snow ©2000 by Colleen L. Reece.
Christmas Cake ©2000 by Janet Spaeth.

Illustrations by Gary Maria

ISBN 1-57748-811-3

Scripture verses are taken from the King James Version of the Bible unless otherwise noted.

Published by Barbour Publishing, Inc., P.O. Box 719, Uhrichsville, Ohio 44683 http://www.barbourbooks.com

Member of the
Evangelical Christian
Publishers Association

Printed in the United States of America.

Christmas Threads

Everlasting Light

by Andrea Boeshaar

Dedication

To my son, PV2 Richard A. Boeshaar—
a hero if there ever was one.
May God continue to be a lamp unto your feet
and an everlasting light unto your path.

Prologue

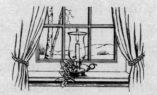

Grandma, why do we put a candle in the window on Christmas Eve?"

Bonnie Myers turned her aging eyes to the questioning nine year old who had volunteered to set up the final Christmas decorations. What a joy young Alaina was to her! Raven hair and ocean-deep, blue eyes—there was a haunting resemblance between the child and her namesake.

"Well, dear," Bonnie replied, gently gliding her rocking chair back and forth, "it's quite a story."

"I love stories!" Alaina declared, her eyes snapping with enthusiasm.

Bonnie smiled. "Then I will tell you." Her blue-veined hand gripped the box in her lap tightly before she opened it, revealing a one hundred, thirty-five-year-old candle. It had obviously seen better days. Large clumps of wax marred the remaining circumference which had been burned down to its last six inches. While once the candle had been an ivory color, it was now yellowed with age. "It all started with this, Alaina."

The girl wrinkled her nose distastefully. "That old thing?"

Bonnie nodded. "This old thing. It belonged to my great-grandmother, Alaina McKenna."

"Alaina? Hey, that's my name!"

"Yes, I know," Bonnie said with a chuckle. "You were named after her."

The girl smiled and plopped down on the carpeted floor at her grandmother's feet, waiting eagerly to hear the story.

"It was Christmastime in 1865, and the War Between the States had just ended," Bonnie relayed. "Your great, great, great-grandmother didn't know if her husband was dead or alive. . . ."

Chapter 1

December, 1865

Desolation. Gray and bleak. As far as the eye could see. Standing on the covered porch of the large farmhouse, Alaina Dalton McKenna hugged a knitted shawl more tightly around her and gazed across the ravaged land while her heart ached. *Yankees. I hate every last one of them.* Even as the thought formed, Alaina could hear Reverend Pritchard's voice last Sunday commanding his congregation to "love your enemies." But that, of course, was easier said than done! Charleston lay in ruins, Fort Sumter had been abandoned by the Confederate army, and much of Columbia had been burned beyond recognition. Surely this was the end of the world.

Looking toward the orchard, Alaina felt like crying for the umpteenth time as she viewed the charred peach trees. Their skeletal remains added even more barrenness to the dull winter landscape. Why did they have to burn everything? Last February when Sherman's troops made their march from Savannah to the sea, they hit South Carolina particularly hard, since the war had started in the state. The Yankees set fire to everything in their paths. The prosperous McKenna farm in Richland County was no exception. As her mother-in-law, Eloise, said, it was a miracle their house still stood, proud and erect. Their barn, animals, equipment, and outbuildings were gone. All gone. However, this past summer, they had been able to grow a few crops which would keep them from starving to death this winter.

If only Braeden would come home, Alaina thought wistfully. *He'd know what to do.*

Melancholy enveloped her as Alaina stepped off the porch only to meet a gust of cold wind that tugged at her dark skirt. Shivering, she strolled down the winding dirt pathway to where a pretty, white picket fence once stood, separating the McKenna property from the road. Only a scant few fence posts remained of it now—another visible wound brought upon this farm and family by those wretched Yankees! Except Alaina supposed the McKennas had fared much better than most in these parts, and she forced herself to be thankful that she at least had a roof over her head. If Braeden would come home, she'd be more than thankful; she'd be absolutely ecstatic! As she glanced down the dusty road, tears of disappointment filled her eyes. She saw no shadowy figure of her gallant husband in the distance, marching home from war. Only more desolation of the countryside.

Oh, God, please bring Braeden home, she prayed for the millionth time. *Please bring him home for Christmas.*

An empty, futile feeling swelled in the pit of her

stomach, and Alaina wondered why she bothered. She had almost given up praying altogether, deciding that God must surely be a Northern sympathizer. Still, she clung desperately to the last remnants of her faith and held fast to her memories. The past helped Alaina endure the present. Now, giving her mind free rein, beloved images suddenly mingled with tears as she thought back five short years ago, to a simple, serene time before this nightmarish war ever began.

"You got an invitation!" twelve-year-old Miranda shrieked, running through the six-room farmhouse and bursting into the kitchen.

Alaina dropped the dough she'd been kneading. "An invitation? Me?"

Breathless, her younger sister stopped in front of her and held out the elegantly folded envelope. "It just came. Open it. Quick. I want to know what it says!"

"No doubt it's from Jennifer Marie Stokes."

Miranda frowned slightly. "She's that rich planter's daughter, isn't she? The one Mama said ain't worth an ounce of your attention."

"Oh, now, Jennifer Marie isn't really that bad," Alaina drawled, wiping the sticky bread dough from her hands and taking the invitation. "She's just lonely and needs a friend. She says I saved her life, and I suppose that's true, but—"

"Mama said, 'pride goeth before destruction and a haughty spirit before a fall,' " Miranda recited, " 'and Jennifer Marie Stokes is headed right that way.' That's what Mama said."

"Hush," Alaina scolded, "or I won't tell you what my invitation says."

Miranda clamped her mouth shut while Alaina tore at the embossed paper. Although her family was what South Carolinians referred to as "plain white folk," Alaina and her sister had been taught to read and write. Scanning the printed type on the invitation now, Alaina gasped with pleasure. "I have been invited to Jennifer Marie's eighteenth birthday party."

"Mama won't let you go. There'll be dancing, and Mama says dancing is a sin."

"I won't dance. I'll just watch everyone else."

"She won't let you go."

"Yes, she will, but don't you dare say a word about it. It's my invitation and I'll do the asking. Promise?"

Miranda shrugged a slender shoulder and tossed her walnut curls over her shoulder. "All right. I promise, but only because you're my only sister and I love you dearly."

Alaina leaned forward and pressed a kiss on the girl's cheek.

In the end, she had somehow convinced both her mother and father to allow her to attend the party. Before she knew it, she was on her way to the Stokes' plantation, riding in a luxurious buggy Jennifer Marie had sent for her, complete with a lady's maid for an escort.

It was a half day's journey from the Dalton farm to the Stokes' plantation, but Alaina was filled with such anticipation that she barely noticed the ruts in the road that threatened to jangle her bones from their joints. Once she arrived, Jennifer Marie insisted she nap before preparing for the party that evening. However, Alaina felt too excited to rest and she dressed carefully, donning a new gown she'd sewn for this occasion.

"Oh, now, honey, you can't wear that old thing!" Jennifer Marie exclaimed upon seeing Alaina's simple blue dress with its high neckline and lacy white collar.

Alaina felt herself pale. "I can't?"

"You look like a ten year old in that outfit. Here," Jennifer Marie said, leading Alaina to her ornate wardrobe and throwing open its doors, "choose one of my gowns. Perhaps this lilac creation will adequately complement your fair complexion."

"I couldn't possibly wear that," Alaina gasped, gazing at the lovely dress with its wide, hoop skirt.

"Why not?" Jennifer Marie's delicate blond brows raised in surprise.

"Because it's. . .it's too. . .*beautiful*," she breathed in reply.

Jennifer Marie laughed. "You goose. Of course it's beautiful. I only possess beautiful things. Look around you. Is this room not the most exquisite bedchamber you've ever seen?"

"It is indeed," Alaina said, casting her gaze on the four-poster, canopy bed with its yellow satiny comforter. The same sunny material hung across the long mahogany windows which overlooked the vast cotton fields beyond the mansion.

"Lending you my favorite gown is the least I can do," Jennifer Marie told her, patting her elegantly coiffed blond ringlets. "Why, you saved my life that day in town, and I shall never forget your kindness."

"You have more than repaid me," Alaina insisted, recalling the incident in which she'd pulled Jennifer Marie out of harm's way as a runaway wagon careened down the main street of Columbia.

"I haven't even begun to repay you," Jennifer Marie said, her hazel eyes sparkling with adoration. "You are my very best friend, Alaina Dalton, and I have a big surprise for you tonight."

"For me? But it's your birthday party."

Jennifer Marie laughed, sounding like a twittering little bird. "Change quickly, and you'll see what I have planned." With that she left the room in a billow of pink taffeta.

Feeling uncertain, Alaina took off her simple frock and allowed Jennifer Marie's maid to help her into the lilac-colored gown. Much to her delight, it fit perfectly, although the neckline was much too low to be considered modest. If Mama saw her, she'd have a fit! But it surely was the most gorgeous thing Alaina had ever set eyes on. Looking into the mirror, she tugged upward on the bodice. Well, perhaps it wouldn't hurt to wear this dress just this once.

Music from the string ensemble downstairs floated to her ears just as Jennifer Marie reentered the room.

"Are you ready yet?" She gasped in delight. "You look marvelous! I just knew that dress would be perfect for you. Nita," Jennifer Marie ordered the lovely, dark-skinned girl, "fix Miss Alaina's hair."

"Yes, ma'am."

"That's not necessary," Alaina replied, but to no avail. So she allowed the young maid to pin up her hair in the most enchanting way. Alaina gaped in disbelieef at her reflection.

"Is that really me?"

"Yes, it is." Jennifer Marie laughed gaily. "I can't wait to see Braeden's face when you walk downstairs with me."

Alaina froze. "Braeden? Who's that?"

A hint of a blush crossed her friend's dainty features. "He's my first cousin on my mother's side, and he's plain white folk, just like you."

Indignation rose up in Alaina, and she was immediately thrust back into reality. She didn't belong here, being waited on by servants or wearing this dress. Who was she fooling?

"Oh, now, I can see I insulted you. I didn't mean to," Jennifer Marie gushed, putting a sisterly arm around Alaina's shoulders. "I only said that about Braeden so you'd feel more comfortable when you meet him." Jennifer Marie smiled warmly. "He's a handsome rascal. I know you'll like him. That's my surprise. I want you to meet my charming cousin." Walking to her bureau, Jennifer Marie lifted her puff from its container and began powdering Alaina's skin. "You simply must stay out of the sun, honey. You are freckling something awful."

Alaina coughed and waved away the cloud of white dust. Then, before she could utter a single protest, she was whisked from the room.

❧

"Alaina!"

A deep, male voice hailed her from her musings,

and Alaina realized she was ambling down the road toward the river. Looking to her right, she saw her neighbor, Michael Wheeler, running toward her. The concern he felt for her was evident in his dark features. Michael. Dear, sweet Michael.

"Alaina! Where are you going?" He caught up to her, panting from his sprint across the wide front yard of his home which stood in sorry disrepair. Bit by bit, Michael was restoring it in spite of the fact he only had one arm with which to work. He'd lost his left arm in the War. "Alaina?" He took hold of her elbow with his hand.

"I was just lost in thought, Michael," she explained. "I guess I walked off aimlessly."

An expression of understanding crossed his handsome face. Still, he gave her a mild reprimanding. "It's not safe for you to walk off alone, Lain."

She sighed. "I know. . . ."

"Any word from Braeden?"

"None," she replied, her heart sinking. "And I know what you're going to say, so save your breath."

Michael shook his head, looking chagrined.

"You're going to tell me Braeden is dead, that it's been over a year and a half since anyone's heard from him. You're going to remind me that you fought with him in the great cavalry battle at Trevilian Station. You took a bullet to your left arm and you saw that Braeden had fallen there in Virginia."

Alaina choked on the sudden flood of emotion. "I can't believe he's dead. I *won't* believe it!"

Michael pulled her close, and her tears spilled

down the front of his woolen tunic. "Why are you doing this to yourself?"

Alaina could feel his warm breath against her ear, and she pushed back, knowing it wasn't right to allow herself this measure of consolation. She was, after all, a married woman. "If Braeden were really dead, I'd know it. I'd feel it in my heart."

Michael's brown eyes filled with both skepticism and pity. "Come on, I'll take you back home."

Chapter 2

After supper that evening, the McKennas gathered around the hearth as was their custom. Eloise read from the novel *Jane Eyre*, and as she listened to the story, Alaina embroidered on the handkerchief she planned to give her little brother, David, for Christmas. Jonathan McKenna, Braeden's father, sat in a nearby armchair, sipping a cup of ground chickory they used as a substitute for coffee. Every so often he set down his cup, stood, and stoked the fire. Eloise droned on without missing a syllable.

Alaina stifled a yawn and paused in her stitching. She was growing tired of hearing about the sardonic Mr. Rochester. Seeking diversion, she gazed into the hearth and watched the flickering flames until she felt almost mesmerized. And then she reflected upon a true romance. The one she shared with Braeden. . . .

Jennifer Marie was in her glory on the night of her eighteenth birthday party. She didn't merely walk across the polished wooden floor of the ballroom, she fairly floated—and she pulled Alaina right along with her.

"There he is! There's that no-good cousin of mine!"

Alaina soon realized the latter had been spoken in jest because Jennifer Marie looked pleased to see the young man they were rapidly approaching.

"Braeden, I'm so glad you came tonight."

"I wouldn't miss your birthday party for the world," he replied, placing a perfunctory kiss on Jennifer Marie's rosy cheek.

"And now I'd like to introduce my very best friend, Alaina Dalton." She gave Alaina's wrist a good yank, forcing her to step forward. "She's the one I told you about, Braeden. And just look at those blue eyes. Why, a man could drown in them, don't you agree?"

"Why, yes."

Alaina quickly lowered her gaze, her face aflame from the flattery.

"It's a pleasure to meet you," Braeden said, taking her gloved hand and bowing graciously.

Remembering her low neckline, Alaina curtseyed cautiously. She lifted her gaze and saw the unique color of his eyes—a honey-brown with golden flecks. In the briefest of moments, they regarded each other with interest.

"I had a feeling you two would get along famously!" Jennifer Marie declared. "And, Braeden, I do hope you brought your devilishly handsome friend, Michael Wheeler tonight. I'll cry if you didn't."

"Oh, he's here. . ." Braeden searched the ballroom. "Somewhere."

"I'll find him," Jennifer Marie said with a deter-mined arch to her winged brow.

Braeden grinned amusedly before turning back to Alaina. "May I get you some punch?"

"Why, yes. Thank you."

A nod of reply, and he strolled off toward the refreshments. He returned within minutes. "Where are you from?" he wanted to know.

"Sumter County. And you?"

"Richland County." Braeden chuckled, and Alaina noted its warm, friendly sound. "We're practically neighbors."

"Very true, Mr. . . .Mr.?"

"McKenna. But, please call me Braeden."

Alaina felt another warm blush creep into her cheeks. "How did you and my cousin become fast friends?"

"Oh, it happened last year," she recounted in an embarrassed tone. "You might say I was in the right place at the right time and just happened to meet Jennifer Marie in the process."

"Hm, I see." He lifted a thick, blond brow. "I think I see."

Alaina laughed softly. "Perhaps someday I'll tell you all the details."

"I'll look forward to it," he said, a promising gleam in his eyes.

The string ensemble began to play another melodious piece and couples waltzed into the center of the colorfully decorated ballroom. "I'd ask you to dance," Braeden began, "but it goes against my religious convictions."

Alaina expelled a sigh of relief. She feared he'd ask her and had been worrying over her response. "I share your opinions that way."

"You don't say?" His skeptical gaze assessed her in two quick up and down motions, and Alaina suddenly wished she hadn't given in to Jennifer Marie's request that she change evening gowns. Beneath Braeden's questioning stare, she grew increasingly self-conscious.

After a few long moments, he changed the subject. "It's a pleasant night. Would you care for a stroll outside?"

"Oh, that would be lovely. I'll get my shawl."

Alaina made her way through the throng of guests and climbed the elegant, winding staircase. Nita, bless her heart, was quick to find the gown's matching lilac wrapper, and Alaina felt grateful to have a convenient cover for her bare shoulders. Descending the steps, she took notice of Braeden standing at the end of the balustrade, waiting patiently.

"I'm sorry to have kept you waiting," she murmured apologetically.

"Miss Dalton," he replied, lifting his strong, square chin, "you are worth the wait."

❧

"Alaina, I'm retiring for the night. Do you hear me, child?"

Shaken from her reverie, Alaina looked up at her mother-in-law. A likeness of Braeden's eyes stared back at her.

"Are you all right, dear?"

"Y—yes, I'm fine," she stammered. "I was just. . . remembering."

"You do that far too often, I think."

"I can't seem to help it, Mother McKenna. I miss Braeden so much."

The older women straightened, a resigned frown etched upon her face. "We all miss him. And I miss Kirk as well. But I cannot bring either of my sons back by pining over what's gone forever. Neither can you. You need to move forward, Alaina. There's no two ways about it."

"You think Braeden is dead, too."

"Foolish girl, of course he is!" Remorse immediately crossed her lined features, and Eloise curbed the sharpness in her voice, "Alaina, it's been over six months since the South surrendered. What would detain Braeden so long? Besides, you heard Michael Wheeler. He's almost certain he saw Braeden fall on Virginia soil over a year ago. And Michael checked the hospitals and searched everywhere for him before he came home, maimed as he is." Eloise shook her white-blond head, wearing a pitiful expression. "The hard truth is Braeden has most likely been buried in some mass grave in some unknown countryside."

"No!" Alaina shrieked, standing to her feet so abruptly that her chair toppled backwards. "No, he's not dead!"

With tears blinding her vision, she ran to her bedroom and closed the door behind her. Minutes later, she heard her mother-in-law's voice waft across the hallway as she conversed with her husband.

"I fear for that girl's sanity."

"She's been through a lot, Ellie. Let her be."

"But I think we should have Braeden legally declared dead so we can all go on with our lives." A heavy-laden silence filled the momentary pause. "Michael Wheeler would marry Alaina in an instant.

Anyone can see he's interested in her just by the look in his eyes whenever they're in the same room."

"That ain't for us to decide," Jonathan replied gruffly. "If Alaina thinks Braeden is still alive, and if she wants to wait the rest of her life for his return, we need to respect her wishes."

"I suppose you're right," Eloise stated in a tone of complete acquiescence. "It's just that Alaina is so young and pretty. Why, I hate the thought of a wasted youth. With Michael, she could have children."

"And that'd be a fine thing for Braeden to come home to—his wife married to his best friend."

Eloise gasped. "So you believe Braeden's alive, too?"

"I don't know what I believe anymore."

Leaning against the door, her cheek right up against the cool wooden frame, Alaina sobbed. *Oh, God, please bring my husband home!*

Collecting herself, she walked to the window and pulled back the filmy drape. Moonlight streamed in through the glass panes, transporting Alaina back to another time when the moon, like her heart, was so bright and full. . . .

"Will you just look at that moon," Braeden remarked, gazing heavenward. "Why, it seems so close, I'd like to reach out and touch it."

Alaina smiled. Her gloved hand was hooked around his elbow as they strolled around the Stokes' well-groomed property.

He looked down at her. "My cousin tells me your father is a farmer."

"Yes, that's right."

"Mine is also. As the firstborn son, I'll be taking over our family's farm soon."

"I have an older brother, David. Like you, he's destined to till the land."

"And what are you destined to do?" Braeden asked, stopping and turning toward her. He took both of her hands in his and gazed down into her face.

"Why. . .I don't know," Alaina replied, surprised by the question.

"You don't have any dreams you're harboring?"

She shrugged and pulled her hands from his, feeling shy. "Well, perhaps, I do have one small dream."

"Tell me what it is," Braeden said as they resumed their stroll.

"No, you'll laugh at me."

"I won't. I promise."

Alaina shook her head. She couldn't possibly tell him her secret ambition. He'd undoubtedly collapse in hysterics as her father and her brother, William, had.

"Tell me," Braeden persisted.

"You really won't laugh?"

"I won't, on my honor as a gentleman."

"Well. . ." Alaina looked at him askance and within a heartbeat, she felt certain she could trust him. Besides, it was about time for some honesty on her part. "Someday," she began, "I'd like to study at the university in Columbia."

"Hm. . .and what's so funny about that?"

"It's funny," she began, "because I'm not who you think I am."

They both halted in their tracks and faced each other. Braeden lifted a curious brow. "How so?"

"I don't come from prosperity. My family barely makes ends meet. This dress I'm wearing—it's not even mine," Alaina blurted. "It belongs to your cousin, and I wish I wouldn't have agreed to wear it."

"Yes, I gathered as much."

"You did?" Her jaw dropped slightly.

Braeden chuckled. "Your blush when we first met gave you away, my dear, not to mention the way you continue to tug on that wrapper."

"Oh, I'm so embarrassed," Alaina gushed, wishing the earth would open and swallow her whole. "Jennifer Marie will never invite me anywhere again."

"There, now. This can stay between the two of us," Braeden assured her, looping her arm around his as they began to walk again. "Jennifer Marie need never know about it."

"Truly?"

"Truly."

Silence accompanied them for a few steps around the garden. It was too early in the season for any blooms, but the evening was so pleasant.

"Have you had any formal education?" Braeden asked.

"I've gone to the Field School some. My mother taught me the rest. She was educated in Charlotte before her family moved to Sumter County. Still, I'd love to learn more." Alaina momentary chewed her lower lip, feeling suddenly ungrateful for everything her parents had done for her. "I will say this about my family," she added, "we may not have a lot of money, but we're happy and we love each other. That's all that really matters to us. Education is secondary when put in that perspective."

"I agree."

"What about you?" Alaina couldn't help asking. "Do you have any secret dreams?"

"Actually, I do," he admitted. "But it's a secret."

"I won't tell," Alaina said, smiling. "I promise."

"Very well, then. I'm fascinated with the railroad."

"You are?"

Beneath the moonlight, Alaina saw him nod. "I think railroads are the future of this country." He paused once more. "Can you imagine the importing and exporting the South could do if only our railroads went all the way to the West Coast?"

"Railroads instead of shipping by sea?"

"Yes, I think once the railways are developed, they'll be a much more efficient means for transporting both goods and people." Braeden smiled. "Have you ever been on a train?"

"No."

He smiled fondly into her eyes. "Then one day I'll take you for a train ride."

Alaina lifted her chin in a challenging manner. "Do you always make promises to perfectly strange young ladies, Mr. McKenna?"

"You hardly seem like a stranger to me," he said in all seriousness. "The fact is, I feel like I've known you my whole life."

Chapter 3

"Mother McKenna, I've made a decision," Alaina said the next morning at breakfast.

"Oh? And what might that be?"

"I've decided that since I'm a burden on this family, I will go home to my mother."

"Burden?" Eloise jolted in surprise. "What on earth are you talking about?"

Alaina picked at the egg and potato on her plate, knowing this was more food than she'd eaten at one meal in weeks. Michael Wheeler, in all his thoughtfulness, brought over a few eggs this morning. Thankfully at least a couple of his chickens survived Sherman's invasion. The potato was one of their own crops from last summer which had endured preservation. However, Alaina had no appetite. She couldn't get herself to confess to eavesdropping, but it was obvious she added to this family's hardship. Why else would Mother McKenna suggest she marry Michael?

"I'm another mouth to feed around here."

"You'll be another mouth to feed at your mother's place as well, and she's no better off than we are."

"Yes, but—"

"Alaina, you are a McKenna as much as I am, and you belong here. Obviously you're inflicting unnecessary guilt upon yourself. Stop it at once."

"Yes, ma'am."

Eloise reached across the scarred, plank table and gently patted her hand. "There now, dear, these are lean times for every Southerner." She sat up straight in her chair once more, looking dignified despite her worn, woolen dress and plain, brown apron. "How is your mother doing, by the way?"

"As well as can be expected." Sorrow filled Alaina's heart. "Mama told me she wishes she would have died of the influenza rather than Papa and Miranda."

Eloise shook her head ruefully. "Such a tragedy."

An errant tear slipped out and ran down Alaina's cheek. She brushed it aside and another took its place.

"Do you feel you need to go to her? Is that what this is all about?"

"No. David can take care of Mama. He's all Mama has since William fell."

"Then it's settled. You'll stay here where you belong."

Alaina wiped away her tears. "Do you really mean that, Mother McKenna?"

"Of course!" She forced a smile through all the anguish that she, too, had suffered. "We'll persevere together."

❧

"I can't believe I let you talk me into bringing you here," Michael said the following Sunday afternoon. "Braeden would have my hide if he ever found out."

Alaina curled her lips into a small grin. "I'd have talked Braeden into bringing me. . .if he were here."

"Bet you wouldn't," Michael teased her, reining in the sorry-looking mule with his one arm. All humor evaporated as the wagon stopped in front of the remains of the Stokes' plantation.

"Oh, Michael," Alaina despaired. "Just look what's become of this place."

"I knew we shouldn't have come," he muttered, wagging his dark head in concern.

"No. I needed to come. . .again."

Before Michael could help her alight from the wagon, she jumped down on her own. She walked through the warped, wrought-iron gate beneath the charred oak trees. Looking ahead, she saw that only two chimneys stood erect, the rest of the mansion had been burned beyond repair.

Heavy-hearted, Alaina tramped through the over-grown brown brush that had once been part of a lovely flower garden. Just beyond it lay a small cemetery with three wooden crosses.

"Oh, Jennifer Marie," she said, leaning over the forlorn, white picket fence that squared off the graves, "I'm glad you can't see what those hateful soldiers did to your home. At least you're with Jesus, strolling the streets of gold."

"Lain," Michael said, coming up behind her and putting his hand on her shoulder. "Why are you doing this?"

"I miss my friend. I miss her so very much." She whirled around to face Michael. "This surely is the end of the world, isn't it? Just like something out of the Book of Revelation."

He grinned sardonically. "We should be so lucky."

Ignoring the quip, Alaina turned back to the cemetery. She'd come to pay her respects. Somebody had to, after all, and Jennifer Marie was family.

She had died from smallpox a year ago today—just weeks before Christmas, just months before Sherman's army burned Columbia. Jennifer Marie's mother had died of the same deadly disease a month later and her father was killed by Yankees when he resisted attack on their home.

"It's time to go, Lain," Michael said, his hand resting on her right upper arm.

"I don't even have any flowers to lay at their graves."

"Come spring, there'll be flowers again," Michael said, leaning closer. "You'll see."

"This surely is the end of the world," she repeated.

"No, Lain. It's just the beginning." Michael forced her to turn and look at him. "We can rebuild our homes. . .and our lives."

Alaina recognized the ardor darkening his brown eyes and tried to take a step backward, but it was no use. She was standing with her heels against the fence. "Michael. . ." She put her palms against his chest to forestall him.

"Admit it, Lain, you're as lonely as I am." His eyes bore into hers.

She swallowed hard. "All right. I'll admit it."

"Then marry me," he said, his tone softening. "I might be maimed physically, but I'm still a whole man emotionally and spiritually. I'll make you happy, I swear I will."

"But—"

"Braeden is dead," he said as if divining her thoughts. "You need to accept that."

"Oh, Michael," she choked. "I. . .I. . ."

"I know it's hard for you." He lifted his hand and caressed her cheek. "But I've got enough love in my heart for the both of us. That, and time, will heal all our wounds."

He dipped his head, his lips lowering toward hers. Alaina closed her eyes in bittersweet anticipation. Then, suddenly, she thought she heard Braeden calling her name.

"Did you hear that?" she gasped, her eyes wide with surprise.

"Hear what?" Michael pulled back and looked around. "All I hear is the wind. What did you hear?"

"I heard—" She closed her mouth, shutting off the rest of her reply. Why, Michael would think she was touched if she hold him she'd heard Braeden's voice. Alaina shook her head. Perhaps she was losing her mind. It sounded so real. Then, again, perhaps it was this ghostly place.

"Come on, Lain," Michael said on a note of resignation. He took her hand. "You've had a long day. Let's go home."

Alaina allowed him to lead her back to the wagon and help her board. Michael climbed up to his perch without a word and seemed pensive all the way to the farm, but Alaina didn't mind. She was busy with her own troubled thoughts. Was she going crazy, or was she enveloped in so much darkness, she couldn't see the light? *Oh, Lord,* she prayed, *where are you?*

She recalled what her father-in-law had said several nights ago. "I don't know what I believe anymore." Somehow the comment seemed to encompass more than just Braeden's whereabouts. Were they all losing their faith?

Chapter 4

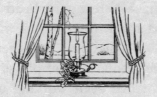

The sunshine warmed Alaina's cheeks as she hung bedding out to air on this exceptionally pleasant December day. Not far off in the distance, she could hear the sounds of her father-in-law's axe *chop-chop-chopping* as he felled the last of the dead trees on the McKenna property. To her far left, remains of miscellaneous farm equipment stood in a great heap, looking like a pile of twisted, metal bones. But Alaina refused to so much as glance in that direction this bright morning and, instead, found something comforting in hearing the thud of another burned out tree trunk as it hit the ground. At last, she would no longer have to see the charred orchard. Scarred as it was, the farmland showed signs of recovery.

"Lain! Lain!"

Hearing the excitement in Michael's voice, she dropped the quilt back into the basket and ran to meet him.

"What is it?" She hoped he had news about Braeden.

"You're not going to believe it!" he cried happily. "It's a miracle."

"What? Tell me."

"I shot a buck this morning!"

Alaina's heart sank. "A buck, you say?" She forced enthusiasm into her voice.

"Yes." Michael threw his head back laughed heartily. "I didn't think there was a wild animal alive this side of the Mississippi. But there he was this morning standing proud as you please just a few feet away from where I've been working on the house. I grabbed my gun and shot him dead with a single bullet. Me! With only one arm!"

"Oh, Michael, that's just wonderful!" Alaina said, fighting back the tears of disappointment. For a fraction of a moment, she'd been certain Michael was bringing her news about Braeden, that he was alive and well and on his way home to her.

Alaina swallowed the sudden lump of emotion. "I'll fetch Papa McKenna. He'll help you skin it."

"No, that's all right. I can fetch him myself. Where is he?"

"Over yonder, by the peach trees. . .what used to be the orchard anyway."

Michael gave her a parting grin before turning on his heel. Once he was on his way, Alaina returned to hanging out the bedding. She tried in vain to tamp down her mounting dismay. A buck was definitely a blessing. Why couldn't she be happy for Michael? Surely he'd share the meat and they would all eat well for the next couple of weeks. As if in line with her musings, her father-in-law came up the path toward the house, shouting his exuberance.

"Ellie! Ellie! It's too good to be true!"

Mother McKenna walked out onto the back porch and stood with hands on her slim hips. "I declare, Jonathan," she drawled sassily, "you're going to wake the dead with all this commotion!"

"Get out your best kettle, woman!" he replied, their handsome neighbor by his side grinning broadly. "Michael, shot a buck this morning, and I suddenly have a taste for venison stew."

"Hmph!" Mother McKenna lifted her chin indignantly, but Alaina could tell the older woman was just as anxious to cook a hearty meal as the men were to eat one.

"My, what a blessing!" Eloise exclaimed as Jonathan and Michael set out across the barren pasture, heading for the Wheeler place. Before the war, there were four strapping, young Wheeler brothers and their widowed father on the neighboring farm, but Michael's siblings were killed, one by one, in various battles. Michael's father, Eloise said, died of a broken heart, and Alaina figured the diagnosis was probably correct. She could see where brokenheartedness could be fatal.

With the bedding on the line, Alaina wandered around the house to the front porch. She suddenly felt like every ounce of energy she possessed had evaporated. Sitting down on the steps which were badly in need of paint, she thought about Michael's marriage proposal. True, he was kind, handsome—even with one arm missing! And he was a hard worker. But he wasn't Braeden.

She leaned her cheek against the wooden railing and stared off into the distance forlornly. She heard the twittering of a tiny bird in a surviving palmetto tree. . .and then she heard something else. Singing! Alaina strained to hear, only to realize the low, smooth-sounding voice crooning "Dixie's Land" was getting closer by the moment.

"O' I wish I was in da land o' cotton,
"Ol' times dar am not forgotton,
"Look away! Look away! Look away! Dixie's
   Land."

Alaina stood up and glanced toward the road. Marching around the curve, she saw the gleaming, dark face of a man in a white shirt and bedraggled, gray pants supported by suspenders. As he neared, she glimpsed the battered, gray cap on his head and the blue kerchief filled with meager belongings that he'd tied to a long stick and carried over his shoulder.

"Ezekiel," she breathed in recognition. She blinked and reality set in. "Zek!" With renewed spirit, she bolted from the stairs and ran across the lawn. "Zek, is that really you?"

"Miz Laina," he said, flashing her his infamous wide grin, "it shore is me. And you's a sight for sore eyes!"

For the first time in months, Alaina laughed. "Where have you been?"

"Been ever'where, I reckon," the former farmhand replied. Then a look of sadness filled his eyes. "I been ever'where and nowhere, but now I be comin' home."

"How wonderful!" she declared, walking alongside him up to the house.

Alaina fretted over her lower lip for several moments before she actually worked up the courage to form the supreme question. "Have you seen Braeden?"

They reached the front porch and stopped.

"You mean he ain't home?" Alaina shook her head ruefully, and Zek's broad shoulders sagged as if in final defeat.

"Last I saw Massah Braeden," he began ruefully, "it was nigh onto a year ago. He got hisself shot at the railroad station in Virginia. Looked pretty bad, but he weren't dead when I seen 'im. I stopped to help, but Massah Braeden tole me to keep goin'. He said, 'Git outa here, Zek, afore you git your fool head blowed off.' I said, 'I ain't leavin' you, Massah Braeden.' So I pulled 'im over to the brush near the tracks an' I lays down beside 'im like I's dead." A sad smile crossed the black man's face. "Well, the war done went on 'round us, and by some miracle o' God we didn't git ourselves kilt. Come nightfall, it looked like the Yankees won that fight. Them mean ol' Bluebelies come walkin' down the tracks like they owned 'em, kickin' bodies to see ifn they's really dead. They come to us, and they give Massah Braeden a kick. He yelped like a hound, so the soldiers done took him 'way and put 'im in a wagon. An' that's the last I seen him."

"Braeden got captured?" She felt the blood draining from her face.

"I reckon so, Miz Laina."

"We should have been notified!" she exclaimed indignantly.

"Shoudda is right. But in this war, nothin's as it should be."

Heavy-hearted, Alaina sagged onto the porch steps.

"I shore is sorry 'bout Massah Braeden."

"I know you are," she fairly choked.

The front door opened and Eloise stepped out of the house. "I thought I heard voices. . .Zek!" she cried happily. "You're home!"

"I shore am, Miz Ellie. I shore am!"

By evening, the tantalizing smell of venison stew drifted from the cookhouse and seemed to permeate every corner of the farm. Alaina and Eloise had worked most of the day, butchering and curing the deer meat. They wrapped up portions for Pastor Pritchard and his family, along with Braeden's sister, Suzanna, and her clan. Then Michael and Zek delivered the goods, but they made quick work of it and returned by suppertime.

"My, but this looks like a feast!" Michael declared after Alaina set his plate down before him. "God truly sees after our needs."

"Amen!" Zek exclaimed, and Alaina dished up a plate for him, too. When she handed it him, he said, "Thank yo', Miz Laina, and now I'll just be goin' to eat out on the back po'ch."

He got as far as the door before Jonathan halted him. "Wait! I want you to eat with us here at the table."

Zek turned, his dark eyes wide with disbelief. "But Massah Jonathan, that ain't right. No Negro oughta eat with Whites at the suppah table!"

Jonathan expelled a weary-sounding sigh. "You went off to war with my sons, Zek. Sure, I know that you were first employed with the cavalry as a servant, but it wasn't long before they put a gun in your hand, too. Your blood's the same color as theirs—as mine."

Zek hung his head sadly. "I shore am sorry for yo'

loss of all them boys yo' raised up. They's good boys, too. Mebbe it shouldda been me who died, 'stead of them."

Tears filled Alaina's eyes, and animosity filled her heart. "No one should have died!" she cried angrily, tossing the serving spoon into the pot of stew. "I hate those Yankees! I hate every one of them!"

"Alaina!" her mother-in-law gasped.

Molten sadness blinded Alaina as she darted from the kitchen into the rapidly cooling December dusk. She sprinted through the yard, past the cinders littering the barn's foundation, across the cold, hard dirt in the garden, and there she leaped over the tiny creek. She ran through a cluster of unmarred oak trees and continued to run until her lungs burned, rendering her breathless.

Sagging to her knees, she sobbed bitterly. "Oh, God, I wish I were dead." She wept and poured out her anguish to the Lord. Finally, there wasn't another tear left.

"Lord, what should I do? How can I go on?"

My grace is sufficient for thee, came the Divine reply, *for My strength is made perfect in weakness.*

Alaina lifted the edges of her apron and dabbed at her swollen eyes. "Yes, yes. . ." She believed it. She'd memorized that passage of scripture as a girl—2 Corinthians 12:9. It had remained in her heart ever since. *". . .and, lo, I am with you always, even unto the end of the world."*

She sniffled and then felt the urge to recite a portion of Psalm 23. " 'Yea, though I walk through the valley of the shadow of death, I will fear no evil: for Thou art with me. . .surely goodness and mercy shall follow me all the days of my life: and I will dwell in the house of the LORD forever.' "

She shook her head and marveled. Never before had she thought she'd feel so grateful that her mother had insisted she memorize selections from the Bible. Now, as the Lord brought His Word to mind, Alaina felt as though she could feel the Savior's arms around her, comforting her, encouraging her to rise from the cold earth and walk back to the house.

"Alaina!"

She heard Papa McKenna's booming voice as she crossed the stream. "Not to worry," she called back. "I'm here. I'm all right."

It wasn't long after Jennifer Marie's eighteenth birthday party that Braeden called upon Alaina and asked her father's permission to court her. At first she feared Papa wouldn't allow it, after all he still referred to her as his "little girl" even though she was seventeen—and even though Miranda was really his little girl! Braeden was twenty. Would Papa think he was too old for her, or too young?

As it happened Samuel Dalton took an instant liking to the gallant young man pursuing his daughter, and he allowed Braeden to visit once during the week and spend Sundays with their family. It was on one of those Lord's Day afternoons that Alaina packed a picnic lunch for herself and Braeden to share under the expanse of a thick oak tree. It was unseasonably warm for the last days of March. "Would you care for another piece of chicken?"

Braeden groaned and patted his stomach. "No, Laina, I'm so full I might just bust."

She laughed softly and watched him stretch out on his back, his blond head close to her lap.

"Did you fry that chicken yourself?"

Alaina felt a warm blush creep up her neck into her cheeks. "No, I must confess, Mama did it, but I helped."

Braeden chuckled under his breath. "I wouldn't care if you didn't know how to set a kettle to boiling."

"Oh, yes you would—when your stomach started to rumble, then you'd care."

"Well," he drawled teasingly, "maybe just little."

Alaina clucked her tongue and smiled. "You!" With that she gave the top of his head a good swipe with her red, checkered napkin.

Braeden sat up and spun around on his tailbone. He bent his legs, resting elbows on knees, and a sudden, earnest expression crossed his face.

"Laina, war is coming to South Carolina."

She let out a huff of exasperation. "I declare! That's all you men talk about these days."

"It's a grave concern. South Carolina seceded from the Union last December. Since then, other states have followed suit, including Texas. The Union has made it clear; it won't stand for what it considers our *rebellion*."

"Yes, I know all that," Alaina replied feeling aggravated. Why did Braeden have to ruin a perfectly wonderful afternoon with this senseless talk about secession and the Union? She heard plenty from her father and older brother, William.

"Laina, look at me."

She refused and continued picking at the imaginary lint on her skirt until Braeden took hold of her chin and forced her gaze to meet his troubled, amber eyes.

"I'm a man torn in two over this, Laina," he said softly, stirring the compassion in her heart.

"Whatever do you mean?"

He appeared both relieved and satisfied that he'd gotten her attention. He dropped his hand and sighed. "I'm a simple farmer but a true-blooded South Carolinian. I was born and reared here, and I love my land. I will fight for this new Confederation of Slave States because my heart is here. Here, where my Irish grandfather carved out a life, a legacy."

"But therein lies the problem," Braeden said, looking off in the distance. "I'm not sure if I agree with all the aspects surrounding the slavery issue. I've seen terrible abuse inflicted upon some Negros by their masters. Then I think of Ezekiel and Abraham, and the opposite is true. Why, we boys all grew up together, and I can recall their Mamie giving me a well-deserved licking or two. We have our differences, but they didn't stop us from working side-by-side in the fields. While I reckon they're our property, I love them as much as I love my family's farm—so much, that I'm prepared to die for the right to keep what's mine."

"Oh, Braeden, don't say such horrid things!" Alaina gasped. "I can't bear the thought of you dying!"

Looking back at her, he smiled wistfully. "Would you miss me if I died, Laina?"

"Silly man, of course I would!"

A mischievous glimmer entered his eyes. "How much would you miss me?"

"Well, I would miss you—"

Alaina suddenly realized he was having fun with her sensibilities. She lifted a brow. "Actually, I wouldn't miss you one bit, Braeden McKenna." She plucked a handful of grass and threw it at him, striking him in the chest.

"You, scamp!"

She laughed and he caught her upper arm, pulling her toward him. He was so close now, Alaina could feel his breath on her forehead. She watched the mirth fade from Braeden's expression.

"Would you really miss me, Laina?" he asked softly, his eyes searching hers.

"Yes," she whispered. "Yes, I would."

Alaina woke still feeling the delicious warmth of her dream. She rolled over and reached out for Braeden— only to feel the cold sheet on his half of the bed.

Stark reality settled upon her. "Oh, Braeden," she sobbed quietly, "I wish I would have known just how much I'd miss you. . . .

"But, then, I would have never let you go!"

Chapter 5

A laina could still recall the brisk morning of April 12, 1861. She was washing clothes in the yard with her mother and Miranda. Patches of snow still covered the ground, residue from the freak snowstorm only weeks earlier.

She heard horse's hooves pounding the gravel road leading up to the house. She exchanged wondering glances with her mother and sister just as Braeden came into view. Another man, tall and dark-headed, rode beside him. He looked familiar, and Alaina recalled seeing him at Jennifer Marie's birthday party. Reining in their animals, the men dismounted simultaneously.

"Oh, my!" Alaina gasped in horror, wiping her wet, soapy hands on her apron. She quickly rolled down the sleeves of her white, cotton blouse and finger-combed her wind-blown hair back into its chignon. "What on earth is Braeden doing calling on me at this hour!"

Her mother chuckled softly and left her wash tub to greet the two well-dressed men walking their way. Miranda stared on in wide-eyed, girlish curiosity.

"Good morning, ma'am," Braeden began with a

polite bow. "Allow me to present my good friend, Michael Wheeler. Michael, this is Mrs. Dalton."

Ruth Dalton nodded. "Mr. Wheeler." She turned back to Braeden, as wisps of her graying, mahogany-colored hair blew across her cheek. She pushed it back with one hand. "This is a pleasant surprise, albeit an unexpected one."

"Yes, ma'am." Braeden's golden-flecked brown eyes peered over Ruth's head at Alaina. He smiled before addressing her mother again. "I wondered if I could speak with you and Mr. Dalton. You see, I received word this morning that the Union has sent out one of its naval vessels with supplies for the men at Fort Sumter, but the Confederate army has the fort surrounded and has no intention of allowing the Union passage into the Charleston harbor." Braeden wet his lips anxiously. "This is likely the beginnings of war, Mrs. Dalton, and it's my desire to be there when that first shot is fired."

"I see. . ." Alaina's mother looked back at her, and Alaina suddenly realized she'd been holding her breath. She let it out slowly as the conversation continued. "What has this to do with your speaking to my husband and me?"

"Michael and I are headed into Columbia to purchase train tickets to Charleston for this historic event. Since my sister and her husband are going along, as is my cousin, Jennifer Marie, I wondered if you would allow Alaina to accompany me. . .us."

Ruth gave him a little smile. "I will call for my husband at once." She whirled around. "Miranda, find

David and tell him to properly water our guests' horses. Alaina, make some lemonade. I'm sure Braeden and Mr. Wheeler are very thirsty after their ride, and I know your father and William will appreciate a drink when they come in from the field."

"Yes, Mama," Alaina replied.

Miranda ran off to find their little brother while Alaina approached the men. Her gaze, however, never wavered from Braeden's grinning face.

"I promised you a train ride, Alaina Dalton, and I'm determine to keep my word."

"So I hear."

Braeden introduced her to Michael.

"A pleasure to meet you, Mr. Wheeler. Won't you both come inside and make yourselves comfortable while we wait for Papa?"

They both nodded and followed Alaina into the house. After seating them in the parlor, she quickly busied herself with preparing the lemonade.

"You're right, Brae, she's a pretty little thing," Alaina overheard Michael remark.

"She's spoken for, so don't get any ideas, my friend," Braeden ground out in warning. Michael laughed good-naturedly.

Alaina felt a heated blush rise into her cheeks. She didn't think she looked "pretty" in her plain brown skirt and white blouse. They were the clothes she typically did her chores in; they were not for entertaining by any stretch of the imagination. Still, she was flattered by Mr. Wheeler's compliment and Braeden's possessive claim.

Minutes later, nineteen-year-old William dashed

into the house. His face shone with excitement and his dark hair was matted with perspiration. His shirt and trousers were soiled from working outside and in all his exuberance he obviously forgot Mama's rule about changing in the mud room before entering her well-kept home.

"Has the War Between the States really begun?" William panted.

"Could be soon," Braeden answered.

"May I come along to Charleston with y'all?"

"Of course. . .that is, if your father will give his consent."

"He already has." William smirked. "He said I could go because I promised to keep an eye on Laina. After all, we can hardly entrust her care to a rake like you."

Alaina grimaced. She'd die an old maid unless her obnoxious older brother learned to curb his tongue.

Much to her relief, Braeden easily laughed off the teasing comment, and when Samuel Dalton strolled into the house with his wife, he stated his intentions once more.

"Where will you stay?" Samuel inquired.

"Jennifer Marie's widowed aunt, Mrs. Stokes, has graciously invited us into her home."

Alaina chanced a peek at her mother, knowing she didn't care for Jennifer Marie. If it weren't for Braeden's influence today, she wouldn't be going anywhere except back out in the yard to wash clothes. Despite her dislike for his cousin, Mama was very fond of Braeden.

"I reckon you can go, Laney," her father said.

"Oh, thank you, Papa!" she gushed, momentarily

forgetting herself in front of their guests. She cleared her throat, regaining her composure, and sent Braeden an embarrassed smile.

He returned an assuring wink. Then, looking at her father, Braeden said, "William is welcome to come along, Mr. Dalton."

"All right boy," he told his first born, "you may go, too."

William let out a whoop of glee, furthering Alaina's humiliation.

"You need to change clothes," Ruth said, obvious displeased that her son had tracked field dust into her parlor. "I'll pack your things."

"If you hurry, Will, we'll wait for you," Braeden promised. "But, Laina, you've got more time to get ready. Jennifer Marie said she'd come for you in the carriage. Except," he added, squaring his broad shoulders, "you'll be sitting next to me on the train."

"Unless, of course, I get there first," Michael teased, earning himself a playful shove from Braeden.

Everyone chuckled while Alaina, feeling a blush to her hairline, took her leave and began packing. Sometime later, Braeden called a good-bye to her before mounting his horse and riding away after Michael and William. Then once she'd changed into simple, but sturdy, beige traveling garb, she met her parents in the kitchen. The noon meal had long since been served, yet they remained in their places across from each other, wearing contemplative expressions.

"What's wrong?"

"Nothing is wrong, dear," her mother replied.

"Papa? Why do you seem so troubled?"

"I'm not troubled." He combed a callused hand through his short, charcoal-gray hair. "It's just that. . . well, you're all growed up, Laney. You're not my little girl anymore, are you?"

She shook her head, frowning in confusion.

After a weighted silence, Samuel pushed his chair back and stood. "Braeden talked to your mama and me privately this morning. He asked for your hand in marriage."

Alaina gasped. "He did?" She couldn't keep the smile from her lips.

"I gave him our blessing."

"Oh, Papa!" Happily running toward him, she threw her arms around his thick neck. "Thank you, Papa! I love Braeden so much!"

"Now, don't you say a word 'til he proposes."

Alaina stepped back, gazing up into her father's weather-worn face. "I won't. I promise!"

In the next moments, Miranda and David burst into the house, announcing the arrival of Jennifer Marie.

"Hurry, Alaina," she said while the driver loaded her bags, "I don't want to miss the train."

Climbing aboard the handsome, black, convertible, four-passenger buggy, Alaina waved to her parents and siblings before settling herself into the front seat. Two female servants sat in the back.

"Oh, we're off at last," Jennifer Marie said with an impatient sigh as she vigorously fanned herself. The temperature had risen remarkably since the morning. Turning, she inspected Alaina's attire in two sweeping glances. "Why, I declare! You look so prim in that outfit."

"Thank you." She frowned. "I think." Alaina knew she was no match for Jennifer Marie's bare-shouldered, billowing, ivory lace gown; however, she'd come to accept her station in life. She was a farmer's daughter, soon to be a farmer's wife. Alaina's heart hammered with dreamy anticipation as she wondered when and where Braeden might propose to her. She could only imagine that it would be somewhere utterly romantic.

"I have a surprise for you," Jennifer Marie crooned, drawing Alaina out of her musings. "I had a new dress made just for you. It's a dark gold silk with black trim, and you'll positively shine in it, Alaina!"

She gasped, bringing a hand to her throat.

"And, not to worry," Jennifer Marie added as if divining Alaina's troubled thoughts, "I insisted upon a high neckline."

Alaina couldn't help but laugh, shaking her head in wonder. "You had a new dress made just for me? Why, that's very generous of you, but quite unnecessary."

"On the contrary, honey. Aunt Sabrina is sure to hold a formal celebration this weekend to show our support for the Cause, and you simply must have something presentable to wear." Jennifer Marie beamed. "I had actually planned to give you the dress for your eighteenth birthday next month, but I decided the gift couldn't wait."

Alaina smiled warmly. "You're a sweet friend, Jennifer Marie."

"Well, I do have a favor to ask. . . ."

"Oh?" Alaina lifted a brow.

"Yes, well, I've had my eye on my cousin's best friend,

Michael Wheeler, for some time now. My father spoke to Michael's parents about a possible match between us. Since I'm the only Stokes heir, there's no one to take over Riverwood once Papa gets old. With Michael's expertise in farming, he'd be perfect." Jennifer Marie pouted prettily. "But the Wheelers' declined Papa's offer, citing the fact that they're Christians and we're not. I've always thought we were Christians—that is, we believe in God, but apparently that's not enough.

"In any event," Jennifer Marie babbled on, "I intend to remedy that small problem at once, and I want you to tell me how to be a real Christian so I can capture Michael Wheeler's heart. I know I've caught his eye on numerous occasions. Furthermore, I've instructed Braeden to purchase a ticket for me beside Michael today on the train. I intend to talk about Christian things all the way to Charleston. Won't he be impressed?" She smiled broadly. "Tell me what I should say."

"Well. . ." Alaina momentarily fretted over her lower lip. She knew Braeden had told Jennifer Marie about Jesus and how He had suffered and died on the cross so that her sins could be forgiven—if only she'd ask and accept God's free gift of salvation. Obviously the explanation hadn't sunk in. Furthermore, Braeden said his mother shared the gospel with her sister, Jennifer Marie's mother, many times in the past. But the answer was always the same: Lucinda Stokes was trusting her own religion, and she'd passed on those faulty beliefs to her daughter.

But, perhaps, things were changing. Maybe God could use Jennifer Marie's desire to be a "real Christian," in spite of her less than pure motives.

"Well," Alaina began again, "you might begin by asking Michael if he's involved in any ministries in his local church."

"Ministries?" Jennifer gave her a quizzical look. "Aren't those the men in long robes who give long, drawn-out sermons on Sunday mornings?"

"No, those are *ministers*." Alaina sighed. It would surely be a long ride into Columbia.

Chapter 6

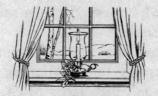

J ust look at this beauty!" Braeden exclaimed walking Alaina past the steaming locomotive.

She gave him a curious look before glancing
back at the snarling, black engine. "Why, I think an
angry bull might be a more accurate description."

Braeden didn't seem to hear the quip as he continued
his inspection. He seemed enthralled. "She's one of
South Carolina Railroad's finest. A true Southern Belle."

"Well, I don't know," she said with a pout, "I think
I'm jealous."

Braeden whirled around, his blond brows raised in
surprise. "Jealous? Of a steam engine?"

He chuckled heartily while Alaina stood by and
bristled. At last, she turned on her heel and marched
toward the passenger car.

"Oh, now, Laina-honey," he drawled, "don't be
cross with me." Catching up to her, Braeden grabbed
hold of her elbow. He matched her strides easily. "You
know I have a penchant for trains."

She sighed audibly. "And I suppose you're going to tell
me that there are worse affinities, so I should be grateful."

"Affinities?" Braeden grinned teasingly. "You've been reading that dictionary again, haven't you? Practicing up for the university."

"Oh, hush," Alaina replied, trying to do her best to sound aggravated; however, Braeden's teasing could always make her smile.

"That's my girl," he crooned, helping her aboard.

Making his way up the narrow aisle, Braeden located their seats which faced Michael and Jennifer Marie's. He nodded to the pair as he assisted Alaina onto the bench.

"Did you ever hear the story about the *Best Friend of Charleston*?" he asked, leaning sideways so their shoulders touched.

Alaina smiled. "No, I don't believe I ever have."

"Well, the *Friend* was America's first passenger locomotive, and it made its debut in 1831 in Charleston," Braeden began. "But one day, its fireman got tired of hearing the hissing sound of the engine, so he closed the safety valve. A most unfortunate thing to do. The locomotive blew up, killing the fireman."

"How dreadful," Alaina said frowning. "I don't like that story."

"Well, here's another one—it's much nicer. . . ."

Michael Wheeler lifted a dark brow. "Why do you insist upon boring that lovely lady?" he asked, his brown eyes twinkling with amusement.

"Mind your own business, or I'll be forced to challenge you to a duel!"

Michael laughed. "May I remind you that you lost the last one?"

Alaina watched a slow smile spread across Braeden's face.

"You lost a duel?" she queried. "And lived to tell about it? How can that be?"

"It's a long story, my dear."

"Oh?" She raised an imputing brow. "I think I'd rather hear that one than another account of trains."

Alaina heard Michael's rumbling laughter, though he obviously fought to contain it.

"Don't mind him, Laina," Braeden whispered.

"All right, I won't," she whispered back. "Now, tell me the dueling story."

Michael was quick to oblige her. "Braeden and I have a history of fighting over women."

"That's not entirely true." Braeden chuckled and looked at Alaina. "We were twelve years old and scrapping over whom Miss Daisy Marshall, our Sunday school teacher, was most fond—Michael or me."

She smiled into Braeden's eyes while across from her, Jennifer Marie giggled daintily from behind her silk fan.

"Miss Marshall liked me best, of course," Michael said, feigning a pompous air, "but Brae and I decided to do the gentlemanly thing and duel it out—with our slingshots."

"I was always partial to the biblical account of David and Goliath," Braeden admitted with a charming grin.

"Oh, you two," Alaina said with a soft laugh.

"All right, show the ladies your battle wound."

Braeden frowned. "Must I?"

"You must," Michael insisted.

Expelling an annoyed breath, Braeden pushed back a thick lock of blond hair from the very top of his forehead. There Alaina saw an almost perfectly round scar.

"Like David, I must be a man after God's own heart."

"Don't flatter yourself," Braeden muttered in fun.

"I rendered him unconscious for a whole five minutes," Michael told Alaina and Jennifer Marie. "But I thought I'd killed my best friend. I was devastated. I knelt down on the ground beside Braeden, crying and pleading with God to bring him back to life. I even went so far as to promise Brae he could have all of Miss Marshall's affections, which at twelve years old consisted of one of her smiles or, if we were especially fortunate, a verbal greeting." He chuckled. "Then much to my astonishment, Braeden awoke. I was ecstatic, and for years, I thought I'd witnessed a miraculous event."

"A duel," Jennifer Marie crooned, casting a long gaze at Michael and batting her lashes ever so delicately. "How utterly romantic."

"I have sworn off women ever since," Michael stated, returning her stare.

Jennifer Marie gasped. "Say it's not true!"

Michael glanced at Braeden, and Alaina saw that mischievous shimmer in his eyes again. She soon decided he was more of rascal than Braeden, but they definitely fueled each other's antics. Alaina made a mental note to mind her p's and q's around those two!

❧

"I declare! I never thought we'd get here!" Jennifer Marie said as the last of their belongings were brought upstairs to the bedroom she and Alaina would share for the entire weekend. "I never saw so many people in my life!" She flounced on the wide, canopy bed. "And that train ride!" Peeking at Alaina from under beneath her feathery lashes, she confessed, "I don't believe I care to travel in that fashion. Why, my backside is positively numb from those awful, hard benches!"

"Mine as well," Alaina replied, collapsing into a nearby arm chair. "Now why can't trains be as posh as this?" She ran her hand along the blue velvet upholstered armrest.

"That would be a sight better, wouldn't it?"

Alaina nodded.

"Well," Jennifer Marie said, standing to her feet, "I suppose we should change and make ourselves presentable. The party has already started on Aunt Sabrina's rooftop. Why, I heard men shouting encouragements seaward, toward Fort Sumter." She smiled. "Isn't this exciting?"

"Extremely." Alaina stood and pulled out her favorite frock, a simple blue-and-white stripe dress, having a stiff white lacy collar that hugged her throat in a flattering way. But what she truly adored was its fashionable, puffy sleeves.

"I never did get to talk to Michael about anything of significance on the way here," Jennifer Marie stated with a pout as her maid helped her into a crimson silk gown with a V-shaped neckline. "Did you see him looking at me during the journey?"

"I. . .I don't recall," Alaina stammered. The real truth was, Michael Wheeler didn't seem very interested in

Jennifer Marie. He only acknowledged her when propriety dictated, but how to convince her starry-eyed friend of that was a dilemma. Perhaps Braeden could discuss the matter with her. Alaina smiled at one of the maids who offered to button up the back of her dress.

"Well, his head will turn tonight," Jennifer Marie announced assessing herself in the looking glass. She ran a hand down the fitted bodice. "If Michael Wheeler is any kind of man, he'll notice me in this gown." She whirled around, facing Alaina, the sound of her crinoline and dress brushing the carpeted floor. "But I don't suppose I'll capture his attention until after this silly battle is over. Why, I declare! Men these days are positively consumed with war talk."

Alaina agreed. It was all her father, William, and Braeden spoke about lately. As they made their way to the door, she glimpsed her modest reflection in the mirror and surmised that no marriage proposal would likely be forthcoming, either, until the Confederates blew Fort Sumter out of the Atlantic.

As it happened, the fort remained intact and there were no casualties on either side. But the sight was spectacular. Cannon fire exploded like fireworks on Independence Day, entertaining all of Charleston. Mrs. Sabrina Stokes' house was a popular place. High-ranking guests mingled about the rooftop and around the lavishly decorated ballroom which overlooked the harbor.

Finally on Saturday, after two days of fighting, Major Robert Anderson surrendered Fort Sumter to General Pierre Beauregard. The Confederates had tasted their first victory! To celebrate, Mrs. Stokes threw a grand party, just as Jennifer Marie had predicted.

"Here is the dress I promised you," she said, holding the lovely golden gown out to Alaina. The bedroom they shared was littered with Jennifer Marie's clothing. She sighed, her eyes drooping with melancholy. "Now if only I could decide what to wear tonight."

"Oh! This is the most. . ." Alaina swallowed hard. "Why! I've never had such a splendid gift."

"I'm glad you like it. Let's just hope it elicits a marriage proposal. . .from Braeden, that is."

Alaina laughed. "Of course from Braeden. Who else?"

"Indeed." Jennifer Marie stepped closer to her. She tipped her blond head curiously. "I've noticed Michael has been keeping you company quite often this weekend."

"Oh, he just feels badly for me because Braeden has been so preoccupied. Why, he told me so. I mean, Braeden is his best friend, and Michael feels. . .obligated."

"Don't be so naive. If Michael felt so sorry for you, he could easily see to it that my cousin, Suzanna, and her husband attended to you rather than taking the task upon himself."

Alaina frowned. "Well, I. . ."

"It's true. Michael Wheeler has designs on you. I just hope you're not planning to encourage him."

"I'd never do such a thing!"

"Perhaps not intentionally."

Alaina chewed her lower lip, reflecting on the last two days. True, she'd spent a lot of time with Michael and had enjoyed his companionship. It had made up for the sting of Braeden's neglect, although Alaina knew it couldn't be helped. Braeden, strong and courageous—he'd joined the cavalry and she couldn't feel more proud of him. He'd report for duty within the next couple of weeks, and Alaina sensed there would be talk of marriage before he left.

She hoped so, anyway.

"Now, honey, take my advice," Jennifer Marie said sternly. "Stay away from Michael Wheeler."

Alaina nodded, but she knew her friend's instruction would be hard to follow. It wasn't that she invited his solicitations; it was that he sought her out, and she couldn't find it in her heart to be rude to the man. He was charming, friendly, and a proper gentleman at all times. And he was ever so interesting. Why, Alaina scarcely believed him when Michael first told her he liked to paint. He promised to show her his collection someday of the portraits, still life, and pastoral scenes he'd created on wood and canvas. Alaina couldn't wait to see them. She fancied artwork herself.

Yes, they'd enjoyed each other's company, but perhaps tonight things would be different. Perhaps tonight she could remain dutifully at Braeden's side—and perhaps tonight he'd ask her to be his wife!

Chapter 7

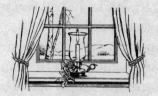

The lavishly-decorated ballroom never ceased to impress Alaina, even though she'd been inside of it quite often during the past couple of days. Looking up at Braeden, she smiled. "You look positively dashing in that gray uniform," she whispered.

"Yes, so you've told me," he replied with a teasing gleam in his brown eyes and a smirk tugging at the corners of his lips.

Alaina blushed and Braeden chuckled. Around them couples made their way to the middle of the parquet floor and began waltzing to the sweet notes wafting from the string ensemble in the far corner of the ballroom.

"Are you sure I can't get you some punch?"

"I'm quite sure," Alaina drawled politely. "Thank you."

Braeden scanned the elegantly clad guests. "Hm, I see my dear cousin has found another suitor."

Alaina gasped. "Really? Where?"

"Over there. See her?"

Following the direction of his gaze, she spotted Jennifer Marie flirting shamelessly with a uniformed officer. "Why, I thought she was sweet on Michael. In fact, I was going to speak to you about that."

Braeden peered at her expectantly.

"I noticed Michael's lack of interest toward Jennifer Marie," she began, "and I hoped you would be the one to break the news to her."

Braeden chuckled. "Alaina, my dear, at least four people have broken the news to Jennifer Marie with regard to Michael. She simply won't believe any of us. Michael, himself, tried to explain his feelings. In a word, he said she's much too bold for his liking."

"And she's not a believer."

"That's the biggest problem, yes."

"Oh, Braeden, I wish Jennifer Marie would come to know the Lord."

"We all do, Laina." He smiled warmly into her eyes. "Keep praying."

"I will," she promised, gazing up at him adoringly. In that moment, no one else in the world seemed to matter except the two of them.

"Braeden! Come quick!" William exclaimed breathlessly, rushing up to him. He, too, had enlisted and wore a crisp, gray uniform.

"What is it, Will?" Braeden asked, a little frown furrowing his brow.

"It's General Beauregard. He's here!"

"Surely, you jest!"

"It's true. Hurry! You must hear what he has to say!"

Braeden turned to Alaina, and her heart sank despite the apologetic look on his face. "I'll return shortly. Wait for me?"

She nodded. Then, watching his retreating form, Alaina gathered her golden skirts and carefully sat on a nearby chair, hoping not to wrinkle the lavish skirts. She determined not to sulk as she turned her gaze to the happy couples gracefully waltzing around the room. Mama always said dancing was a sin, and as Alaina observed how closely Jennifer Marie's partner held her in his arms, she decided Mama had a good case.

"I don't suppose you waltz, Miss Alaina."

Looking up to her right, she spied Michael Wheeler. He wasn't in uniform but looked dapper in spite of his somber attire. He'd told her it was the best suit he owned and he saved it especially for funerals. Alaina had laughed at the humorous remark. "No, I don't waltz," she replied in answer to his question. "I don't dance at all."

"You're a fine, Christian woman." Michael sat in the chair next to hers. "I don't dance all the dances, but I'm partial to a brisk reel."

"Reel? I don't know what that is."

The music stopped and the ensemble announced their short intermission.

"It's a lively dance," Michael explained, "and involves two or more couples. They hook arms and swing around from partner to partner, moving in a figure-eight."

"Hm. . ." She gave it but a moment's thought. Smoothing out her skirt with gloved hands, she considered Michael with a sardonic grin. "And why, may I ask, aren't you listening to illustrious General Beauregard?"

He pondered the inquiry for several moments. "Guess I don't care to hear him gloat over this first victory. Call me a skeptic, call me a pessimist, but I just don't believe the South is going to have such an easy time of it. We're farmers. We're gentlemen. We're not soldiers."

Alaina stifled an indignant snort. "Well, I declare! You're the only man in all of South Carolina with any sense!"

Michael chuckled.

"But I hope you won't misunderstand," Alaina added seriously. "I am extremely proud of my brother and Braeden for volunteering."

"And I have every intention of doing my part," he assured her, gazing out over the consorting crowd. Then he turned and faced Alaina and a kind of wistfulness entered his dark brown eyes. "But not just yet. I need to make certain that Pa will be able to run the farm since I know my two brothers will enlist—if they haven't already."

She nodded understandingly. He'd already informed her that he was the youngest of his brothers, all just a little more than a year apart. His mother had died when they were young, and his two older brothers had been in and out of various scrapes, although they appeared to be showing signs of settling down. But of the three Wheeler boys, Alaina gathered that Michael was the most loyal to his father. In fact, it sounded to her like Michael was the one who held his family together.

"I have every confidence that you'll do what's right," she said, smiling.

An expression crossed his face that hinted at his chagrin. He stood. "Shall we get some air?"

Alaina nodded and Michael helped her to her feet.

"That's a lovely dress," he said, escorting her through

the opened double doors and out to the verandah.

"Why, thank you. Jennifer Marie had it made for me—for my upcoming eighteenth birthday. Wasn't that just the sweetest thing for her to do?"

"Yes, it was. She can be very thoughtful." Michael glanced over his shoulder before backing up against the wrought-iron rail. "I see she's found another diversion."

"Seems you're off the hook," Alaina quipped. They shared a laugh. "Oh, now, that wasn't nice of me to say, was it?" she stated in self-admonishment. "Jennifer Marie has only been gracious and kind to me, and I had no cause to speak of her in that dim light."

"I'll take it to my grave, Alaina," Michael whispered, leaning close to her ear. "I swear."

She felt her face flush as she gripped the railing and stared out over the black expanse of the Atlantic Ocean. Jennifer Marie's warning about Michael having designs on her rang in Alaina's mind. Was she encouraging his attentions by standing beside him out on the verandah? But there were others around. It wasn't as if they were alone and unchaperoned.

"It's a nice night," Michael remarked.

"A bit chilly."

"Just look at all those stars. . . ."

Alaina glanced up at the sky and smiled, thinking about how her father liked to create all sorts of stories about angels riding through the galaxies.

Michael turned and his coat sleeve brushed against her satin-clad arm. "You're quite fetching in the moonlight," he murmured. "Braeden's a lucky man."

She opened her mouth to question his motives, but

suddenly an enthusiastic melody accompanied by hardy applause captured her attention. Michael listened a moment, then dropped his head back and laughed. "Come on," he said, grabbing her hand.

Alaina balked. "Michael, I—"

"It's harmless. Here watch for a minute."

He stood behind her, his palms resting on her shoulders, while Alaina watched a couple skip up a row paneled with ladies on one side and men on the other. When they reached the end, the couple locked elbows and swung around one way, then the other, before making their way behind the group and standing at the beginning of the line. The women stepped forward and curtseyed. The men stepped forward and bowed. Then next couple proceeded in the same manner, but when they reached the end, they did a different jig before returning to the beginning of the queue.

"See, it's easy," Michael said. "When a couple reaches the end of the line, they do a dance step of their choosing. Let's join in."

Alaina still had reservations, but before she knew it he had pulled her into the middle of the ballroom and they were folded into the clapping, chanting throng.

"Alaina!" Jennifer Marie called, sporting rosy cheeks, "isn't this fun?"

She wasn't sure yet, but nodded nevertheless.

Respectively, Alaina followed the other ladies and stepped forward and curtseyed. Directly across from her, Michael stepped forward and bowed. He gave her a rascally wink, and she arched a dubious brow.

Finally it was her turn with Michael. Arm-in-arm,

they promenaded up the middle of the row of humanity and at the end, he pulled her into his arms and they twirled around in a close embrace before he released her.

"That was shameful," Alaina scolded him under her breath once they'd gotten back into line.

He feigned a curious frown. "You think?"

"I know."

Michael chuckled.

"Michael, you dickens!" Jennifer Marie exclaimed. The gaiety of her tone was laced with disbelief.

Alaina mouthed the words, "told you so," to Michael.

He smirked, his dark eyes shining with amusement. However, he was much more a gentleman on their next turn when he simply took her hand and led her into a pirouette. Alaina couldn't help giggling as the room spun around her. When it stopped, she found herself staring into a pair of very unhappy, golden-flecked eyes.

"Braeden!"

"I believe you and I have some talking to do." He took her elbow and unceremoniously led her from the ballroom.

At last they stood, face-to-face in a darkened hallway.

"What do you think you're doing?" he demanded in a hushed but angry voice.

"I, um, well. . ." Alaina swallowed nervously. "It was all quite innocent, really."

"Is that so?" Braeden narrowed his gaze. "Well, I have a notion to confront my *innocent* best friend about this scandalous incident."

"Scandalous?"

"What else would you call it?" Braeden narrowed

his gaze. "You have disgraced me in front of family and friends alike. You, *dancing*, of all things. And then I come to learn from my sister that you and Michael have been quite chummy ever since we arrived in Charleston. Is that true?"

Alaina shifted uneasily. "Yes."

He released an audible sigh. "Laina, I thought you were above all this nonsense." The disappointment in his voice was quite evident. "And here I thought you'd be a good example for my cousin. But just exactly who is influencing whom?"

Alaina gasped at the indirect insult. "Well, it's your fault that Michael and I have kept company. Why, you've spent scarcely ten minutes with me this whole weekend, what with all this war business. For all your indifference, I wish I never would have come. Dancing with Michael is the most fun I've had in days!"

Fury swelled in her chest as she pushed past Braeden, avoiding his attempt to grab her arm. Angry tears blurred her vision as she took to the staircase. She heard Braeden call her name, but ignored him. Reaching another shadowed hallway, she ran to the bedroom she shared with Jennifer Marie and closed the door soundly behind her. Two startled maids gaped at her untimely arrival.

"You in fo' the evenin', Miss?" one of them asked.

Doing her best to swallow her emotion, she could only shrug. At her back, the door pushed open, and Jennifer Marie entered the room. She waved off her servants then gushed all over Alaina.

"You poor thing. That cousin of mine is an absolute

scoundrel. When I saw you two leave the ballroom, I followed, and I heard every harsh word he spoke to you. But, I declare! You handled the likes of him just fine."

"On the contrary. I've muddled up everything. My attitude was all wrong," Alaina lamented. "I didn't have that meek and quiet spirit every godly woman should possess. I acted like a bona fide shrew!"

"Well, knock me over with a feather," Jennifer Marie replied, wearing a shocked expression. "You're the first Christian I ever did know to make a mistake. Why, I thought Christians were holier than God Almighty."

Alaina shook her head. "That's our standard, but we fall far short of it."

"You mean you're not perfect?"

"Did I ever claim to be?"

"Well, no. . ." Jennifer blushed slightly. "It's just that you're always so. . .good. My cousin Braeden is the same way. He's genuinely good. Why, he's the only one on my mother's side of the family who's ever cared about me."

Alaina wiped away an errant tear. "Well, he will never ask me to marry him, seeing what I've done."

"Oh, he'd be a fool to let a little thing like this—"

A knock sounded followed by Braeden's voice, calling for Alaina to come out and speak with him.

"I'll handle the brute," Jennifer Marie promised with an artful grin. She sashayed to the door and opened it very slowly. "Go away, Braeden."

"I want to talk to Alaina."

"She's. . .well, she can't talk."

"Why not?"

"She's crying her eyes out, that's why. Shame on

71

you. You're a veritable beast!"

"Jennifer Marie," he began in a warning tone. "I insist that you—"

"As for Alaina and Michael," she continued, cutting off his reply, "well, I don't know why you're so upset. It isn't as if you've *proposed marriage*," she stated emphatically. "Alaina doesn't belong to you. You have no claim on her."

Behind the door, Alaina chewed her lower lip apprehensively. She could practically hear Braeden seething out in the hallway.

In that moment, Jennifer Marie looked her way and winked. "There, there, honey, don't sob like that. Your sweet face will get all red and blotchy." She turned back to her cousin. "Excuse me. I must tend to Alaina. She's distraught."

"Then I ought to do the tending," Braeden stated brusquely, sticking his booted foot in the doorway so Jennifer Marie couldn't shut him out.

"You? Why, you're the cause of her suffering!"

A pause.

"Alaina?" he called despite the feminine blockade of white silk and ruffles between them. "Laina-honey, now I didn't mean to make you cry. I was just. . .well, I was jealous! Now come out here and talk to me where I can see you."

Jennifer Marie donned a winning smile. She turned and, taking Alaina's wrist, hauled her toward the threshold. "I think you two ought to kiss and make up this instant," she drawled sweetly. "You're splendid together, can't you see that?"

Alaina chanced a peek at Braeden, her handsome, blond Confederate soldier who stood staring back at her with thoughtful, questioning brown eyes.

"Is that true, Laina?" he asked softly. "Are we splendid together?"

She nodded out a subtle reply, feeling her chin quiver ever so slightly. "I'm so sorry I disgraced you," she blurted. "I didn't mean it. Truly, I didn't."

"I know. I guess some things between Michael and me haven't changed since we were twelve years old." Braeden held out his hand to her. When Alaina took it, he drew her into an snug embrace. "I love you so much, Laina. I've loved you since the first night we met."

"I love you, too," she murmured into his shoulder.

Watching, Jennifer Marie sighed dreamily, although the couple was scarcely aware anyone else on earth even existed in that moment.

Braeden pulled back, holding Alaina at arm's length. "Will you marry me?" he asked, searching her face beneath the soft glow of the wall sconce. "Will you be my wife?"

"Yes, I will," she replied in a heartbeat.

Lowering his head, he kissed her with promise while beside them, Jennifer Marie clapped her gloved hands and declared, "Why, this is the happiest day of my life!"

Chapter 8

Alaina scanned the deserted, dirt road and distinctly remembered the last time she'd seen her husband; it was going on two years.

It was in the spring of '64 and Braeden was faithfully serving in the cavalry on South Carolina's coast. He'd been granted a couple days' leave—a reward for reenlisting. Sipping strong coffee on the back porch as the nippy, April wind swirled around budding treetops, Braeden filled her in on everything the newspapers had failed to report about the war. He said it was amazing that most of the state remained untouched by all the fighting. He still believed the South could win despite its devastating loss eight months earlier at Gettysburg.

A great sadness enveloped her now as she turned her gaze to the dreary, December sky. Zek confirmed that Braeden had been wounded, but he wasn't dead. . . until the Yankees captured him. Alaina closed her eyes against the horrors she'd heard about Federal prison camps and emaciated Confederate soldiers. There was little hope that Braeden made it out alive—especially since he'd been injured first. The hardiest of men returned from Yankee prisons resembling mere shadows of their former selves. Surely Braeden was dead.

"Alaina!"

She glanced over her should at the sound of her mother-in-law's voice. Moments later, Eloise appeared at the doorway.

"What are you doing out there? You're liable to catch your death."

"I'd welcome it." She looked back out toward the road, ignoring Mother McKenna's exasperated sigh.

"You've been more melancholy than ever since Zek came home with news of Braeden's capture. Well, my dear, you need to develop some backbone. I've lost two sons, but do you see me wallowing in self-pity? No. Now, here. . ." The older woman stepped onto the porch and thrust a jar at her. "Take this vegetable soup over to the Wheeler place and make yourself useful. Jonathan and Zek are over there trying to help Michael out, and I promised those men I'd fix supper."

Alaina obediently took the large container.

"And while you're on your way," Eloise added as wisps of her faded blond hair blew onto her aging cheek, "you might try counting your blessings for a change. Our home wasn't burned. The Yankees didn't find our personal valuables. We're luckier than most."

"Yes, ma'am."

Alaina's eyes filled at the sting of her mother-in-law's rebuke. She crossed the yard tearfully and started down the road. Off in the distance, she heard hammering as Papa Jonathan and Zek attempted to help Michael rebuild his home. The task was a daunting one. Half of the

Wheeler house had been ruined by fire and since timber and sundry other supplies were no longer available, reconstruction was nearly an impossibility.

As she walked on, Alaina suddenly thought about Jennifer Marie. One of the more precious memories she held dear to her heart was the day her friend became a Christian. It was back in '62 and Jennifer Marie had just learned that the man she'd fallen in love with, Major Uriah Perkins, had been killed. He was the one she'd met at her aunt's party the night Braeden proposed, and it wasn't long after Alaina's marriage that Jennifer Marie was making great wedding plans of her own.

But on that particular day, her buggy had rolled up the gravely road to the McKenna's house and lurched to a halt. Out she'd stepped, wearing a stunning black ensemble that caused Alaina's knees to weaken in trepidation.

"It's not Braeden, is it, Jennifer Marie?" Alaina had asked, her chores all but forgotten. "Please, tell me it's not Braeden."

"No, it's. . .it's Uriah!" she cried. "A neighbor brought this to me last evening, and. . .look!"

Alaina took the crumpled, sheet bearing a list of names of the dead. Yes, Uriah's name was among them. Braeden's was not. Feeling relieved for herself and a deep, heart-piercing sadness for her friend, Alaina burst into tears. "Oh, I'm so sorry for you."

They embraced, then Alaina led Jennifer Marie into the house and made her a cup of tea. Mother McKenna joined them in the parlor, fussing over her niece like a hen. Jennifer Marie, however, would not be consoled.

"D—do you th—think Uriah's in h—heaven?" she stammered in between sobs.

"I couldn't say," replied Mother McKenna. "I didn't know the man."

"He was good and kind. . .the most wonderful man on earth. Why, Uriah hated the thought of killing— even killing Yankees. He was an upstanding, moral person who never even once tried to take liberties with me—even when I wished he would."

Alaina couldn't help smiling inwardly at the remark.

"Those are fine characteristics for a man," Eloise began, "but they don't guarantee a home in Heaven. Only faith in the Lord Jesus Christ can do that."

"But Mama said she took me to the church when I was an infant and had me baptized. She told me that makes me a Christian."

"No, I'm afraid it doesn't. If being baptized as an infant could save a person's soul, our Lord would not have had to go to the cross and suffer for our sins." Eloise stood and fetched her worn, leather-bound Bible. Sitting back down, she ruffled through its delicate pages. "Here. . .listen to this. It's from the Book of Romans, chapter three: 'For all have sinned, and come short of the glory of God; Being justified freely by his grace through the redemption that is in Christ Jesus: Whom God hath set forth to be a propitiation through faith in his blood, to declare his righteousness for the remission of sins that are past. . . To declare, I say, at this time his righteousness: that he might be just, and the justifier of him which believeth in Jesus.' "

Looking up from God's Word, Eloise gave Jennifer

Marie a warm smile. "It doesn't say a person ought to be baptized in order to enter the kingdom of God, does it? It says that Jesus is the justifier for all who will believe in Him."

Jennifer Marie dabbed at her swollen eyes with a lace handkerchief. "I don't know if Uriah believed that or not."

"My dear, it's not our place to judge. But you can choose your eternal destination here and now."

Alaina snapped from her musings as Michael's house came into view. Walking up the stony dirt road, she smiled to herself remembering how Jennifer Marie had accepted God's free gift of salvation—His Son, Jesus Christ.

You're so lucky, Jennifer Marie. You're in Heaven with the Savior!

"Well, look who's come to pay me a social call," Michael said, his voice carrying across the wintery brown lawn. He jumped from the two foot ledge on which he'd been working and dropped his hammer. The left side of his white shirt sleeve was pinned halfway up and Alaina marveled at how much Michael accomplished despite his disability. "If I knew you were coming, Lain," he said with a grin, "I would have set out the tea cakes in the parlor here." He nodded toward the scorched end of his home.

Alaina shook her head at him, wondering how he could make such a flip remark about something as dreadful as a burned out parlor. "I brought you, Papa Jonathan, and Zek some soup." When she reached the porch, she handed him the jar.

"Very kind of you. Thanks. But you just missed your father-in-law. He started back to your place through the field several minutes ago."

"I guess Papa Jonathan will have his soup at home, then."

Narrowing his gaze, Michael searched her face. Alaina turned away, brushing a few dark strands of hair off her cheek.

"You've been crying again," he observed.

"What's not to cry about?" She stepped onto the porch, inspecting the site for new repairs. "But let's not talk about it. How are things coming along here?"

"They're coming, but very slowly."

Alaina nodded, still aware of Michael's concern for her.

"If I could finish getting these windows boarded up, the cold winter wind won't be able to howl through the rest of the house." He looked skyward. "I think we're in for some weather. Rain, maybe snow."

Alaina pulled her woolen cape around her more tightly. "You could always stay with us, Michael."

He fixed his gaze on her and grinned. "Jonathan said the same thing just this morning. He said I could have Kirk's room. But, I. . .well, I don't think that's a wise idea, considering how I feel about you, Lain."

She felt herself blush, yet her heart crimped painfully. While evidence seemed to indicate that Braeden was dead, she didn't want to accept it. But perhaps it was time to force herself to do so. Maybe Mother McKenna was right—maybe she needed to "develop some backbone" and get on with her life. She turned to Michael, noting his ardent expression and the light of sincerity in his chocolate-brown eyes. He loved her. It was obvious. Maybe she should just marry him and make up her mind to be happy again.

"Why, Miz Laina, I didn't know you was here," Zek said, coming to stand in the front doorway.

She looked away from Michael and smiled wanly into Zek's dark face. "Mother McKenna made some vegetable soup. She had me run it over."

"Warm soup. . .that shore sounds good." He glanced at Michael and grinned. "I'll take that soup fo' you, Massah Michael." Michael held out the container to Zek who took it then motioned Alaina inside. "C'mon, now, it's mighty col' out here!"

Alaina followed him in and glanced around the house. There were stairs to the immediate right which led up to the second floor. To the left, the parlor and dining room were boarded off to keep the December wind at bay. She walked down the corridor where pieces of salvaged furniture and Michael's damaged paintings lined the wall. He was so talented, and to see his artwork in such state caused Alaina's heart to sink. Entering the kitchen, she saw the charred remains of the cookhouse.

"One of the bedrooms upstairs is now safe enough for me to sleep in," Michael said, coming in behind her, "so I don't have to sleep in the kitchen anymore."

"Such devastation." Alaina expelled a huff and whirled around, facing Michael. "Those Yankees had no cause to do this to our homes and our land."

He smiled at her indignation. "It's war, Lain. What

do you think happens in a war?"

"Well, women ought to run the next war, that's what I think. Things would be a sight better."

Michael hooted. "Now *that* would be a phenomenon—women running a war. Let's see. . .you'd stab the enemy with your vicious tongues and confuse them so greatly with gossip and rumors they wouldn't know which direction they were moving in."

"Oh, hush." She gave him a leveled stare. "And I do not gossip or backbite. Not all women do, you know."

"You could always render the enemy senseless with your parasol or throttle them with your lace shawl."

"Why, Michael Wheeler, you stop mocking at once!"

He laughed some more. "Oh, now, I'm only teasing, Lain."

In the far corner of the room, Zek was chuckling softly as he spooned the soup into bowls. "You best be careful, Massah Michael. My mama used to say ain't no fury on God's green earth like that of a woman scorned."

Michael feigned an expression of dread, and Alaina gave him another severe look in reply. "Aw, Laina, don't be angry with me," he said, sobering. "It's just that you're so pretty when you're riled. Your cheeks get all rosy. . . ."

Michael touched the side of her face with the backs of his knuckles, but Alaina slapped his hand away in aggravation.

"I done warned you, Massah Michael." Zek chuckled heartily, bringing three bowls of soup to the table.

"Oh, Zek, I didn't want any," Alaina started to explain.

Suddenly the sound of horse's hooves could be heard out front. Alaina froze. No one had horses anymore, except for the. . .

"Yankees!" she cried, turning to Michael as wild, icy fright coursed through her veins.

"It's all right. Don't panic."

"What if it's more raiders? Why, you heard what they did to poor Mary Baily—and then they killed her husband!"

"Shh, Lain. . ." He looked over her head at Zek. "You know where my gun is."

"Yessuh, and I knows how to use it, too."

Michael nodded and then gave Alaina a little hug around the shoulders. "I'll go see what this is all about. You stay right here."

She inclined her head weakly.

Zek already had Michael's gun in his hands as he made his way to the front of the house. In spite of her promise, Alaina followed. Peeking over Zek's broad shoulder, she saw Michael walk out and greet two Federal officers, clad in crisp, blue uniforms. They each sat astride a sleek roan.

"Shoot them, Zek!" she ordered spitefully.

"Now, Miz Laina, that'd be cold-blooded killin'. I cain't do that."

"But they've taken so much from us. . .burned our fields, our farms, looted our homes then set them on fire, killed our cattle. They murdered William, Kirk. . . Braeden." Alaina fairly choked on her sudden tears. "I despise the very sight of those horrid men!"

"Look at them, Miz Laina," Zek answered softly.

"They's just like us. They's lost brothers, too."

"I don't care. I hate them!"

"That's cold-blooded killin', too, Miz Laina. Jesus said so. He said hatred's the same as murder."

She swallowed her next bout of wrath, knowing Zek spoke the truth. She had a heart full of bitterness. In shameful silence, she watched as Michael conversed with the officers.

"You gots to forgive. I did. An' as fo' Massah Braeden, well, I been thinkin'. . ."

Alaina turned toward him expectantly. Zek had his gun pointed directly at the two soldiers and his trained, dark gaze never strayed from the potentially deadly situation outside.

"I been thinkin' it'd be just like Massah Braeden to hear what Sherman did to pore So' Carolina, and it'd be just like him to go West to Texas like most folks is doin'. Why, Massah Braeden probably tried to write or wire y'all 'n' let you know he's alive, but with them Yankess ever'where, his messages didn't get through no-how! But he's got hisself a plan for him 'n' us an' it'd be just like him git home fer Christmas so he can tell us all 'bout it."

"Oh, Zek," Alaina replied dejectedly, "I'd like to believe that, but how would Braeden have ever survived—wounded and in prison camp? It's not possible."

"Anythin's possible. With God all things is possible."

Alaina didn't argue but shifted her gaze and watched curiously as the two officers galloped away on horseback. She felt certain the men were headed to the McKenna farm, and she was suddenly glad that Papa Jonathan had left earlier. On his way back to the house now, Michael was reading a parchment of some sort. Zek lowered his gun and murmured a prayer of thanks.

"As if I didn't already know my tax bill is due," Michael groused, entering the cluttered foyer. He grunted in disgust. "And by the first of the year! Well, I don't have the kind of money they're asking for. Who does? The Confederate dollar is only worth a little more than one cent to the Union dollar. Who can even afford a sack of flour these days—five hundred dollars for flour? Such an atrocity! They're trying to break us. Break South Carolinians because the war started here. Can't they see we're already broken?"

"Mercy," Zek muttered, shaking his dark head.

"Oh, Michael. . ." A little sob caught in Alaina's throat.

"Now, Lain, don't cry." Michael's tone changed as he stepped forward and slipped his right arm around her waist, pulling her against him. "Don't cry," he whispered against her temple. "We'll think of something."

"I think Miz Laina gots to go home," Zek announced sternly. "That's what I think." He took a firm hold of her elbow and fairly tore her out of Michael's embrace.

She gave Zek a startled look, but the angry fire in his eyes kept her from arguing. "I be takin' you home right now. C'mon."

Alaina complied. On the way out, she glanced over her shoulder and saw Michael's mystified expression. She was certain it matched her own.

"I'll come back, Massah Michael, don' you worry,"

Zek called from the porch, guiding Alaina down the steps. "I said I'd help with rebuildin', an' I won' go back on my word. But Miz Laina's gotta go home this minute or Massah Braeden. . .he gonna have my hide!"

Chapter 9

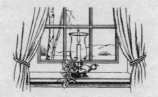

"Zek! Don't walk so fast!" Alaina cried breathlessly. The large man slowed his pace. "For pity's sake, what's gotten into you? And what did you mean by, Braeden will have your hide?"

He stopped on the road and faced her. "I knowed Massah Braeden since we was born. We gots our whuppin's together when we was naughty boys. Why, we didn' even care we's a different color 'til Massah Braeden went to school and someone tole him different. After awhile, Massah Braeden said he didn' care I's black and he's white. And I didn' neither.

"And I know Massah Michael, too," Zek continued. "I know he's Massah Braeden's best friend, but Massah Braeden and me. . .we's tighter than best friends. I know how Massah Braeden thinks, and I know there's some things he won' share with his best friend, no how! One o' them things is his woman. And if I stood by and let that happen, I'd get mine. . .right after Massah Michael got his!"

"Now, wait a minute, Zek," Alaina said with hands on hips, her chin lifted defensively. "Michael says he loves me and he wants to marry me. Everyone else says Braeden is dead. Mother McKenna thinks he's buried in a mass grave somewhere. She tells me to get on with my life and stop pining for my husband who's never coming home. Michael's told me the same thing."

Zek stood there listening to her argument, staring off into the distant, charred remains of woods across the road.

"For so long, I've been the only one who's had any hope, but it's rapidly diminishing." Alaina heaved a weary sigh. "I almost believe that if Braeden hasn't come home by now, he never will."

"Miz Laina," Zek replied, bringing his gaze back to hers, "I cain't explain how I know this, but I know Massah Braeden ain't dead. When I saw Massah Michael touch you jest now, I knowed it wasn' right jest as if Massah Braeden could walk through a door any time and see it fer hisself. Then we'd all be in fer it."

The remark gave Alaina pause. Her husband's possessive nature had always caused her to feel loved and cherished. Nevertheless, she wouldn't want to reckon with it.

They began walking again, but this time at a more leisurely stride.

"Miz Laina, I think if'n Massah Braeden is alive, he'll be sure to get hisself home fer Christmas. He wouldn' want to miss another one with his family. Massah Braeden always loved Christmas."

"Yes. . ." Alaina recalled the only Christmas she and Braeden shared. He had been as excited as a child, picking at the goodies his mother baked and teasing his brother Kirk about presents, and yet the holiday's true meaning wasn't lost on him. He had always kept his focus on the Savior's birth and why it was so significant to mankind.

Contrition swelled in her chest at the memory. If Braeden came home for Christmas this year, what would he find? A faithless wife who'd been self-absorbed in sorrow and bitterness? Well, perhaps she'd had a right to her feelings, but she'd given them free rein for far too long.

"Zek," she said in a broken, little voice, "tomorrow's Christmas Eve."

"Yes'm, it is."

"I haven't begun to prepare."

"No, ma'am."

"We haven't even cut down a tree. . .supposing there's an evergreen somewhere to be felled."

"I could check down by the swamp."

"Would you?"

Zek nodded.

"And we should find something to take to the neighbors. Why, they're in dire straits just like us. Perhaps there's some venison left, and Mother McKenna and I could cook it up into little meals to pass out."

"That sounds awful good, Miz Laina."

"And then, of course, there's our own Christmas dinner to think about." She quickened her step. "I've got so much to do!"

Zek chuckled. "Yes'm."

Alaina made her way up to the house. If the soldiers had been there, they'd come and gone. *Help me forgive them, Father,* she silently prayed, entering in a flurry. Her busy thoughts suddenly fueled the enthusiasm Alaina had thought died with her loved ones.

"Mother McKenna! I just realized tomorrow's Christmas Eve and I haven't done a single thing to prepare for the occasion."

"Oh, hush, child," Eloise said in mild reprimand. "Christmas won't visit our house this year."

"But—"

"How can you even think of celebrating? My sister and her husband are dead. Jennifer Marie is gone, Kirk died in battle, and Braeden. . .Braeden is gone, too. The Yankees disposed of our cows and chickens. Our land has been depreciated by fire. These are dark times and all we can do is survive one day to the next as God sees fit, doing our best to accomplish what we can. But celebrate? That's out of the question."

"You told me to count my blessings, Mother McKenna," Alaina said before casting a curious glance at her father-in-law who sat at the dining room table with his balding head in his hands. "At least we've got our home."

"Not for long," Jonathan replied, lifting his gaze. His eyes beheld a vacant, defeated look. "We can't pay our taxes."

"No one can."

"Is that supposed to be a consolation?" Eloise charged. "We'll all be homeless. So what?"

Suddenly Alaina saw her in-laws for what they had become. Once a kind, gentlewoman, her mother-in-law was now calloused. Her father-in-law, always capable and cheerfully robust, had turned forlorn, brokenhearted.

But, then again, hadn't they all?

"Couldn't we forget our suffering for the next two days?" Alaina asked, tears springing into her eyes. "It's Christmas. There'll be plenty of time to fret over the tax bill afterward."

The older couple glanced at each other, considering the request.

"I guess it wouldn't hurt to be cheerful for a while," Eloise stated at last.

Jonathan agreed, albeit reluctantly. "Grief isn't all that easy to let go of, but I'll try."

"Wonderful!" Alaina declared, feeling as though she had some purpose to her life again—and that purpose was to bring Christmas into the hearts of others. And, perhaps, Lord willing, the joy of the season would stay with them and see them through their future trials. Perhaps it would even bring Braeden home!

❧

"Miz Ellie! Miz Laina! Look here what I found!"

The two women turned from where they stood at the kitchen table, mixing up cornmeal, and gaped in surprise as Zek hauled in a large tree.

"Goodness!" Alaina gasped.

Her mother-in-law smiled.

"An' guess what else Massah Jonathan and me found down by the creek?"

"What?" Eloise asked, tipping her head and looking amused.

"A cow. A real-live milkin' cow. Don' know who it

could belong to. Massah Jonathan is out askin' neighbors if'n it's theirs. And she milks real good. Don' look sick neither."

"Maybe some fool Yankee turned her loose, not knowing cows will die if they're not milked."

"Milk," Alaina said wistfully. "I haven't had milk since Mrs. Tanner brought over a pail for us weeks ago."

Eloise turned toward her. "Do you know what we could make if we had milk? And maybe an egg or two?"

"Johnnycake." Alaina grinned.

"Go see if Michael's chickens laid any more."

Alaina nodded, but Zek stood in her way, holding onto the end of the tree trunk. "I best be the one goin' to Massah Michael," he told her with a worried frown knitting his thick, black brow.

"That's not necessary, Zek," she replied firmly. "I know my place. I'm Braeden's wife."

He grinned broadly. "Yes'm."

With their newly-chopped Christmas tree out of the way, Alaina took to the winter-barren field and the well-worn trail that cut through both properties. The Wheeler farm came into view, and she strode purposefully to the house. "Michael?" she called through the door.

He appeared within moments. "Lain. . .what brings you here?"

"Eggs. Might you have any to spare?"

"Haven't checked recently." He leaned against the doorjamb, his one hand tucked into the pocket of his trousers. He seemed in no hurry to do her bidding. "I've made up my mind. I'm going West. There's land for the taking out there."

"You're leaving South Carolina?"

He nodded. "I've been thinking about it for a while now, but only just decided today." He paused, his gaze darkening earnestly. "I want you to come with me."

She shook her head. "I can't."

"Braeden's dead."

"We don't know that for sure, and until we do, I'm a married woman."

"Oh, Lain. . ." Michael looked heavenward and sighed in exasperation. "What if you never know for sure?"

"Then I can never remarry."

He narrowed his dark gaze at her. "You would deny us both happiness just to be true to a. . .a memory?"

Alaina looked down at her shabby, leather shoes and chewed the corner of her lower lip in dismay. She didn't want to hurt Michael, yet she had to somehow make him understand.

"You're a wonderful man," she said, meeting his probing gaze once more, "and you deserve to marry a woman who loves you. But it's not me. I love Braeden. . . and I always will." A wounded expression flittered across his swarthy features and Alaina knew her words had met their mark. "I'm sorry," she murmured.

"I know I could change your mind if you'd give me the chance."

Alaina shook her head.

"Well," he said on a dejected sigh, "then I guess there really isn't any reason for me to stay in Richland County."

"Will you stay until after Christmas at least?"

"Would it make a difference to you?"

Alaina shook her head once more. "I've decided to wait here for Braeden—for the rest of my life if I have to."

He clenched his jaw and gazed out over the ruins-strewn yard. He seemed to be fighting his emotions. The very sight made Alaina want to weep, but she held her tears in check.

Finally, Michael composed himself enough to face her once more. He reached out to touch her cheek, but Alaina drew back. At his puzzled, injured look, she said, "I'm a married woman. Remember?" She felt wretched, adding to his misery; however, she'd made her decision. Better he grieve now than marry a woman who didn't love him—or worse, marry a woman who was still his best friend's wife!

She tipped her head and forced a smile. "Now, what about those eggs, Michael?"

Chapter 10

A fine, freezing mist began to fall on Christmas Eve morning. Beneath the gloomy skies, Michael had loaded everything he owned into his wagon before driving over to say good-bye to the McKennas.

"You sure you don't want to spend Christmas with us before you go West, son?" Papa Jonathan asked, a sad expression on his face. "We're going to miss you 'round here."

"I'll miss y'all, too," he drawled, and Alaina knew he purposely avoided her gaze.

"Weather could get worse," said Mother McKenna. "Won't you wait until the storm passes?"

Michael shook his dark head and gave them each a parting smile. Finally he turned to Alaina. "You tell Braeden that I'm sorry I missed his homecoming."

"I will," she promised.

A wistfully amused gleam suddenly entered his eyes. He grinned. "You know how I'll always remember you, Lain? In a golden dress with black, brocade trim, twirling around and laughing like you don't have a care in the world."

Embarrassed that he should recall the sorry incident, Alaina threw him a quelling look.

He chuckled, and taking up his mule's reins single-handedly, he slapped its backside and started off toward the road.

"Bye, Massah Michael," Zek said, looking misty-eyed.

"I'll write if I get a chance," he replied. "Maybe y'all can come out and visit me on my ranch someday."

"God be with you, Michael," Alaina called. "We'll be praying for you."

"I love you. . . I love you all!"

They stood on the front porch, Alaina, Zek, Jonathan, and Eloise, and watched Michael's wagon roll down the lonely, winding road.

"It's a horrid day to travel," Mother McKenna said. "Why, that boy is liable to catch his death."

"He'll be all right," Papa Jonathan replied. "He's lived through worse than a little cold rain."

Alaina shivered and walked into the house. Soon everyone was back inside and Zek was stoking the fire. There was still much to be done in preparation for Christmas, but the dreary weather and Michael's departure had dampened their spirits.

Until Zek started singing.

"Hark! The herald angels sing,
" 'Glory to the newborn King;
"Peace on earth, and mercy mild,
"God and sinners reconciled!' "

Then Alaina joined in. Soon Mother McKenna was tapping her toe and Papa Jonathan was humming along.

That afternoon, Suzanna and her family came to visit, bringing with them two plump pheasants ready to roast. God had provided their Christmas dinner. Later, they went to the evening service. Afterwards, Alaina and Eloise handed out venison stew and cornbread to families—some having had nothing to eat in days. The gifts of food were accepted with much gratitude.

"My, but that did my heart good," Eloise said as they rode home in the back of the Reynolds' wagon. Suzanna and her husband were travelling in the other direction to their farm and since Michael left, the McKennas no longer had convenient transportation. But the Reynolds insisted their place wasn't too far out of the way. Though there was a biting chill to the wind, the rain had stopped for now making the ride bearable. . .even slightly enjoyable.

"Let's sing a Christmas song!" one of the little Reynolds girls exclaimed. So they did. They sang all the way home. Finally, John Reynolds halted the wagon. Alaina and her in-laws climbed down and bid the other family a merry Christmas.

"It's so dark," Alaina murmured. "Why, the house is barely visible from the main road."

Her comment went unnoticed, but it troubled her throughout the rest of the evening. *What would You have me to do about that, Lord?* she asked in silent prayer. She worried that if Braeden came home, he wouldn't know they were waiting for him. In fact, he might not be able to tell the house was still standing. Many in the area were not.

"I'm going to turn in for the night," Papa Jonathan said a good while later. Crossing the room, he leaned over the armchair in which Alaina sat and kissed the top of her head. "Merry Christmas."

She smiled. "Merry Christmas."

"Aren't you going to bed, Dear?" Eloise asked her, following her husband.

"Yes, I'll be along shortly."

The older couple took to the stairs and the room grew deathly still. Zek had returned from attending church with his people, but had long since gone to sleep in the lean-to that he and Papa Jonathan constructed outside the back of the house. The cabin he'd grown up in on the far end of the farm had been destroyed like the other outbuildings.

Suddenly, she thought about what Zek said yesterday. "If'n Massah Braeden is alive, he'll be sure to get hisself home fer Christmas. He wouldn't want to miss another one with his family. Massah Braeden always loved Christmas."

Where is he, Lord? Where is he?

Alaina shook off her melancholy and stood. Tomorrow was Christmas Day. She'd see Mama and her youngest brother, David—that was something to look forward to. Standing, she blew out the light perched on the table beside her. Darkness descended like a thick drape, and she couldn't see her own hand in front of her face. Feeling around until her fingers found a matchstick, she relit the candle and replaced its glass lamp.

Then she had an idea: *Why not put a candle in the window so if Braeden comes home, he'll see a bit of light?* Like the star that guided the shepherds on the very first

Christmas, the light in the window might guide Braeden home. The notion grew. Why not put a candle in every window facing the road so Braeden wouldn't—couldn't—miss it.

Alaina set to task, placing a single candle on each wide sill of the four front windows, both downstairs and up. Mother McKenna might accuse her of wasting a precious commodity, but it was Christmas, and Alaina couldn't think of a better use for the wax tapers than to light her beloved's path back into her awaiting arms.

The last candle she lit was in her bedroom.

Nodding in satisfaction, she readied herself for bed. She pulled the pins from her hair and brushed it vigorously. She could hear the wind outside, whistling through the treetops. She heard a soft rain pelting the house. She heard a low rumble of thunder.

Thunder?

She listened more carefully. No, it was a horse—horses. More than one. Alaina stood apprehensively, her hairbrush still in her hand. Suddenly she felt very foolish; because of her, the house was aglow. Why, it was a veritable invitation for wayward soldiers, ruffians, and thieves. She should have realized it sooner.

Cautiously, she glanced out the window and by the light emanating from the house, she saw a shadowy figure dismount. She glimpsed the beard and realized it was a man. She could make out a second horse tethered behind the first, but it was loaded with satchels. The man was obviously alone.

In that moment, he looked up at Alaina and she gasped in horror. But when he stepped closer to the house, smiled, and removed his wide-brimmed hat, recognition immediately set in. "Braeden!"

Dropping the brush, she whirled from the window and hurried out of the bedroom, nearly colliding with Papa Jonathan in the hallway.

"Put the gun away," she said, noting the rifle in his hand. "It's Braeden. He's come home!"

She ran down the stairs and flung open the front door. He now stood on the porch. "Braeden!" she cried, throwing herself into his outstretched arms.

He was soaked to the skin, and the pungent smell of wet wool, horses, and leather assailed her senses, but Alaina could have cared less. With her arms around Braeden's neck she hugged him fiercely.

"You're home. . . ."

He kissed her hard before folding her into a snug embrace. "Alaina," he breathed against her cheek. "I thought you were dead."

His beard scratched and tickled her face, and Alaina brought her head back, curiously examining the growth with her fingertips. But then his words took root. "Dead?" She shook her head in wonder. "I feared you were dead, Braeden. I. . .I don't understand."

"It's a long story, my love. One I'll save for later." Lowering his mouth to hers, he kissed her soundly once more.

"Braeden! Is it really you?" Eloise breathed.

He reluctantly loosened his hold on Alaina and shifted his focus to the small group now gathered on the porch. He smiled "It's really me, Mama."

"Praise the Lord."

Papa McKenna echoed the words.

Within moments, they shared hugs and kisses, and then Zek appeared just in time to join in the welcome.

"My faithful, valiant friend," Braeden said, clasping Zek warmly.

"I done tol' ever'one you'd be back fer Christmas."

Braeden chuckled. "You were right." He turned to his parents. "Where's Kirk?"

Papa McKenna shook his head sadly.

"No. . .no, not Kirk. . ."

"It's true, son." Mother McKenna said grimly. "He's dead."

Braeden swallowed convulsively. "Michael?"

"Lost an arm, but he's alive. He left for Texas just this morning." Papa McKenna shuffled his feet, his gaze lowered. "He got discouraged. . .like us all, I'm afraid. The Wheeler place is in sorry shape and. . .well, much of our farm was destroyed, too."

"Well, things are going to change now," Braeden stated decisively. "We'll build this farm back up. I've got the funds. Mama, Papa, I'm going to build you a nice house of your own." He grinned sheepishly. "See, Laina and I are going to fill this one up with children."

She blushed, her heart swelling with joy.

"And, Zek, you're a free man now. You need a place of your own and, I'm thinking that it's high time you found a pretty woman and settled down on your own plot of land. And it's only fitting that you take a share of the McKenna property. You love it as much as I do."

"Yessuh!" Zek's wide, toothy smile shone like moonlight.

"You have. . .funds?" Alaina asked incredulously. "Braeden, where have you been?"

He took her hand. "I'll tell you all about it if Mama will make some good, strong coffee to warm my insides."

"There's no coffee, Braeden," Mother McKenna announced apologetically.

"Then it's a good thing I brought some. I bought a sack of flour, too. And sugar, butter, and—"

"How on earth did you do that?" Eloise gasped, her right hand over her heart in all her surprise.

"Bought it, Mama." Braeden laughed. "It's part of the story."

"Well, first things first," Papa McKenna said. "You need some dry clothes. Come along with me, son, and I'll search some out for you."

Alaina watched Braeden follow his father up the stairs, and it was all she could do to restrain herself and not run after him. Instead, she helped Mother McKenna unpack Braeden's saddlebags. They both marveled at the extraordinary bounty.

"We can have biscuits tomorrow with our Christmas dinner!" Alaina declared.

"I can bake a blackberry pie." Eloise shook her head. "This truly is amazing."

Zek stood to one side, wagging his head in wonder. Soon Papa McKenna returned and exclaimed over the goods as well.

Finally Braeden reentered the room, and Alaina's pulse quickened. They smiled at each other, but Braeden's expression said he couldn't quite believe what he was seeing. Had he really thought she was dead?

Suddenly, he looked at the cold hearth. "No fire? A man could freeze to death in this house."

In no time, it seemed, a fire was blazing, and they all gathered around it, Alaina sitting close to Braeden. She thought he looked different. . .older, and that reddish-blond beard certainly added a distinction. But he looked no worse for wear. His shoulders were just as broad as she remembered, his forearms, strong and powerful. He hadn't come home half-starved as most Confederate soldiers, and he certainly hadn't lost his zest for life.

"Like Zek told you, I got wounded in Virginia," he began. "I took a bullet in my right side, but it went clean through out my back without hitting any major organs. Then I got captured. The Federal commander, however, was a Christian man and took pity on the Confederates who were wounded. He ordered his doctor to tend to our injuries and allowed us to rest two days before we made the march north to the prison in Maryland. Prison camp," Braeden said, shaking his blond head and staring into his coffee, "was an unspeakable horror, but I survived."

Inhaling deeply, he continued. "We'd all read about Sherman's march through the South, the burning of Columbia, and I worried about you all." He looked pointedly at Alaina. "Shortly thereafter, Ambrose Powell, a good friend of Jennifer Marie's aunt in Charleston got captured. When we met up in prison, he told me that Jennifer Marie died of the small pox, and that—" Braeden paused to choke down the obvious emotion. "He told me, Laina, that he heard you'd died, too." He glanced across the way. "And, you, Mama. . . Papa."

"Oh, Braeden," Alaina said on a deep sigh, "how awful for you."

For several moments, a heavy silence hung in the air. Then Braeden started speaking once more. "When the war ended, and I got released with all the others, I was as skinny as a reed and weak as a kitten. I knew I'd never make it back to South Carolina alive. From the information I'd been given, I figured there was nothing to come home to. I managed to straggle into the nearest town, and as I was sitting on a bench despairing about my situation, the Union commander who'd apprehended me on the battlefield crossed the street to shake my hand like we were old friends. I hated him for a good long minute, until he said we were brothers—brothers in Christ. We were brothers against brothers in this awful war, but now, he told me, it was time to reconcile. I ended up forgiving him, and he offered me a job. Working on the railroad, repairing track."

"The railroad!" Alaina smacked her palm to her forehead. "I should have known."

Grinning broadly, Braeden slipped his arm around her shoulders and drew her nearer. "I got two hundred dollars in gold just for signing on. I accepted a six-month term and earned one hundred dollars a month. I was fed three hearty meals a day and soon got my strength back. At first I wondered if my position was traitorous, but soon decided quite the opposite since the railroads will eventually help the South get back on its feet.

"Then finally my contract was up, and the Lord prompted me to head home. I couldn't guess why, because I expected nothing to be left, no family, no house, no farm. But God wouldn't allow me to do anything else. I felt no peace until I decided to make the trek back here. I purchased a couple of horses and supplies along the way. As I got closer to Columbia, the devastation I witnessed made me sick. These last few miles were the worst. I mourned all over again the loss of the love of my life." His arm tightened around Alaina, and hot tears filled her eyes. "And I mourned my parents whom I thought were dead, too. I had hoped maybe I'd find Kirk, Michael, or Zek."

"But then, as I came around the bend. . ." Braeden chuckled, although Alaina saw the moisture pooling in his amber-brown eyes. "I saw the house lit up, and I couldn't believe it. The lighted windows shone right into my soul."

"Lighted windows?" Mother McKenna asked with a frown of confusion.

"Candles. I put them there," Alaina said. She turned to Braeden, reveling once more in the very sight of him sitting there beside her. "It was my prayer that their special light would guide my husband home."

He leaned sideways and kissed her. "They did. They surely did." He smiled. "Merry Christmas."

"Merry Christmas." Then, like an added blessing from Heaven, Alaina recalled a passage of scripture from the Book of Isaiah that sent her heart soaring: "For the LORD shall be thine everlasting light and the days of thy mourning shall be ended."

"I'm so thankful we're reunited, Braeden. God led you home where you belong. This is truly the best Christmas ever!"

Epilogue

W ow, what a cool story, Grandma!"
"Yes. . ." Bonnie sighed on its happy ending.

"So whatever happened to Michael Wheeler?"

Bonnie smiled warmly at nine-year-old Alaina. "From what I've gathered, he made a new home for himself out West. But he sent back this portrait of your great, great, great-grandmother. See the signature and date at the bottom right corner? It says *Wheeler, 1872.*"

On the far side of her bedroom, Bonnie stood behind Alaina as they scrutinized the painting on the wall.

"She's wearing that golden dress, Grandma—the one her friend gave her."

"Uh-huh."

Alaina whirled around, her uplifted face a mask of wonderment. "I love that story. It's a part of me, isn't it?"

"Yes. And now it's now up to you to pass it on to your children someday. . .and to your grandchildren. . . great grandchildren." Bonnie glanced down at the long, narrow box she still carried in her hands. "And it's up to you to pass on the tradition of putting a lighted candle in the window each Christmas Eve."

The child took the box and reverently touched the scarred candle inside. "It's a symbol of God's light."

"And His everlasting love through our Lord, Jesus Christ."

Alaina smiled, awe and understanding shining from her deep, blue eyes. "Merry Christmas, Grandma."

"Merry Christmas."

ANDREA BOESHAAR

Andrea was born and raised in Milwaukee, Wisconsin. Married for twenty years, she and her husband Daniel have three grown sons. Andrea has been writing for over thirteen years, but writing exclusively for the Christian market for over six. Writing is something she loves to share, as well as, help others develop. Andrea recently quit her job to stay home, take care of her family, and write. She has authored nine **Heartsong Presents** titles of inspirational romance.

As far as her writing success is concerned, Andrea gives the glory to the Lord Jesus. Her writing, she feels, is a gift from God in that He has provided and "outlet" for her imagination. Andrea wants her writing to be an evangelistic tool, but she also hopes that it edifies and encourages other Christians in their daily walk with Him.

Yuletide Treasure

by Gail Gaymer Martin

Favour is deceitful, and beauty is vain:
but a woman that feareth the LORD,
she shall be praised.
PROVERBS 31:30

Chapter 1

A cloud of black smoke curled past the window of the Chesapeake and Ohio locomotive. As the shrill whistle sounded, Livy Schuler snuggled deeper into her travel cloak and studied the changing winter scenery. Scattered buildings stood along the tracks and she sighed, sensing their lengthy journey neared completion.

She gazed at her four-year-old nephew as he lay fast asleep, his blond curls bobbing against the stiff seat cushion as the locomotive swayed through the countryside. "Davy," she murmured, "wake up."

The child shifted against the seat, but did not wake. Her heart ached for the boy. Christmas was no time for a child to be away from his parents, but his mother's illness necessitated the journey. And when her brother, John, asked for her help, she acquiesced. With Ruth's unfortunate stroke, how could she refuse?

The trip from Detroit stretched into hours with stops for passengers and when an occasional cow wandered onto the tracks. She had amused Davy with toy soldiers and storybooks. Later, when he drifted off to sleep, she found a discarded newspaper and read about President Grant's fight against the greenbacks and the resurgence of Queen Victoria's popularity.

"Next stop, Grand Rapids," the conductor called, moving along the aisle.

Opening his weighted eyes, Davy shifted and released a soft whimper.

"We're nearing the station, Davy. We're going to have such fun with your Aunt Helen and Uncle Charles."

Only sadness filled his face, and she hoped Helen and Charles would understand the child's lack of enthusiasm. Ruth's brother, Charles, had been gracious to invite Davy for the holiday. Livy pictured her brother John's somber expression when he had no other choice but accept their offer.

Livy could only imagine the Mandalay home and life among the wealthy. Charles owned one of the largest furniture-making businesses in Grand Rapids, which, after the war, became the furniture capital of the world. And Charles had found success on the coattails of inventive, skilled craftsmen like George Pullman and William Haldane. Livy shook her head in wonder at the life the Mandalays must lead.

Anticipating their arrival, Livy returned Davy's lead soldiers to her satchel. With the bag open on her lap, she looked at the small package John had asked her to deliver to Helen.

Shameful curiosity overtook her, and she felt through the paper. Wood, perhaps, and a strange shape —rounded on one end, pointed on the other, one side smoothly curved, the other a jagged zigzag. She couldn't determine what lay hidden within the paper. Guilt needled her, so she withdrew her hand from the satchel and latched it. The package didn't belong to her, and as curious as she was, she had no cause to look inside.

A whistle blast jarred her back to the present. The train slowed and came to a shuddering halt. Livy rose, buttoning her dark gray travel cloak, then hooked Davy's coat and, grasping his hand, led him down the aisle.

With the conductor's assistance, she stepped to the platform while soot from the smoke stack showered down in a fine spray of drifting black flakes like ebony snow. Her gaze swept along the station's visitors, looking for Charles's son, Andrew, whom she had never met. Seeing no likely prospect, she turned and lifted Davy to the ground and headed toward the small depot, searching for warmth.

"Hello. Miss Schuler?"

She pivoted, hearing the voice, and looked into a pair of glinting, ice blue eyes. Her pulse lurched as radically as the chugging locomotive had. "Mr. Mandalay?"

"Yes, but please call me Andrew." He paused, bending at the waist. "And this must be Davy."

The child peered at him and nodded.

"How do you do, Davy? I'm your cousin, Andrew." Straightening, he focused on Livy. "How was your trip? Too long, I'd guess."

Livy drew her gaze from his delightful smile. Six hours, yes, but tolerable."

"Leaving your friends and family during the holidays is very generous of you. I'm sure Uncle John was grateful."

"Yes, but I had no choice. John and Davy needed me."

"No matter, it was very kind. Well then, it's much too cold on the platform. The carriage is this way." He motioned behind him, then reached for her satchel. "I'll carry that for you, Miss Schuler."

"No need, thank you. It's light, and please call me Livy." She turned, pointing to the two small trunks sitting on the baggage cart. "But those cases are ours, if you don't mind."

"Aah. Then I'll retrieve those," he said. "Wait here for one moment."

As he darted down the platform, admiration rose within her. Besides his dazzling eyes, Andrew had been graced with other handsome features. His fair hair contrasted with his darker skintone, likely the result of his days at the logging camp. John mentioned Andrew had only arrived home for the holidays.

Watching him return with their baggage, she noted his tall stature and broad shoulders, dwarfing her own petite frame. She imagined his muscular arms swinging an axe to fell a pine tree or hoisting a log onto a large logging sled. As he approached, she caught her breath. His firm, square jaw was softened by his deep dimples and generous, captivating smile on his full, sensitive mouth.

"Ready?" he asked, moving to her side. "Follow me."

Tucking Davy's hand in hers, she hurried behind Andrew, following his long strides. He stopped beside a carriage, a claret-colored Dearborn pulled by two matching bays, then opened the door and slid their baggage inside.

"Come, Davy," he said and lifted the boy into the coach. Then he reached for Livy's hand. As she stepped to his side, his gaze swept across her face and heat rose to her cheeks. They stood so close, the scent of his damp woolen coat and peppermint filled her senses. He assisted her into the conveyance and spread a thick robe across their laps.

"That should keep you warm," he said, his dimples glinting with his steady gaze. "The ride is short."

She swallowed, finding her voice. "Thank you."

He grinned again and closed the door. Livy nestled against Davy, her thoughts shifting back to Andrew's earlier comment, "Leaving your friends and family during the holidays is very generous of you." *Leaving my friends? If the situation weren't so pitiful, I would laugh.*

Lately, her life rose before her in a dismal, gray picture like the winter day. At twenty-eight, she was a spinster, a word she detested. Looking in a mirror, she saw no reason for her lack of beaus. Though she would not be considered a beauty by most, her features were pleasant, her figure was trim, and she earned a suitable income as a music teacher. But single, she was.

Though the Bible said God would provide, "ask and you shall receive," she had long given up asking God for a husband. The Lord, from all she could comprehend, desired her to remain the detested word—a spinster. But she had other plans.

Recently, Henry Tucker, owner of the neighborhood mercantile, delayed her in the shop with casual, genial conversation. She sensed his interest, and though she had little attraction for him—*none,* if she were honest—he was a likely candidate as a husband. Not God's plan perhaps, but her own.

Sadly, Henry's young wife and baby had died in childbirth. Now at forty, he told her he longed for a wife and family. Each time she entered the shop, he looked at her with yearning, and she had begun to wonder if this were the man for whom she might set her cap.

Heat rose to Livy's face, recalling her deceptive words to John as she boarded the train earlier in the day. She explained a commitment to the church choir influenced her to hurry back to Detroit. But in truth, a different reason motivated her.

Shame filled her at the deception. Telling a lie, no matter what color, was a sin. But she couldn't admit to John that Henry indicated he'd come to call during the Christmas holiday. That was the true reason she needed to be home. Though she hadn't extended an invitation to him directly, Henry was most persistent. And he was a man of his word.

A chill shivered through her as she felt the icy air and considered her possible future—a loveless marriage. Why? She asked herself the question many times. Why did she long for marriage if it wouldn't be filled with love and contentment? The answer that marched into her head was always the same. She recalled Noah. God guided the animals to the ark two by two. She was a *one*. And besides, if God had a change of heart, her amiable feelings for Henry might grow to love.

Livy pulled the lap robe higher around Davy's shoulders and her own chilled body. The carriage jolted, and she slid sideways as the horses trotted around a corner. Elegant houses stood along the rutted roadway, and she huddled closer to Davy, as much for her own comfort as for his.

Picturing her handsome driver, Livy admired Andrew's splendid frame. A strange sense of longing rose in her chest. She closed her eyelids and wondered what the next days might bring.

Chapter 2

Andrew snapped the bays' reins, and the carriage lurched forward. He adjusted the heavy blanket across his legs and veered the animals onto the rutted roadway. To satisfy his father's wishes, he'd been genial to the guests. More than genial, he'd been pleasant. Yet, he hoped his own plans weren't thwarted by their stay.

Three months at the logging camp left him eager for feminine companionship, and with four more months to follow, he was unwilling to sacrifice his own plans to entertain a child. His memory drifted to a flirtatious young woman he had met at a house gathering in the autumn, and he looked forward to seeing Rosie Parker again.

His mother discouraged such relationships, prompting him to find a suitable young lady from the church, particularly the music director's sister. He'd seen the prim and proper young parish women dressed in their demure, somber gowns but found himself drawn to Rosie. She was so like her name—curly blond hair, crimson dress, musky perfume, and a spirited wit.

He grimaced, recalling the biblical missive ringing in his mind: women should dress modestly and decently, not with gaudy jewels or expensive clothes, but with good deeds. Despite the verse, Rosie's image filled his head. She didn't fit God's description, but he'd live for now with his sinful desire. Rosie beguiled him.

Yet, his mind drifted to his passengers inside the carriage. He recalled the sad, frightened face of his young cousin, Davy. The poor boy had been forced to leave his home at Christmas. Then, Livy—Olivia Schuler, John's unmarried sister. A spinster, they called her. He noted she dressed in somber colors like the young church women he knew. Still, the shy sparkle in her green eyes hung in his memory.

As the house appeared, Andrew slowed the bays. He drew the carriage to a halt beside the long pillared porch and climbed down. After hitching the horses, he opened the coach door. At the same time, his mother, wrapped in a fur-trimmed cape, stepped from the house.

"Here we are," he said, assisting Livy to the ground then swinging Davy beside her. "I hope you were warm enough."

"We were fine." Livy's gaze swept across the wide expanse of house. "Your home is lovely."

"Thank you," he said, grabbing her satchel and guiding them up the steps. "A servant will see to your luggage," he added.

Livy forced her mouth closed after she gaped at the vast structure before her. The lovely home of broad, white clapboards and black shutters was graced by a sprawling porch.

As she headed toward the entrance, John's sister-in-law, Helen waited for her. They'd met only once, years earlier. Livy had forgotten how lovely she was. It was clear that Andrew, with his fair hair and blue eyes, had inherited his mother's good looks.

As Livy approached, Helen stepped forward, her arms opened wide in greeting. "Davy, Olivia, welcome." She swooped down to wrap Davy in her arms, but he slid behind Livy's cloak and peeked out at the gracious woman.

Livy took the woman's hand with a gentle squeeze. "Thank you, Helen." She motioned to Davy. "He's a bit shy, but he'll adjust with time." Livy caught her nephew's hand and pulled him out from behind her skirts. "Davy, this is your Aunt Helen. Say hello."

A soft greeting fell from his lips, but instead of looking at her, his focus riveted to the expansive dwelling.

"Won't you come in?" Helen moved forward while a servant pushed the heavy door inward and gave them wide berth.

Livy scooted Davy ahead, and they entered the central hall. A broad staircase rose to the second story, and a door stood open on the right where Livy could see a fire burning on the hearth. "Come," Helen said, motioning toward the fireplace. "Warm yourselves. We'll have tea and chocolate."

The word "chocolate" seemed to motivate Davy. He hurried ahead of her, wide-eyed as he took in the scene. After the servant brought in a heavy tray, they sat in the parlor sipping hot chocolate and nibbling on tea cakes.

"We're having a small dinner party this evening in

your honor," Helen said. "Our young choirmaster, Mr. Daily, and his sister will join us."

"How nice," Livy said. As she spoke, Andrew's expression drew her attention. He grimaced and his reaction aroused Livy's curiosity.

When teatime ended, Andrew left the room, and shortly thereafter, Helen led them up the stairs to their bedrooms where the baggage had been placed. After unpacking Davy's trunk, Livy left him playing with his toy soldiers and headed for her room next door.

She made quick work of hanging her few garments. As she emptied her smaller satchel, her hand settled upon the keepsake John had given her, and she lifted it from the bag. She recalled John's discomfort as he asked the favor. "Would you. . .slip this trinket to Helen? I'm sorry I can't explain, but it's a keepsake from long ago. She'll understand."

Livy had eyed the package with curiosity and agreed to deliver it safely, but as John slipped her the parcel, he added, "And. . .er, I'd appreciate the utmost discretion. The memento is nothing, really, but. . ." He had faltered without finishing his sentence. With his fervent request for tact, she wondered how she might secretly deliver the gift to Helen.

As if her question were heard, Helen tapped on her open door. "I hope everything is satisfactory."

"The room is lovely," Livy said, admiring the deep rose and delicate blue decor and the elegantly carved bedstead. "Thank you."

"I suppose leaving home during the holiday season was difficult. It's very kind of you to bring Davy here."

"I hope to return to Detroit before Christmas—if Davy seems settled," Livy said, clutching the small package.

"I see. John didn't mention your plans. I'm sure Davy'll be fine after a day or two. We've asked Andrew to spend time with him. I hope that'll help."

Livy smiled. "I imagine Andrew has other plans for his holidays, but I appreciate everyone's kindness. Davy is a good boy, but he's never been away from his parents before."

"How is Ruth?" Helen's face knit with concern.

"It's sad. She can't speak or use her left limbs properly. But praise God, the doctor expects a good recovery."

"I pray that's true," Helen said. "She and I were best friends when we were young."

"Best friends? I didn't know." She hesitated. "You knew my brother, John, then." She ran her finger across the jagged edge of the memento clutched in her hand.

Helen plucked beneath her collar at the pleats of her bodice. "Oh, yes, John and Charles were school friends. To Charles, I was only his younger sister's friend. But one day, he noticed me." She paused for a moment. "Your brother and I were dear friends even before Charles."

"I wondered," Livy said, extending the tissue-wrapped parcel toward her. "He asked me to give you this package. He said you'd understand."

Helen stared at the gift without moving. When she took it, her fingers followed the erratic shape beneath the tissue and a faint smile rose to her lips. "Yes. Yes, I believe I do understand. Thank you." Her fingers

curled around the tissue, and her sh _____
a sigh. "Well, then, I'll get back to the _____
ments. Our guests are expected at sever _____
toward the door. "Please, let me know if yo _____
thing," she said, before she disappeared dow _____

Livy sat on the edge of the carved oak _____ her mind filled with questions. Being twelve years younger than John, she didn't recall his friends. "Dear friends," Helen had said. She chided herself for her blatant curiosity.

Rising from the bed, she opened the chifforobe and rifled through her gowns. Nothing seemed suited for a dinner party. With the holiday season at hand, why hadn't she planned ahead to bring a few party dresses? She chuckled at herself. Party dresses? She really had nothing particularly "festive" in her wardrobe. A spinster's need for party frocks was minimal.

She pulled the garments from the closet one at a time. A tailored, navy wool skirt and brilliantine shirtwaist seemed inappropriate for a dinner party. Livy examined her three dresses and settled on a brown day gown with shoulder piping and deeper brown velvet trim on the sleeves and peplum. She would have to make do.

When she'd finished dressing, Livy went to Davy's room. Earlier in the day, he seemed listless and ate his dinner in the kitchen. Now, when she peeked into his room, Davy had already fallen asleep. She left a small lantern burning in the hall outside his room, for fear he'd waken and be frightened in the strange surroundings.

As Livy descended the stairs, the fireplace glowed through the doorway, and voices drifting from the parlor ned as warm and inviting as the flames. When she entered the room, Charles stepped forward to greet her, but Livy's attention was drawn to Andrew. Her face warmed with the greeting. She stifled her emotions and focused on Charles. Taller and sturdier than Andrew, his imperious size awed her. "It's been a long time, Charles. Thank you for having us."

"You're entirely welcome, Livy. Anything for Ruth and her family." He brushed his thick mustache with long fingers and turned to the guests. "Livy, this is Mr. Daily and his sister, Miss Daily."

"Roger and Agatha, please," the young man said.

"How do you do? And please call me Livy," she responded, admiring the young woman who greeted her. She was trim and attractive, dressed in a rich brocade gown of deep lilac with a fashionable bustle. Her bowed lips curved slightly in greeting, but her interest was not on Livy.

Dressed in a brown worsted suit, sporting a tan corduroy vest, Andrew looked dashing. Tonight his tall stature and broad-chest were more impressive than in the afternoon. He paused in the soft lamplight that brought out red highlights in his golden hair. Livy understood Agatha's gawking on his appearance. A feathering of longing rippled through Livy, and she struggled to keep her admiration hidden.

"You look refreshed, Livy," Andrew said, his gaze sweeping her from head to toe. "Have a seat and let me bring you some warmed cider."

"Thank you," she said, sinking into the sofa cushion across from the two dinner guests. In a moment,

Andrew returned and slipped a cup into her hands. She wrapped her cold fingers around the mug, enjoying its warmth and hiding the slight tremor awakened by his touch.

"And how was your trip, Livy?" Roger asked.

"Fine, thank you." Livy studied the pleasant-looking young man, admiring his gentle face and friendly smile.

"I understand you gave up your holiday to bring your nephew here," he added.

"No accolades, please. With Ruth's illness, my brother needed my help with Davy. Besides, I must admit I'm returning to Detroit before Christmas. . . that is, if Davy seems well-adjusted here."

"Ah, I see," Roger said.

An unexpected look of disappointment shot across Andrew's face. "But you must stay," he blurted. "Who'll entertain Davy?"

His sudden explosion caught Livy by surprise. When she looked, a pinkish hue crept to his neck. Embarrassment? His first words had sent a ripple of pleasure through her, but the next comment that shot from his mouth dampened her hope. He wasn't anxious for her stay, in particular, only for someone to watch over Davy.

But Roger's next words softened the tension of the moment. "I had hoped to coerce you into joining our choir for the services. I understand you teach music. Singing, I'm told."

"Yes, voice and piano. Though I must admit, piano is really not my strength."

With a sheepish grin, Andrew bounded from his seat to the spinet in the parlor alcove. "Please, play for us, Livy." He raised the cover from the keys and pulled out the bench. "Maybe, a carol."

"Yes, do play," Agatha gushed, moving to Andrew's side. Her hand captured his arm. He looked at her fingers gripping his forearm, and a covert frown flew across his face. Unobtrusively, he lifted her hand and stepped back to his chair. Agatha's lips pursed a delicate pout.

Livy grinned inwardly at the silent antics. Though she was unaccustomed to flirting herself, Agatha's pursuit of Andrew was straightforward. When the amorous drama ended, Livy accepted Andrew's invitation to play. She preferred to sing than play, but rather than refuse his request, she stepped to the piano. A collection of sheet music lay on a small cabinet beside the spinet, but she needed none for carols. Livy played them without a musical score. She slid onto the bench, fingered the keys for a moment, then struck the first chord. The rich tones of the instrument drifted through the room, and in her head, she sang the familiar song, "Good Christian Men Rejoice."

As the music ended, Helen swept into the room and graciously announced dinner. When Charles took his wife's arm, Livy's heart thudded as Andrew approached, but before he reached her, Agatha anchored herself to his side. With a lavish bow, Roger smiled and guided Livy to the table.

The scrumptious meal was served on translucent Haviland china in an elegant rose pattern and genuine silver. Livy had never tasted such succulent roasted pork. Helen served the meat with sweet potato pie and apple butter. Genial conversation filled the room, and when they finished, Helen guided them back to the living room for dessert.

"What a fine meal, Helen," Roger said, leaning back and patting his lower vest where the buttons strained against the cloth. She thanked him with a smile and continued to pour coffee from a silver pot. "I'd like to return the invitation. Perhaps, next Friday you could join us for a holiday dinner."

Livy glanced at her hosts, waiting for their response. Though Helen sent Roger a bright smile, Andrew responded before his mother. "Sorry, Roger. I have a previous engagement, but thank you for the invitation. Hopefully, the others can join you."

Livy's heart tumbled with disappointment.

A desperate look on Agatha's face seemed to curb her brother's response. "Let's find a time agreeable to everyone," Roger suggested with haste. "Would Saturday or Sunday accommodate everyone?"

Livy waited. After a quick discussion, Saturday evening was accepted, so she would be included in the dinner. If the train schedule cooperated, she had planned to be on her way home by Sunday afternoon. Now, though, Livy felt differently. She looked at Andrew with masked longing. Why did she allow herself to dream such foolish dreams? Must she spend her entire life yearning for the impossible?

Henry's less-than-perfect frame rose in her mind. Though not handsome, he was a kind man, owned a business, attended church regularly, and wanted a child. *I must stop tormenting myself with wishes. A kind, gentle family man is best. And Henry shows interest in me.*

She chided herself for her wavering emotions. *Use common sense, Livy. If God wants something else for you, He will let you know.*

God? Perhaps it wasn't God who wanted something else for her. She faltered and looked toward Andrew's captivating face, then bit her lip, knowing the truth that tugged at her heart.

Chapter 3

On Thursday morning when Andrew came down the stairs, Helen beckoned him into the morning room. "You know, Andrew, Livy is returning home on Sunday and we'll need help with Davy. He's a good boy, but your father and I can't spend the complete holiday entertaining him."

Andrew clenched his teeth to keep himself from blurting his frustration. Though he always showed respect to his parents, he wanted to remind his mother that he had personal plans, too.

"You do understand?" she added.

He unlatched his tensed jaw. "I understand, Mother. I'll do what I can. . .though I wish we could convince Livy to stay."

"She warned us when she arrived that her intention was to leave before Christmas. She must have a reason."

Andrew looked at his mother, his mind searching for a solution. Would he have the pluck to ask Livy why she wanted to return home? "Maybe she'd change her plans if we entice her to stay."

"Andrew, that would be manipulative. We need to

respect her wishes."

Though he heard her, Andrew's mind reeled with schemes. What would keep Livy in Grand Rapids? He examined his own motivation, and his stomach tightened as he pictured Rosie. While he pondered the question, an idea crossed his mind. Could he be a matchmaker? Roger Daily was a good-looking fellow. Yet, Andrew had noticed during dinner how she looked past Roger, and afterward in the parlor, she looked everywhere but at him.

"You will cooperate, Andrew?"

His mother's voice brought him back to the present. "Yes, I'll do my best."

"Thank you," she said and left the room.

Playing cupid with his imagination, he envisioned Livy and Roger together, a perfect pair: restrained, quiet, musical. Yet, the idea aroused an ominous constriction in his chest. He didn't like the picture. But why? Livy and Roger were perfect for each other.

Livy's pensive face filled his mind. His thoughts drifted back to the family dinner party, and he envisioned Livy in her subdued brown dress. Though she wasn't as colorful as Rosie, Livy had many appealing qualities.

He pictured her dark brown hair and clear, ivory skin. Most of all, her gentle, gracious nature filled his mind. Picturing Livy with Davy, Andrew was touched by her gentle kindness.

Andrew hesitated and his mouth sagged at his recollections. He sounded like a lovesick school boy, mooning over a girl. What had gotten into him? Tomorrow he would see Rosie again. Then he'd know the pleasure of a vivacious woman's company.

He struggled to push Rosie's image into his mind. Instead, her blue eyes transformed to large, green emerald ones. Livy. A shudder rifled through him. "Control yourself," he whispered aloud.

"Pardon me."

Andrew jumped at the soft, feminine voice. As if she had stepped from his vision, Livy stood in the doorway, dressed in a white shirtwaist and dark blue skirt.

"Good morning." He forced a lighthearted chuckle. "Apparently, I was talking to myself, but now you're here, so I can talk with you." His mind raced. "Have you eaten?"

Her delicate hands were folded at her waist, and she focused on her intertwined fingers. "No, I was on my way to breakfast when I heard you."

He latched onto the pause in conversation. "Then let's go together." He rested his hand on her arm, feeling the warmth of her skin through the soft airy cloth. As they headed down the hall, his plan gathered momentum, hoping to arouse her interest in staying for the holiday's duration. Inner pleas filled him. He so rarely prayed, and today he was praying for God to manipulate a situation. If he weren't so desperate, he'd be ashamed. Still, he had no interest in spending his vacation playing with soldiers or wooden puzzles.

Walking beside Andrew, a spicy aroma like cloves or bay rum soap filled Livy's senses. The pressure of his hand on her arm sent a warm jolt to her fingertips, and her chest fluttered with the sensation.

In the dining room, a sideboard was spread with sausage, bread, butter, and baked apples. Livy filled her plate, completing her meal with a cup of hot tea, then sat at the table with Andrew across from her. "Would you like to ask the blessing?" Livy inquired.

Andrew bowed his head and murmured a brief prayer. Then without lifting his fork, he leaned back and stared at her. "So, you're hoping to return to Detroit for Christmas."

His riveting gaze left her suspended for a moment. Lowering her head, Livy caught her breath. "Yes, I have a commit. . . . I should say, I have an engagement."

"Engagement?" His mouth curved to an appealing grin.

Discomfort bound her. "Well, not an *engagement*, exactly," she said. "A friend is to come calling."

Andrew forked a piece of sausage. "A gentleman?"

His boldness surprised her, and she answered without thinking. "Yes, Mr. Tucker. . .Henry."

"Is he a beau?" A frown flashed across his face before he turned it to a smile.

"No, well. . .Andrew, your questions are rather inappropriate."

"Forgive me, Livy. I wondered what called you back home. Mother would love to have you. . .*we* would love to have you stay for the holiday. New Year will be fun."

Did he mean "we"? And why? His blunt question had confused her. "Won't you be with your friends on New Year?"

"Yes, a few friends."

"And will *you* spend time with a lady?"

He faltered, and a hint of discomfort settled on his face. "I have many friends. . .male and female."

Since he circumvented her question, she suspected he had a special young woman in mind. "Then, the answer is, 'yes.'"

"Perhaps one. A Miss Parker."

Livy blanched at his admission. The woman had a name, and the name made her real. "Then, you should understand why I'm anxious to return home."

His jaw tensed, and his full lips compressed without a response. Instead, he focused on the food that remained on his plate.

A sense of loneliness washed over her. She was sorry she had confronted him. The silence echoed in her head until, finally, she cleared her throat. "Besides, I neglected to bring appropriate gowns for the holidays. My dresses are much too plain for holiday dinners and parties. So you see, I need to return anyway."

His face relaxed and a sparkle lit his eye. "I'm sure Mother could solve that problem. She owns a million gowns. With a few nips and tucks, you'd have no worry." He placed his napkin on the table edge and slid back, the chair legs scrapping the wooden floor. "Will you excuse me?"

"Certainly. I'm finished, too." She folded her napkin, dropping it on the table, and rose. Without another word, she turned and darted from the room, chastising herself. Why had she tempted herself with dreams again? Shame lifted in her chest. A young Christian woman had no right to lust after a man.

She whispered a prayer of forgiveness for her sin

and pushed her attention to Henry. But nothing stirred in her, except memories of his pleasant demeanor and his kindness.

An amazing awareness blossomed in her mind. She understood, now, why God had not given her beaus. She couldn't control her covetous nature. Unbridled passion rose in her when she looked at Andrew. Instead of being angry at God, she thanked Him. The Lord knew she needed restraints and God provided them. Henry Tucker was the answer. She'd hurry home, assured Henry was the Lord's plan for her.

As Livy retraced her steps to her room, Davy filled her with concern. She hadn't seen him yet this morning. She hurried down the hallway. Listening at his door, the room was silent. When she stepped inside, Davy still lay in bed. Livy rushed across the room to his side. His cheeks burned a fiery red, and beads of perspiration ran from his hairline. She placed her hand on his forehead. A fever. Her heart skipped. She'd never nursed a sick child before. What should she do?

Without question, she turned toward Helen's room. Tapping on the door, Livy waited only a moment before Helen answered her knock. "Livy, good morning. Oh, dear. Is something wrong?" Helen asked as she set something on the nearby dresser. It was a small wooden heart. A jagged line ran from top to bottom where the two halves were joined together like a jigsaw puzzle, forming a complete, unbroken heart.

"Yes, Davy is ill. He has a fever. Would you come and see?"

"Certainly."

Inside Davy's room, she studied him for a moment,

then pressed her cheek against his. "Yes, a high fever, I would say."

Davy's eyelids fluttered and opened. A soft moan left his lips, followed by a deep, rattling cough. Livy pressed her hand against his cheek. "You don't feel well, Davy?"

He shook his head and tried to speak, but he coughed again.

Helen rose. "I made cough elixir not long ago. I'll mix it with warm lemonade." She looked at the child. "You'll like it, Davy. Perhaps, I should make a poultice for his cough," she said to Livy. She darted through the doorway.

Livy wet a cloth and cooled Davy's cheeks, then poured a glass of water from the nearby pitcher.

"What's wrong?"

Livy peered over her shoulder. Andrew stood in the doorway.

"Davy's ill. A fever and cough." She lifted the child's head with her hand as he sipped the water.

"Nothing serious, I hope?" He stepped into the room and approached the bed.

"I pray it's nothing serious. Maybe, a winter cold." She lowered Davy's head, setting the glass on the table.

"A winter cold. Yes, I'm sure that's it."

Helen hurried into the room, carrying a mug. "Here it is." Steam rose from the cup and the scent of lemon filled the air. She sat on the edge of the bed. "Davy, try some of this drink. It will help your cough."

He sipped, and when he tasted the acrid contents, he puckered his lips, but he drank without complaint. The liquid ran from his chin.

"Livy, you give him a bit more, and I'll prepare a mustard plaster. It'll do wonders to ease the cough."

She did as Helen asked while Andrew stood nearby. Gooseflesh rose on her arms with the sense that he was watching her. She longed to make him stop. . .or, better yet, to halt her rising emotions.

Davy sipped the liquid again. As she eased him to the pillow, his eyes drooped closed. She studied the boy, caressing his cheek while Andrew watched her.

"You look like a mother," Andrew murmured. "The picture fits you."

She looked downward to gain control, then faced Andrew. "Thank you," she whispered, "but I don't think God means for me to be a mother."

He tilted his head. "I think you're wrong, Livy. You're gentle and loving. Look how you care for the boy. You were meant to be a mother." He moved beside her and placed his hand on her shoulder. For a brief moment, his fingers kneaded the tense cords in her neck. Then, he was gone.

A sigh quivered from Livy's chest at his familiarity. She eyed the empty doorway. Resting her hand on Davy's arm, she listened to the raspy breathing and waited.

When Helen returned, she carried a folded cloth. The pungent odor of mustard permeated the air. She peered at the concoction in Helen's hand, two pieces of muslin cloth with a dark ocher paste spread between them.

"It's ground mustard and meal mixed with hot water," Helen said. She pulled down the cover and opened Davy's nightclothes, pressing the poultice to his chest. His eyes fluttered open then closed. "There now, if this doesn't work, we'll send for the doctor."

Livy gazed at the sleeping child then pulled a sturdy rocker to the bedside. "Thank you, Helen."

"You're very welcome, Livy."

"I believe I'll sit here for a while," Livy said, her focus on Davy.

"Remember, worry helps nothing." Helen patted her arm. "If his fever doesn't break, the doctor will come."

As Helen left the room, Livy sank into the rocking chair. While Davy slept, she rested her gaze on the gentle fall and rise of the blanket. *A mother?* Was she meant to be a parent like Andrew said? Her present life was free, unburdened, and—to be honest with herself— self-centered. Would she have patience to care for little ones who needed her totally? The questions tumbled in her head.

Children meant marriage. She sighed, imagining a life with Henry. She would live above the mercantile and, perhaps, work in the store. But she would teach her music lessons, as well. A life with Henry? Somehow the idea did not settle well in her mind.

And what about love? Must marriage and love go hand in hand? She was fond of Henry. Were fondness and love the same? *What is love?* Perhaps, her fondness for Henry *was* love. Then, what was it she felt for Andrew? *Passion?* The dreaded word rose in her mind again.

Suddenly, an image appeared. The wooden pieces in Helen's room—two jagged sides pushed together to form a perfect heart. With its peculiar shape, she felt positive that it was half the wooden heart she had carried to Grand Rapids. John called it a keepsake. A keepsake? But why did he return the remembrance to Helen? Her pulse accelerated at her conjecture. What did it mean? Would she ever know?

Chapter 4

Andrew left the carriage with the attendant and mounted the wide porch steps. The music reverberated through the brick exterior. When the door opened, a cacophony of sound billowed out into the quiet night—music, voices, and pandemonium.

Leaving his outer wrap with the servant, he turned to the large parlor. Matthew's parents had stored pieces of their fashionable furniture somewhere. Tonight, chairs and sofas lined the walls, leaving the bare wood floor open for dancing.

Across the hall, friends waved to him. They gathered around a piano, its tinkling notes blending with the music across the way. He stepped toward the smaller parlor as a hand nabbed his arm. "Why, Andrew, how lovely to see you again."

Without looking, he recognized Rosie's voice, and a shiver raced up his arm to his neck. He turned and looked at her. Dressed in a fashionable vibrant purple gown of velvet, her bustle and peplum were designed in a deeper shade like a polished plum. Her neckline scooped to reveal the soft white skin of her neck and shoulders, and for a moment the view startled him.

He had longed to view her lovely feminine frame, yet his subconscious thoughts reminded him of God's Word, "Favour is deceitful, and beauty is vain: but a woman that feareth the LORD, she shall be praised." Livy would never wear a gown cut as low. Her dresses were modest.

Rosie smiled at him, and a lilting laugh rose from her throat. All eyes turned from the small parlor to watch them in the hallway. She was a beauty. Her eyes sparkled and her lashes fluttered like a coquette. Yet he liked to think she flirted only with him. He pushed the Bible verse from his mind, assaying the admiring crowd, and she followed him into the small parlor.

Gathering around the piano, the crowd clapped their hands and sang to the merry music. When Rosie tugged on his sleeve to divert him to the dance floor, Andrew took a step forward to follow her; but at that moment, a gentleman slid onto the bench, and instead of the popular songs, he struck a series of introductory chords. The voices around him lifted in a Christmas carol. "Good Christian men rejoice with heart and soul and voice."

Andrew lingered, turning again to the music. Rosie spoke his name, but he quieted her. His mind soared back to the day Livy arrived and, sitting at the spinet, played the same carol. He had yet to hear her sing, and she said that singing was more her talent than playing. He longed to be with her now, to hear her sweet, sensitive voice raise in song.

He closed his eyes and pictured Livy seated at Davy's bedside. Her dainty hand probably rested on the child's arm. Did she sing him lullabies when no one listened? He shook his head in wonder. God meant her to be a mother. He had no doubt. She had all the attributes: gentleness, compassion, love, generosity, and kindness.

A pressure on his sleeve brought him back, and he turned to gaze into Rosie's pouting face. "I thought you enjoyed my company," she mewled.

"I am sorry, Rosie," he responded. "Would you please me with a dance?"

She nodded and her bright yellow curls bobbed at the fringe of her upswept hair. He took her arm and lead her across the hall to join the dancers in a lively polka, but his thoughts crept back to a quiet room with a sick child and a gentle woman.

As she rubbed the cords in her neck and shoulders, Livy studied the sleeping child. Her eyes drooped as if weighted, and she struggled to dispel sleep. A soft sound through the window alerted her that Andrew had arrived home. She had no idea of the time, though hours earlier, the grandfather clock in the upper hall chimed ten o'clock.

She waited until she speculated Andrew had retired for the evening, then rose. A cup of tea might relax her so she, too, could climb into bed and sleep. For the past two nights, she had keep vigil at the boy's bedside, praying for improvement. Though he had gotten no worse, his cough and fever lingered. Tomorrow she would recommend they send for the doctor.

Her plans to return home seemed thwarted by

Davy's illness, but she had not given up hope. She felt it imperative to receive Henry's Christmas call. The visit could be the beginning of their relationship, and though she questioned her motive, she believed that God's will might be done after all.

Stepping quietly through the doorway, she tiptoed down the upper hall, not to awaken those asleep, and edged her way down the darkened staircase. The glow of a softly burning lantern lit the foyer. A bright moon shone through the fanlight above the door, as well.

Moving with caution, she made her way to the kitchen. Coals still glowed in the range grate, and to Livy's surprise, a pot of heated milk sat on the top cover. Grace must have warmed a cup for herself. Livy sprinkled sugar and cinnamon into a mug and stirred the warmed liquid. As she turned, her heart leaped to her throat, and her hand flew to the neck of her shirt-waist where she had loosened a button. In the dim hall, a shadowy figure watched her.

"I'm sorry I frightened you." Andrew stepped from the darkened hallway into the kitchen with a mug in his hand. "I didn't hear you come down."

Her speeding pulse slowed as Andrew spoke. "I thought you'd gone to bed. The time sitting with Davy has been stressful, and I hoped to calm myself with a warm drink. But I'm afraid I have taken your milk."

"Please, it's not a problem. I made far more than I wanted."

She lifted the pot from the range. "Would you like the rest?"

He stepped forward, and she drained the simmering milk into his mug. "Let's sit in the keeping room," he suggested.

He turned, and she followed him down the hall to the keeping room.

A warm glow shimmered from the hearth, and she slid into a cozy chair, wrapping her skirt about her legs. "Did you enjoy the party?" Livy asked, sipping the sweet liquid.

"Yes, as party's go, it was jolly. Music, dancing, and singing Christmas carols." He leaned forward, staring into the glowing embers. "I thought of you, Livy."

He lifted his gaze to hers, and her pulse tripped at his directness. "Thought of me? But why with so many friends around you?"

"The singing, perhaps. I have yet to hear you sing, and I'd like to. I hear it's lovely."

Her heart hammered with confusion, and she was convinced he might hear it in the room's silence. "You embarrass me, Andrew. You've only heard idle chatter."

"Tell me it is not lovely, and I will believe you."

She pondered how to respond. Others told her she sang like an angel, but she was no judge of her own voice. "I cannot answer you. I have never heard my own voice except in my head. I only know what others say."

"And do *they* say it is lovely?"

The heat rose again to her cheeks.

"Then I am correct."

His gaze captured hers until she lowered her head to quell the pounding in her chest. Her vindictive nature sneaked out of hiding. "And how did you find Rosie this evening? As charming as ever?"

His lips pressed together as if in thought, then his mouth curved to a droll smile. "Why yes, she is an alluring woman."

Livy's heart quieted then fell like a weight. "I'm glad. You are a handsome man, Andrew, and I pray God will bless you with an equally handsome wife."

"God? You believe God's working for me, Livy? I'm afraid you are looking in the wrong direction." His dimples deepened with this wily chuckle. "God's Word leads me to a woman pure in *deed*, not one who is flirtatious. No, Miss Parker is not God's choice." He tilted his head, gazing at her. "Nor my mother's."

His mother? Livy struggled with his meaning. And who did Helen choose for him as a wife? Apparently, someone "pure in deed." Her mind shifted to Agatha. Was the dinner invitation as much to bring Agatha and Andrew together as it was "in her honor" as Helen had stated? She smiled at the idea.

"And what makes you smile?"

"Only a private thought."

"Private? Well, my sweet Livy, you should have 'private thoughts' more often. The smile lights your face and puts diamonds in your emerald eyes."

A tremor rushed along her arms to her chest, and her breath escaped in a short gasp. No man had ever said such bold, yet lovely, words to her before. Like the devil, Andrew beguiled her. She needed to be wary. When she caught her breath, she murmured a thank you, having no idea how to respond to his compliment.

"I need to go to bed. It's very late."

"Yes, I know. You've had a trying day. How is Davy this evening?" he asked, concern blanketing his usual grin.

"The same, I'm afraid."

"I admire you, Livy. You and your selflessness. You sit at the boy's bedside with rare devotion."

"Me? Thank you, but no, Andrew. I am ashamed at my selfish thoughts. I was resentful coming here with Davy. As a spin. . .an unmarried woman, I have only myself to consider."

"Perhaps, but you have changed. Your concern is for the boy alone."

"I do feel a responsibility. Davy is my brother's only child. I would do everything in my power to keep him safe and healthy."

"You see? What I have said is true."

His words amazed her. Perhaps she had changed for the better. "Though he's no worse, I think we should send for the doctor in the morning. . .to be certain."

"The doctor, yes. Rest, Livy. I'll go for him at sunrise." She rose. "Thank you, Andrew."

"You are welcome." He stood and, with one stride, stopped beside her. He raised his hand, tilting her chin upward, and his gaze locked to hers. "I'm right. They are emeralds. Beautiful." He brushed her cheek as he lowered his hand. "Time for bed, and I'll rise early as I promised."

He turned and sped from the room with Livy peering at his shadowed form ascending the staircase. When he vanished into the darkness, she brushed her cheek where his hand had rested. A sense of pleasure washed over her, and she lifted her eyes toward the ceiling spangled with light from the hearth. *Dear Lord, guide my path. Clear my mind. Rein my unbridled passion to self-control in Your Son's Holy Name.*

Chapter 5

Andrew kept his promise, and by nine in the morning, Dr. Browning arrived. Livy rose from the rocker at the sound of the footsteps. When he entered, he greeted Livy and set his bag on the rocker she'd abandoned. Andrew and Helen hovered in the doorway.

"What have we here?" he said, leaning over Davy and peering into his eyes. "How are you, lad?"

Davy stared at the stranger. "I cough," Davy said, his voice raspy from his hacking.

"How is his appetite?" the doctor asked as they hovered near.

"He's taken broth and some bread with apple butter. Little else."

The elderly man nodded, then leaned over his patient. "Open wide, lad."

Davy dropped his jaw, and the doctor peered inside, then pulled a stethoscope from his bag. He pressed the instrument against the boy's chest. "His lungs sound congested, but nothing serious."

He straightened his back, placing the stethoscope

in the bag, and looked at Livy. "I'd like you to prepare some alum and honey mixed with sage tea. It's a valuable gargle. Continue with an elixir for his cough, and keep him warm to sweat out the fever."

He turned to Davy. "And lad, you must eat." The doctor pulled the blankets around Davy's shoulders, tucked them in, then grabbed his bag. "I see nothing serious. He'll be fit again in a few days."

"What do I owe you, doctor?" Livy asked, sliding her hand into her pocket where she'd tucked her currency.

"Four dollars," he said.

She pulled the paper money from her pocket and laid bills into his hand. "Thank you for coming."

He looked at the crisp dollars and nodded. When he passed through the doorway, Andrew followed him. Helen hurried into the room. "Olivia, please let us pay for the doctor's expense. You shouldn't use your savings."

Livy shook her head. "Thank you, Helen, but I've paid him this time. If he visits again, I'll let you pay."

Helen acquiesced with a nod. "I'll ask Grace to stay with Davy tonight while we're at the dinner party."

Livy rubbed her temples. "I think I'll excuse myself and stay at home. If he wakes, he may be frightened with a stranger."

"Grace is no stranger, Olivia." She leaned over the child. "Davy, you know Grace, don't you?"

He nodded. "She gives me pudding," he said in his raspy voice.

"You see," Helen said. "I insist you come with us. Tomorrow you'll leave and all you'll remember is sitting in this chair."

"I've enjoyed myself, Helen."

If Helen knew the truth, Livy's heart flew heavenward recalling the time she'd spent with Andrew. Leaving Davy. . .and Andrew tomorrow weighed in her mind. And though she longed to stay, she felt driven to leave. "I'll see how Davy is in the morning. I'm not comfortable going unless he's totally well."

Helen pressed her arm. "You know you're welcome to stay, Olivia. More than welcome. We'd be delighted if you changed your mind."

"Yes, delighted," a voice echoed from the doorway.

Livy swung toward the sound of Andrew's voice.

"Please, convince Olivia to join us this evening, Andrew," Helen said. "She says she'd rather stay home to sit with Davy."

"Nonsense. What would a party be without you, Livy? You've had no fun at all. In fact," he volunteered, "I'll stay home, and you go along with mother and father."

Livy drew back in surprise. "You? Thank you, but no. If anyone stays home, it'll be me. "Anyway, your mother said Grace would stay with Davy. If he's well enough, I'll join you. I promise."

Helen nodded. "Then, let us do as the doctor said." She rested her hand on Davy's arm. "I'll send Grace up with some soup, and I want you to eat. Do you understand?"

"Yes," he said, his head bobbing against the pillow.

"That's a good lad."

Helen swept from the room, but Andrew remained and ambled to the bedside. "Livy, Father suggested I go out this morning and cut the Christmas tree. I'd like you to come along. If you go bundle up, I'll sit with Davy until Grace comes with his soup. What do you say?"

"I'd like to. It sounds nice. I saw the snow falling from the window."

"Good. Dress your warmest. I'll meet you at the side door in a few minutes."

Livy nodded, and Andrew turned to Davy. "Would you like me to tell you a story of the lumber camp? How about a tale of Paul Bunyan and his great blue ox, Babe?"

Davy's face brightened, and he scooted his head upward on the pillow. "Paul Bunyan? Is he a logger man?" His voice grated, but the cough seemed to have vanished.

Andrew chuckled. "Paul Bunyan is the greatest lumberjack around. And his ox, Babe, is so large he measures forty-two ax handles and a plug of chewing tobacco between the horns."

Livy inched her way to the door. Though she was eager for a break, she'd love to stay and hear the tales of the mythological lumberjack. Guilt tugged at her, too, knowing she had little time for the luxury of a sleigh ride; but Andrew asked, and she couldn't refuse.

"One day when Paul Bunyan came to the logging camp," Andrew continued, "he spied a giant tree that. . ."

In the hallway, Livy peered a final time into the room as Andrew sat in the rocker, his animated hands detailing the story of Paul Bunyan. He had captured Davy's interest, and Livy was grateful.

As Livy exited, Andrew's gaze followed her to the doorway. To his amazement, his chest fluttered like an inexperienced oaf when she agreed to the sleigh ride. He forced himself to concentrate on the tale of Paul Bunyan, and when Grace arrived with the soup, he darted from the child's bedside, anxious to meet Livy.

Dressed in his warmest attire, Andrew gazed through the window, watching snow flakes drift to the ground, and outside, he hurried to the stable. When the sleigh was ready, he grabbed the ax and gathered the buffalo robes, then guided the bays to the side door. Livy waited, her face framed by the window, and he bounded up the stairs to meet her.

Settling into the sleigh, he tucked the heavy lap robe around their legs and steered the horses onto the road. The brisk wind whipped across their faces. Gasping in the icy air, Livy laughed at their adventure, chattered about his Paul Bunyan tale, and then asked about being a lumberjack.

Andrew studied her and, realizing she was sincere, told her about the life of a logger.

"That's a long time away from home," Livy said, her voice reflective. "Months."

"Lumberjacks are home from spring to autumn. Many are farmers and come home in time for planting. It's a life we learn to accept."

"But what of the wives?" she murmured, then continued without waiting for his response. "And what do you do for fun in those long evenings?"

Andrew laughed. "Getting up at four in the morning,

I'm in bed early; but after dinner in the bunk-houses, they sing endless ballads, share personal stories, and tell folk tales. I hate to tell you about their trips to the nearest town. Some get mighty wild." He glanced at her. "You can rest assured, I'm not one of those."

"Rest assured?" she repeated, returning his grin.

When they reached the evergreens at the edge of the frozen river, Andrew secured the bays and helped Livy from the sleigh. He held her arm as they wandered through the fir trees. "What do you say, Livy? Which one? We need something that'll fit in the alcove of the parlor."

Livy's face glowed, and she pivoted in a circle, gazing at the myriad of trees. "There are too many, Andrew."

"Which do you like? Balsams? Douglas firs? White pines?"

"Which is which? You tell me what tree is best for decorating, and I'll pick the prettiest."

A smile perched on his lips. *Livy* was the prettiest, so pretty, he couldn't drag his attention to the trees. They marched through the snow, slipping and sliding, grasping each other for balance. Each time, he longed to hold her at his side, yet he feared she'd resist. Instead, he forced himself to let her go with each laughable mishap.

Finally, like a young girl, she darted between the trees to a shapely one, circled its branches, and returned to his side. "This one," she said. "Look at its color and shape." She bounced like a happy child while he pointed to the snow-laden limbs.

"Good choice, Livy. It's a blue spruce." The tree stood at least seven feet high with well-shaped branches that would hold the candles safely.

She touched the sleeve of his heavy coat. "It's perfect, Andrew."

He swallowed his heart and lay his hand on hers. "But not as perfect as you. Your size, your color, your fragrance. You're much more lovely."

Her face paled, then a rosy flush heightened her coloring. "Please don't say things you do not mean, Andrew. I'm not a young woman who knows how to handle your teasing." Her eyes pleaded with him. "I'm twenty-eight, not a young woman at all."

His hand slid around her shoulder, and he drew her to him, his emotions swaying like a pendulum. "You're young, Livy. What about me? I'm thirty." He dropped the ax and tilted her face with his thumb beneath her chin. "When I watch you with Davy, I don't know, you're. . .perfect, like an angel."

As she lowered her chin, she turned away. "No one's ever spoken to me like this. I don't know what to say."

He'd embarrassed her, and he admonished himself. Where was his self-control? Still, he doubted her words. He couldn't believe she'd never heard such words before. So many questions filled his mind. Reining himself, Andrew dragged his hand from Livy's shoulder and crouched down to clear the snow from the spruce's base.

When he swung the heavy ax, Livy gasped then cheered him on. No longer flustered, her lighthearted demeanor warmed his heart. Though felling trees was a daily chore at the logging camp, Andrew had never felt such pleasure with each stroke of the ax. Livy clapped her hands as the tree tilted, and for her amusement, he yelled, "Timber."

As the spruce toppled to the ground, Livy bolted to his side, and he nestled her in his arms. Silence wrapped around them, and he held his breath. "I want to kiss you, Livy."

Anxiety filled her face. "Please, Andrew, I'm terribly confused. Your life is so different from mine. I can't respond until I know my mind."

"I'd never do anything against your will. Believe me. But I'll ask you again, Livy. You can be sure." He had dampened her pleasure. For that, he was sorry. Grabbing the ax and hoisting the base of the tree, he pulled it to the sleigh and heaved it onto the back. He tucked Livy beneath the lap robes and joined her.

Before he called to the horses, he paused, turning to Livy. "I assume you think I'm forward. But I want to tell you something. When you first came, I found you attractive, but you seemed like the parish women, prim and proper. Yet I've changed and now, I see a different side of you."

She lifted her head, and the sunlight glinted in her eyes like the diamonds sparkling in the snow.

"I don't know why you've never married, but you're meant to be a wife and mother. It's clear to me. You belong with a loving husband who'll support you with a good business. One who wants children and loves you with all his heart. I believe that's what God has planned for you."

"I don't know if you're right, Andrew. For the past few years, I believed that God has no husband for me.

Some days, I think about taking the matter into my own hands. Then, I'm ashamed of my frustration with the Lord."

Andrew couldn't hold back his grin. "Livy, you're not alone. We've all tried to sway God to our thinking. I've done it myself. . .too often, I'm ashamed to say. Wait and see. Put your life in God's hands, and I'll do the same."

"I'll try," she whispered.

He prayed she understood his obscure message and moved the bays back onto the path. He'd say no more.

Livy's mind spun with all that had happened. As if Andrew knew Henry, he'd described him with perfection. A business man eager for children. A Christian man who understood the commitment of marriage. Yet, it wasn't Henry, but Andrew, whom she wanted to opened his heart and tell her he loved her.

A logger's life didn't seem adapted well to marriage. Lumberjacks were away from their homes for months at a time. Not a welcome life for a new bride. Still, she could imagine keeping a pleasant home and awaiting her husband's arrival. Each time he returned, she pictured how she would open her arms and greet him.

Life would be lonely when he was at camp—as lonely as her present life as a spinster—maybe worse. No, she wouldn't be content, married to a logger. And Andrew was a lumberjack. Better to have a life with a businessman, a man like Henry Tucker.

Livy bowed her head, sensing something was wrong. What would the Lord want her to do? Was a spinster's life what God meant for her? Or maybe a life tending orphaned children? Was safe, faithful Henry Tucker the man for her? Or Andrew? Could she trust him, knowing his taste for alluring, flirtatious women? No, she'd never attract a man like Andrew. Why even think about it?

Chapter 6

Returning home, Andrew dropped off Livy at the door. After leaving the horses and sleigh with the stable boy, he came back to the house and brushed the snow from his boots. When he entered the keeping room, his father sat in his favorite chair, reading the *Grand Rapids Eagle*.

"Good evening, Father."

"Andrew, sit and listen to this," Charles said, motioning to the newspaper. "The newfangled Christian Women's Temperance Union is holding a rally tonight." He released a boisterous chuckle. "I wonder if Governor Bagley will be forced to deal with the issue. Pressure's coming from all over."

"I don't know. Did you read about the lobbyists in yesterday's *Detroit Free Press?* They're fighting for exclusive river rights for running their logs to the sawmill. Now, that worries me."

Charles peered over his spectacles. "Could be a serious problem for the small logging camps."

"Like mine," Andrew said, thinking of his young lumber camp. Though his business had grown, he wasn't eager to pay heavy costs to boom logs on the river. He had a distance to go before becoming a lumber baron, but the title was inevitable, and he had to use good judgment. He'd noticed many young women fawning over him, and he guessed it was his future wealth that appealed to them. He hoped that wasn't cause for Rosie or Agatha's obvious attention. Andrew didn't question Livy's friendship, certain that her intentions were pure.

"I suppose, son, you should try to keep a positive attitude." He pulled his gaze from the newspaper to Andrew. "You have mail on the hall table, and there' a letter for Livy, too, I noticed."

"Thank you," Andrew said returning to the foyer. On the table, he found the two envelopes.

He opened the mail addressed to him and scanned the enclosed invitation, a New Year's Eve gathering hosted by Rosie Parker's family. Days earlier he would have smiled with pleasure, but now confusion tugged at his conscience. He wanted Livy to stay for the holiday, and he wouldn't have her sit home while he attended a party.

Yet, if Livy were determined to leave, sitting home on New Year's Eve would be twice as long and lonely, knowing his friends were enjoying the evening. He fingered the card, contemplating his decision. He decided to wait before accepting the invitation, wait until he knew what Livy planned to do.

Holding his invitation, he carried Livy's letter up the stairs. When she opened the door, the scent of ironed linen and soap filled the air. Livy smiled, and he delivered her mail, hoping it was good news from her brother, then went to his room to prepare for the evening.

Inside her room, Livy read John's letter which was filled with satisfactory news. Though Ruth hadn't fully recovered, she'd made progress. He hoped they would bring Davy home within the next two or three weeks. Thrilled with the good news, she was anxious to share it with her nephew.

Placing the letter on her dresser, she peered again into the chifforobe, pondering what she might wear. Tonight, if she attended the dinner party, she'd select her most fancy gown, a light blue dress of voile with embroidered Valenciennes lace. The modest neckline wasn't stylish, but her unassuming personality made it most appropriate.

That evening, Davy seemed content with Grace's company, so Livy slipped on her pale blue gown, tucked her hair into a chignon ornamented with blue ribbons, and joined the family. When she descended the stairs, Andrew observed her with an admiring smile, causing her heart to flutter like birds' wings.

"You look striking this evening, Livy," he said.

His words nestled into her memory. "Oh, it's nothing special, thank you. It's the most festive gown I have."

Without comment, he grasped her hand and brushed it with his soft lips. As Helen added her own compliments, Livy's heart danced.

With everyone ready, a servant held open Livy's cloak, and after each donned his outerwear, they departed.

A light snow drifted from the sky, sparkling in the brightness of the rising moon. The coachman helped them into the carriage, and soon, they were rattling down the rutted lane. Livy nestled beneath a heavy lap robe beside Helen. Charles and Andrew sat on the seat across from them. Facing Andrew's broad shoulders covered by his chesterfield, her memory drifted to the sleigh ride earlier in the day. The day's events took her breath away.

In the growing snowfall, the bays halted before an attractive dwelling. Though smaller than the Mandalay home, the house glowed with candles in the window, and through the pane, firelight flickered on the hearth. Livy climbed from the carriage and followed the others into the foyer with smells of spices and roasted meat filling the air.

"My, my something smells wonderful," Charles boomed as he pulled off his heavy coat then removed his steam-covered spectacles.

"Cloves and cinnamon," Agatha simpered as she took their wraps and hung them on the hall tree. "You smell my mulled cider." Then, leaning closer to Andrew, Agatha added, "And maybe, a bit of lavender."

"Yes," Livy agreed, "lavender is lovely. My favorite is lily of the valley."

Agatha dismissed her with a nod and motioned for them to enter the parlor. Livy sat on the divan, and to her pleasure, Andrew joined her. Agatha took note, evidenced by her frown.

Roger arrived with a tray of steaming mugs and, after greeting his guests, handed each a cup of the warm brew. The heat permeated Livy's hands, and as she sipped, it warm her chilled body.

After dinner, the conversation flitted from one topic to another until Roger slid onto the piano bench. "Now, Livy, won't you sing something for us? A hymn or carol."

Comfortable with singing, Livy rose and stood beside him at the piano. After a brief moment to agree upon a song, Livy looked at her small audience. "I hope you'll enjoy one of the newer carols. Have you heard 'O Little Town of Bethlehem'?" No one had, and they listened with interest as Roger played the introduction.

Livy drew in a deep breath and began the words of the less famous carol. Singing to this intimate group of friends, Livy's knees trembled before she gained courage. From her vantage point, Andrew sat enraptured, his gaze riveted on her.

When she finished the carol, they assailed her with compliments. "Sing another," Andrew said. "Anything, please."

"That was lovely," Helen added. "Truly lovely."

"One more," Livy agreed. "This is another new carol telling the story of our recent war, I think you'll like the refrain, and when you catch on, please join in."

Roger played, and Livy sang. "I heard the bells on Christmas Day, their old familiar carols play." As she reached the end of each verse, her spirit lifted as the voices joined hers with the words of hope, "of peace on earth, good will to men."

When the song ended, Livy returned to her chair. Then, together they sang familiar carols which ended when Agatha rose to bring in dessert.

"Livy, you must sing in church for Christmas if you decide to stay. Your voice could be enjoyed by the whole congregation, not only the few of us here," Roger said. "Will you stay for the holiday?"

She peered from one to the other, wondering what her answer would be. "I'm still not sure. In the morning, I'll see how Davy is feeling."

"If you do stay through the holiday, I'd enjoy your company on New Year's Eve," Roger said.

Livy's heart sank to her toes. If she extended her stay, she prayed that Andrew would be her escort for the evening. "Davy's health will make the determination," she said again.

"Well, then, we'll wait and see," Roger said. "Andrew, are you up for a New Year's Eve celebration?"

"I've received an invitation already, Roger. . .but, don't let my plans ruin your own."

"We'll decide later, then. If Livy stays, we'll find an agreeable time for everyone to celebrate the New Year."

Hearing Andrew's answer, Livy made an immediate decision. Tired of wishful thinking and useless dreams, she prayed Davy would well by morning. She refused to stay another minute in Grand Rapids with her uncontrollable, romantic fantasies. She guessed his invitation was from Miss Parker. No matter what Andrew said to Livy in private, his heart seemed tied to the vivacious woman.

No matter what compliments Andrew dropped in her presence, she'd block them from her hearing. Andrew wanted only one thing: for her to care for

Davy. She was certain. No matter how many sweet things he said, he had no interest in her whatsoever.

Her mind sent up a silent prayer, asking God, once again, for forgiveness. Andrew's captivating personality and good-looks aroused feelings she should never have. God expected chaste thoughts, and Livy assumed that her longing for Andrew's hand on hers and his lips pressing against her mouth could be nothing but sinful.

At twenty-eight, her inexperience embarrassed her. With no older sister, she wished she could garner courage to talk with Helen about love and romance before she returned home. Even though Ruth lived nearby Livy in Detroit, her illness made her seem an unlikely candidate to discuss romance. John certainly showed his wife affection, but Livy had a difficult time imaging Ruth feeling the strong emotions that wielded through Livy's thoughts.

Helen seemed an appropriate counselor. Remembering the wooden heart, Livy was certain the keepsake held a tale of love.

Determined to leave on the next train, Livy packed her bags before the sun had fully risen the following morning. She hurried to the kitchen where Grace was mixing a large pot of oatmeal for the family's breakfast.

When she entered the kitchen, Grace turned. "You're up early, Miss Schuler. Would you like some warm oatmeal?"

"Yes, and tea, Grace, if it's ready."

Livy downed her quick breakfast then returned to the second floor, eager to see Davy. When she entered his room, the boy looked at her with sleepy, reddened eyes. He lifted his head from the pillow, squinting at her traveling gown. "How are you feeling today?" Livy asked, sitting on the edge of his bed. "Did you have fun with Grace?"

"She told me about Joseph and Mary and the baby Jesus. Mama tells me the story sometimes when she's not sick."

"I know. And she's feeling better, according to your papa's letter. You'll be going home in awhile."

Davy placed his hand on the sleeve of her traveling dress. "Are you going away?" His mouth pulled downward, and his coloring appeared mottled.

"I'm catching the train this morning."

"With me?"

A pang of regret caught like a knot in her chest. "No, Uncle Charles and Aunt Helen want you to stay for Christmas, but I have reasons to go home."

"I want to go with you."

"No, Davy, your mama isn't well enough, yet. In a couple more weeks."

"Please, don't leave."

A soft noise from the doorway caused Livy to turn. Andrew leaned against the door frame, observing them. "You're leaving?"

"I'm ready, yes, but. . ." She tilted her head toward Davy. "I seem to have opposition."

"It doesn't surprise me." He stepped into the room and sat beside her at the foot of the bed. "You want your Aunt Olivia to stay here, Davy?"

The child turned his head back and forth, not sure

where to concentrate his attention.

"You're much better now, Sweetheart," Livy persisted.

Wide-eyed, he didn't response.

"I have no reason to stay," she said, turning to Andrew. "Would you ask if a servant could drive me to the railroad station? I'm sure a train is scheduled for today, sometime. I'm willing to wait."

"You're determined to go?"

"Yes, it's for the best." She rose, patting Davy's arm. "I'll see you before I leave." She paused at the door and spoke to Andrew. "I'll be in my room when the driver's ready."

Andrew watched her bolt through the doorway. His folded hands rested on his knees, and he stared at his boots. Why did she insist upon rushing away? He'd believed for a while that she might change her mind. He eyed Davy, noticing a skin rash. He pulled his nightshirt away from his neck. Not sure of the illness, he knew one thing. Davy's problem wasn't a cold. He stepped to the doorway and called to Livy.

Her door opened, and when she saw him, she rushed into the hallway. "What?" she asked, peering toward Davy's room.

"Take a look. The fever and cough were only symptoms."

"Symptoms? I don't understand." She followed him inside. Andrew pulled back the neck of Davy's nightshirt. Livy eyed the red spots. "Scarlet fever?" she gasped.

"I'm not sure," Andrew said. "Maybe, only the measles. I'll call Mother."

Livy nodded, sinking to the edge of the bed. "Please, Andrew. . .there's no need to arrange a ride for the station. I'm staying here with Davy."

Chapter 7

Andrew rose from his bed and ambled across the room to the window seat, his mind on Livy. Two days earlier with the discovery of Davy's scarlet fever, she decided to stay in Grand Rapids. Davy's illness, he thanked God, seemed a light case, according to Doctor Barlow, but Livy was nailed to the boy's side.

To his frustration, Livy was with Davy or did all she could to avoid Andrew. Her most direct conversation came when she asked him a favor. He agreed and had gone to Western Union to sent John a telegraphic message, alerting him of her change in plans and alleviating their fears with the doctor's positive prognosis.

Since that day, Andrew's plans had changed, too. Strange visions somersaulted in his mind. Marriage had evaded him for the past years. First, he was busy building his lumber business. Then, he avoided women, fearing their interest was in his money. Finally, he'd enjoyed his freedom, the unfettered life of a single man. Now, he could think of nothing else but Livy.

Today, he opened his Bible and stared at the scripture. The Testament had lain in a drawer for many months. . .years, if he were honest. But since Livy stepped into his life, he'd been driven to God's Word.

He was thirty, no longer prompted by his parents' guidance, yet his mother's teachings clustered like a litany in his mind. "Marriage is a blessed union, guided by God. A happy man loves his wife, but as important, he must respect her. She instructs and loves his children and supports her husband. A Christian wife is a wonderful gift from God."

The words his mother uttered for years described Livy. He pictured Rosie, but her allure had vanished. Since her arrival, Livy had, with slow assurance, invaded his mind. . .and more, his heart. He admired her grace and compassion, and she radiated beauty despite her reserved appearance. Her face glowed, and her mouth curved to a warm smile when she looked at him.

Andrew looked down at the scripture verses open on his lap. His fingers had guided him to Proverbs 31, and he lifted the leather volume and stared at the words rising from the page. *"Who can find a virtuous woman? for her price is far above rubies. The heart of her husband doth safely trust in her, so that he shall have no need of spoil. She will do him good and not evil all the days of her life."*

Andrew contemplated Livy's gentleness and intelligence. He returned to the page. *"She riseth also while it is yet night, and giveth meat to her household, and a portion to her maidens. . . . She girdeth her loins with strength, and strengtheneth her arms. She perceiveth that her merchandise is good: her candle goeth not out by night."*

He envisioned her sitting at Davy's side, empathy and love shining in her eyes.

"She openeth her mouth with wisdom; and in her tongue is the law of kindness. She looketh well to the ways of her household, and eateth not the bread of idleness. Her children arise up, and call her blessed; her husband also, and he praiseth her." Andrew felt as if God were describing Livy in His Word.

He read further, letting the Lord's lesson take hold. *"Favour is deceitful, and beauty is vain: but a woman that feareth the LORD, she shall be praised."*

Andrew recalled the same verse entering his thoughts at the Christmas party. Was God speaking to him that evening? The question sent gooseflesh galloping along his arms. Though he'd never been a religious man, today his faith pushed against his heart.

He bowed his head, thanking God for the realization that flooded through him. He had to win Livy's love. It wasn't only God's will, but his own.

For two days since she'd changed her plans, Livy dashed from one task to another. Besides nursing Davy, she had approached Helen about appropriate garments for the holiday.

On Tuesday afternoon, Helen searched her closets for frocks that might fit Livy with simple alterations. Livy was amazed at the number of fashionable gowns hanging in Helen's closet.

"Now, Olivia, this one is ideal for you. A few tucks and it'll fit perfectly. And the shade will look wonderful with your coloring. Look in the glass."

Olivia steered her around, and Livy eyed herself in the mirror. The hunter green taffeta gown cinched her narrow waist and draped in graceful folds to the floor with a wide ruffled hem. Livy agreed, the color brightened her eyes and highlighted her dark hair.

"Well," Helen asked again, "will it do?"

"Do? Helen, it's beautiful. More than I could ever afford. I'm sure it's an expensive Worth gown, isn't it?"

"Yes, but I want you to have it. We'll ask the tailor to take in an inch or two, then it will be ideal. No one would ever recognize the dress. And this orchid gown is lovely, and you'll look so beautiful in it. This is fun!"

Livy's mind raced. After the tailor, she had to visit the local mercantile to purchase Christmas gifts.

Once Helen had collected the gowns, Livy and she headed for town to complete their holiday preparations. While Helen lingered at the shop, Livy visited the general store and selected gifts for each family member: a leather brush set for Charles, a gilt-finished sewing box for Helen, a cashmere scarf for Andrew, and a wooden horse and carriage for Davy. Choosing a black velvet reticule and green ribbons for herself, she returned to the tailor shop to meet Helen.

"Olivia, I can't wait for you to see the gown Mildred finished for me. It'll be delivered with yours tomorrow. And not a minute too soon."

"I waited too long to make my decision, Helen. I'm sorry."

"Don't worry yourself. Everything will fall into place." She rested her hand on Livy's arm. "Now, do you think we have time for tea?"

"Whatever you say," Livy said. "The bells sounded three a few moments ago."

"Then we have time. Come. I'll take you to Birdie's Tea Shop." She beckoned Livy to follow. "She serves the most delicious tea cakes."

Outside in the brisk winter air, Livy struggled to keep up with Helen's brisk pace to the tea shop. Before they were seated, Livy gaped at the elegant display of breads and cakes.

When they were seated, they nibbled and chatted like old friends. Sensing the time pass, Livy struggled to muster her courage. She'd wanted to speak with Helen about many personal concerns, and today, the opportunity seemed perfect. Drawing a deep breath, Livy began, "I have a confession to make, Helen. When I arrived here with Davy, it was really against my wishes. My life is usually my own, but I pushed my plans aside to help my brother and Ruth."

Helen's brow creased. "You were being kind, Livy, but I can understand, though my life hasn't been my own for years." She fingered her teacup, and a gentle grin rose on her face. "I'm not certain I'd have it any other way."

With Helen's admission, Livy's heart lifted. "And that's why I'm confessing, Helen. I've want to talk for so long with someone. . .someone who might offer me advice."

Helen's expression melted to tenderness. She rested her palm on Livy's hand. "Please, treat me as you might a sister. If I can help you, I will."

Livy sighed. "I've had so little excitement in my life. For twenty-eight years, I hoped God would lead me to a loving husband, but I'm afraid my hope and God's plan don't match; so earlier this year, I decided to take the matter into my own hands."

Helen's eyes widened. "Your own hands? What do you mean by this?"

Livy sensed disapproval in Helen's expression, and she lowered her head. With careful detail, she described her relationship with Henry Tucker. "Helen, my real wish to go back to Detroit is that I want to be home for Henry's Christmas visit. As I said, I'd longed for a husband who I could cherish. . .one who'd stir my heart. But as you can see, I wasn't meant to be in Detroit for the holiday."

Guilt edged up Livy's neck as Andrew flew to her mind. "I was trying to find someone on my own. Then I wonder if Henry's the husband God has chosen for me."

Helen stroked Livy's arm. "Olivia, we can't force the Lord's will. God's plan for each of us is revealed in His good time, not ours. I understand your eagerness for a home and family. The problem is, we don't see God's full plan."

"But Helen, look how perfect your life is. You and Ruth were childhood friends. . .and her brother fell in love with you. It seems the plan was laid out so carefully. But I don't have a friend with a handsome, loving brother—"

Helen pressed her arm, her face drawn. "Olivia, my story's not that simple. Not that simple at all. Love didn't come as easily as you think. We all must accept God's will and guidance by opening our eyes and our hearts."

Livy searched Helen's face, wanting to understand the message tangled in her words. Questions spilled to Livy's tongue, but she waited for Helen to continue. The only sound was the clerk's voice speaking to a customer.

"You mentioned love," Livy said, after the silence lingered longer than she could bear. "I've asked myself so often, 'What is love?' I have a fondness for Henry. A tender affection, maybe. He's a cordial, kind man who'd be a faithful husband and loving father. Is that love, Helen?"

Helen's tensed mouth relaxed. "I suppose love is different for each of us. . .and remember, Olivia, love can grow. A small spark becomes a flame. A flame can kindle a fire that warms our days." She quieted. Then, a flush rose beneath her collar.

Livy's skin heated at her burning questions. "If I'm too direct, Helen, please tell me." Livy leaned toward her and lowered her voice. "Are love and passion the same? Does love ripple through your chest and take your breath away?" Amusement grew on Helen's face, but Livy didn't care. The questions bubbled from her. "Does your heart dance and long to. . .? I am embarrassed to say it." Her hands knotted against the table, and she lowered her head.

"To be kissed and caressed?"

The words jolted her. "Oh, yes. To be kissed. Is that passion or love?"

"I can't answer that, Livy. Marriage is a warm intimate relationship between two committed people—a sharing of mind, body, and spirit. It's a gift from God."

"A gift from God. I've never thought of marriage in

that way." Livy's mind raced at her own foolishness. Taking matters into her own hands wouldn't be a gift from God.

"And that's why," Helen added, "you must let God be in charge. Wait for the gift. . .whatever it may be. Be assured, Olivia, if you really listen, God will guide you. He'll show you the way. . .even if it's not the path you'd planned to travel."

Not the path you'd planned to travel. The words sent a ripple of excitement down Livy's spine. "Like my trip here, Helen. It wasn't my plan to travel. Was it God's?" Her pulse tripped on its rushed path.

"You have to decide that for yourself. I won't second guess God. But I will say, we've enjoyed your company beyond words. And maybe your visit has answered *my* prayers."

"Your prayers? In what way, Helen?" Without delay, the wooden heart leapt to her thoughts.

"Time will tell, Olivia. Time will tell."

Chapter 8

"You seem a little better, Davy," Livy said.

"May I watch Aunt Helen decorate the hall?"

"We'll see. Maybe, for a while. Would you like to sit in my room and play? We'll see how well you feel then?"

He nodded and swung his legs over the edge of the bed. Livy tugged his heavy stockings over his chilled legs and wrapped a coverlet around his shoulders. "Follow me." Her spirit soared seeing him up and about.

With Davy seated at her desk with a pencil and paper, she sat nearby, wondering what the next days would bring. Celebrating the holiday with the Mandalays had introduced Livy to new customs like cutting the tree. This afternoon, they'd decorate the hall and parlor. Helen promised tomorrow, Christmas Eve, would be filled with surprises.

When Livy rose to admire Davy's artwork, a tap sounded against the door. In a step, she pulled it open, and Andrew peered in at her. "Mother asked me to knock. The servants are bringing in the greens, and she wondered if you'd like to join us."

"Thank you. I'm looking forward to it."

He peered beyond Livy to the desk. "Well, look who's out of bed."

Davy turned with a smile, and Livy pulled back the door. Andrew stepped through the doorway and strode to Davy's side. "You don't look like a leopard any longer."

Davy giggled. "Aunt Livy said I might be able to watch Aunt Helen decorate the hall."

"If you do, Davy, you should only come for a little while. You must stay well. Tomorrow evening, we'll open gifts by the tree. You don't want to miss that."

Excitement spread across Davy's face. "Gifts? Are there gifts for me?"

"Certainly." Andrew brandished a smile. "And gifts for Aunt Livy, too."

An unexpected excitement rifled through Livy. "You shouldn't have."

"But why not? Everyone should enjoy the fun." He rested his hand on her shoulder. "Will you be down soon?"

"Yes, I'll help Davy dress and be there shortly."

"I'll see you later." Gently patting her arm, he turned and left the room.

As he closed the door, Livy pressed her hand against her bodice, calming the riot in her heart.

❦

Davy sat on the bottom of the staircase, his face flushed.

"I hope Davy's reddened cheeks are from excitement and not a fever." Livy touched his face and laughed at herself. "I sound like an overprotective mother."

"Your cheeks are rosy, too," Andrew said. "Or are the red ribbons throwing a reflection?"

She pressed her palms against her heated skin, hoping to hide the truth. "Too much excitement for both Davy and me. Everything looks so beautiful."

She pivoted around the foyer, admiring the wreaths hanging at the front windows, the garland and ribbons draping the staircase, and the swags of cedar displayed over the doorways. Unable to control her enthusiasm, Livy burst into song. "Deck the halls with bows of holly. . . ."

"Fa-la-la-la-la. . . ," Andrew joined her.

One by one, the others followed. Charles grabbed Helen's hand as she stepped from the keeping room, then Andrew clasped Livy's hand, and forming a ring, they circled in the center of the foyer. Davy jumped up from his perch to join them.

With the unfamiliar words in the second verse, their voices faded except Livy's until they roused again at the end of each line, booming the refrain.

"Follow me in merry measure," Livy sang, twirling them faster and faster. "While I tell of Yuletide treasure." The spirited circle broke rank with laughter as the final refrain died away.

Gasping for breath, Helen fanned her face. "I'm much too old for all of this," she said, "especially since we need our energy to finish the tree." The sound of a playful groan echoed against the high ceiling. "We have a reprieve. I believe it's nearly dinnertime. We'll finish after we eat."

As if hearing Helen's words, Grace announced the

meal, and the troupe turned to the dining room.

Davy's presence added a special spark to the family meal. They lingered over dessert until Davy yawned, and Helen offered to take him up to bed. Charles rose, saying he needed to ask the stable boy to bring in a fresh load of logs for the fireplace.

With the others conveniently gone, Andrew faced Livy, knowing the moment had come. Hurrying to her side, he pulled her from chair. "Follow me, Livy. We have one more decoration to hang before the others arrive."

Her face filled with question, but he left her to wonder and headed to the foyer. He heard her brisk footsteps behind him, and he feared to look at her because he'd give himself away. Beneath the parlor archway, he stopped and beckoned. "Come here. I'll lift you up to find the tack."

She frowned but did as he asked. Grasping her small waist in his hands, he swooped her into the air level with the upper door frame. "Do you see it?"

"Yes," Livy gasped.

With caution, he held her against him with one arm and handed her a sprig of mistletoe bound with a red ribbon. "Hang the string over the tack, please."

She grasped the bright spray of white berries and raised it above his head. "Finished," she called.

His stomach knotted as he lowered her, and when her feet touched the floor, he kept her close in his arms. She faced him and hesitated. What if she resisted him? He swallowed the anxiety that rose to his throat. It tumbled downward, tangling around his heart. As the possibility filled his mind, she tried to step backward, but he kept his grasp firm, binding her to his chest.

His fear faded. She didn't struggle or cry out. Instead, a look of wonder filled her face. "I don't have to tell you what happens now, do I? It's tradition."

Livy's lips parted with a gasp of surprise. As if in suspended motion, he lowered his lips to hers.

At his touch, Livy closed her eyes and savored the sweetness she had only dreamed about. A roar grew in her ears. Her knees weakened. Would she faint? Would she die?

His gentle lips lingered on hers until she sensed she would scream. Warmth spread through her, growing and swelling, until she felt ignited with a dazzling glow. *Sparks. Flame. Fire.* Helen's words burned in her mind.

As tenderly as their lips had met, he drew away, and when she lifted her lids, his looked as weighed as hers felt. A heated flush burned on her cheeks and spilled down her neck, and she released a sigh.

"Oh, Livy. Dearest. I've wanted to kiss you for so long. Have I offended you? Please, say no."

She stumbled backward, her hands clutching at the folds in her dress. "Only surprised me, Andrew. I've never. . .no man has. . .I'm—" No words expressed her feelings.

"You're beautiful." He tilted her chin upward with his thumb while a finger caressed her lips. "And you're loved."

Loved? But what of Miss Parker and his logging career? And what of Henry Tucker and. . .? Livy halted her racing mind. "Andrew, please, don't say things you don't mean. I can't bear it."

"I mean every word. I know we've only met, Livy, but sometimes God speaks in ways we never imagine. God's guided me to you. I believe that with all my heart."

"But. . .I'm not sure of my heart. It's beating so fiercely, I think I'll die."

He slid his arm around her shoulder and nestled her against his chest. "You won't die, Livy. You've only begun to live. Me, too. I won't press you, Livy. I only ask you to pray that God's will be done. If you do, I know you'll love me as I love you."

The thundering of her heart drowned his next words, but Livy didn't need to hear more. She'd heard all she ever longed to hear. *You'll love me as I love you.*

Chapter 9

Livy avoided Andrew throughout the evening as the family adorned the tree with apples, strings of cranberries, candy, cookie ornaments, paper creations, and candles. Not that she didn't care about him, but that she cared too much. As soon as possible, she took her leave, hurrying to her room to ponder the day's events.

Sleep evaded her, her thoughts rushing and surging throughout the night. If she hadn't kept her wits about her, she would've awakened Helen from a sound sleep to lay her tangled heartstrings before her. Livy cared deeply for Andrew, yet she couldn't forget all the difficulties she'd bear, especially his months away at the logging camp. Trying to push her fears aside, she reminded herself that God would guide her through the difficult times.

Livy felt bleary-eyed when the sun's golden rays sneaked through the window. During the night, the joyful song they had sung lingered in her mind. *"While I tell of Yuletide treasure."* She recalled, again, Helen's treasure, her keepsake, and longed to know its meaning. Finally,

Livy pulled herself from the bed and faced the day.

With the holiday at hand, Livy joined Helen, adding the final touches to the decorations, dinner menu, and gifts. The parlor door remained closed, awaiting the evening's festivities. And Davy, feeling stronger, hovered near Livy, not giving her a moment of privacy.

Finally before the dinner hour approached, she coaxed Davy to nap, explaining he'd enjoy the evening more fully. With him safely in bed, Livy knocked on Helen's door. Hearing nothing, Livy turned away, but as she did, the door opened, and Helen freed a soft chuckle.

"It's you, Olivia. Charles and Andrew are like children trying to peek at their gifts. I assumed you were one of them. Come in."

Livy entered, her eyes shifting immediately toward the wooden heart. "I'm sorry to disturb you. I didn't sleep well last night. Since you offered to listen, I'd like to take a few minutes, if I could."

"Please, sit, Olivia. I meant what I said. Whatever your worries, my ears are open."

Helen sank into a cozy armchair, and Livy situated herself on an adjacent settee. "So many things are banging in my head, I don't know where to begin. When I spoke to you yesterday, I concealed some of my strongest feelings. . .out of embarrassment, I suppose. Since I arrived, Andrew aroused my interest, and now, I'm very fond of him."

To Livy's astonishment, a smile lit Helen's face.

"I tried not dream about it. He's handsome and fun, and many attractive woman vie for his attention.

I'm quiet and restrained, not his type at all. Yesterday, he made me blush like a schoolgirl."

Helen frowned. "Nothing inappropriate, Olivia, I pray."

"Oh, no, compliments. Lovely things no man has ever said before."

Helen chuckled. "Ah, I feel better."

"But yesterday, Helen, after dinner, he asked me to help hang the mistletoe. . .and he—"

"He kissed you!"

"Yes, the kiss was wonderful, better than I've dreamed, but it was more than a kiss. He said he *loved* me."

Helen bounded from her seat and wrapped her arms around Livy. "This is even better than I dreamed. At tea when I said maybe your visit had answered my prayers, this was my hope—that Andrew and you would fall in love."

Livy's mind spun. She'd been so certain it was the heart that had answered Helen's prayers.

"I saw a spark of interest in Andrew's eyes when you arrived," Helen continued. "I've always hoped he'd find a charming, Christian woman, but he had his own mind. And he's an adult. I couldn't sway him. But I prayed that God would. And you see, my prayers are answered." Helen quieted, then peered at Livy. "You do love him, Olivia? I pray you didn't spend the night wondering how to tell him you don't love him."

"No, no, that's not my problem. I'm afraid I love him *too* much. That my feelings are only passion and not real, lasting love. I've imagined his lips on mine and his arms holding me close—emotions that I know God doesn't approve."

Helen sank onto the cushion beside her. "Don't you know that God created both love and passion? He directs a man and wife to share the intimacy of their lives. It's only when we step beyond our marital beds that God becomes angry. Weigh your feelings for Andrew, Olivia. Do you think only of his lips on yours? Or, do you picture a life together, sharing all the joys and sorrows of marriage?"

Livy's clenched hand covered her heart. "I've compared it all: sickness, health, trials, joys, work, play, everything that happens."

Helen patted her hand. "Then if you can accept it all, God's blessed you with both love and passion. Not all marriages are built on both."

Livy released a deep sigh. "I should talk with Andrew. I didn't respond very well to him." She paused, her interest drawn to the dresser top. As the keepsake tugged at her curiosity, a shiver rippled down her arms. "Helen, when you said, my visit might be an answer to your prayer, I suspected you referred to the package I brought you from John. It was half the heart on your dresser, wasn't it?"

Livy expected anger or distress, but a tender smile rose to Helen's lips. "Yes, it was the heart, but it wasn't the keepsake that I referred to. My prayer was you and Andrew. The heart's a different story altogether. Would you like to hear it, Livy? It might explain what I was talking about the other day."

"Please, tell me, Helen," Livy said, edging forward, eager to hear her explanation.

"I think it makes a rich closure to our discussion."

She settled into the chair. "Your brother, John and I knew each other *before* I became Ruth's friend. We were neighbors and played together as children. But when we became aware of each other as a man and woman—I should say boy and girl—things changed. We fell in love." She smiled. "Or so we thought."

John and Helen? Livy's pulse raced.

"He was a wonderful woodcarver, like Charles, and maybe, that's what brought about their friendship. For a birthday gift when I was fifteen, John carved the heart and divided it in half. We shared each other's heart, he said, and when we married our hearts would become one."

"Helen, I never knew John to be so romantic."

"Oh yes, he was. Very romantic. But the story continues. Around the same time, Ruth came into my life. So she became part of John's life, too. Ruth was frail. She had a weak heart, and John—you know how kind he is—was always around to help her or encourage her on.

"Soon, John spent more time with Ruth than with me. I was angry, I'm ashamed to admit, and wished terrible things on Ruth. But one day, I realized that God guides our walk in life. John, with his patience and quiet gentleness, was a perfect husband for Ruth, not for me. Then, I noticed Charles. . .and Charles noticed me."

The story had captured Livy's imagination. "Was he the spark that became a flame?"

"Ah, yes, like a match struck to yellowed paper. Our love ignited about as quickly. We were young, but God guided us to marry. And, Olivia, I'll never be sorry. Not for one moment. God's will was best for me. . .and for Ruth and John, too. He's made her a fine husband."

So caught in the story, Livy gasped for air. "But what about the heart? Why did he return it now?"

"Oh, I suppose he found it after all these years, tucked somewhere in his belongings. I don't know, but I was touched when I saw it. Touched because he gave back my heart. He reminded me in the dearest way that we're both whole and complete in our lives as we live them now."

"You don't think he's loved you these past years?" Livy whispered.

"My, my, no, Olivia. He's loved Ruth forever. Your brother is such a gentleman, a good man. He would never be unfaithful, nor would I. God guided us as I believe He's guided you."

Livy flung her arms around Helen's neck. "Like you said, sometimes God sends people on a path they hadn't planned to travel. I think my path was here."

Helen squeezed Livy's hand. "And I can't tell you how happy I am."

❦

A tap on Livy's door brought her to her feet. When she opened it, Andrew grinned, holding a large package. "Delivery from the tailor shop," he said, his dimples deepening. "I imagine you've been waiting for this."

"Or I'd be wearing rags this evening," she said. For the first time, she looked at Andrew without a nagging fear or frightening questions.

She moved away from the door, and he stepped inside, placing the large parcel on her bed. As she moved past him, he caught her hand. "Have you been thinking, Livy?"

"I have. A great deal. . .in fact, all night long."

"Me, too," he said, laughing. "And can you tell me your thoughts?"

"I might," she said, "and then I might not."

"Livy, your smile takes my breath away. I'll wait. You'll tell me when you're ready. . .but I know your answer. You can't hide it from me." He strolled from the room, leaving a portion of his happiness lingering behind.

Livy unwrapped her gowns and hung them, choosing the violet frock for the evening. Time was short, and she saw to Davy, and then dressed for the Christmas Eve celebration. Tonight was one to truly celebrate—a night of love, God's gift of love, His Son born to save the world, and her own gift of love for Andrew.

When she'd completed her toilette, she took Davy's hand, and they descended the stairs. As they reached the bottom step, Grace called the family for dinner. Though the meal was tasty, Livy felt like a child, waiting for the moments following dinner.

Finally, Charles stood, offering a Christmas prayer, and they followed him to the hall outside the parlor. In anticipation, Davy jiggled from foot to foot. When Charles swung the French doors open, Livy reveled in the spectacular Christmas tree.

Davy rushed forward while Livy controlled her desire to join him. She marveled at the candles glowing from every branch. She felt childlike as she approached the towering tree that radiated light, reminding her of the star of Bethlehem. Beneath the tree, packages stood wrapped in brown paper, cloth, or lace all tied with ribbons and bows. Nearby a water-filled bucket stood with the rag mop to douse any possible fire.

"Livy, would you lead us tonight? Why don't we sing a carol," Charles suggested, stroking his mustache. "What will it be, Helen?"

" 'Silent Night,' " she said, stepping forward and taking Charles's hand, then Davy's. "It's my favorite."

Livy grasped Davy's free hand, and Andrew stepped to her left and slid his fingers through hers. As they clasped hands around the tree, Livy sang the first notes of the carol, and they joined her. Tears welled in Livy's eyes. She'd never experienced this kind of happiness. Her life seemed complete.

When the song ended, Davy was the first to open his presents. From the first wrapper, he pulled a strange contraption that Charles explained was a stereopticon. Livy had heard Queen Victoria had taken fancy to them, but this was the first she'd seen.

"See the cards, Davy," Helen coached. "Put one in the machine and look at the picture."

Livy removed a card from the package and slid it into the brackets. Davy held it to his eyes and let out a squeal. "It flew at me," he said in wonder. "Look, Aunt Livy."

Livy lifted the contraption and gasped while laughter rang around the room.

When Livy finished her last gift, Andrew slipped another into her hand, a small package wrapped in brown paper tied with a lace ribbon. Inside the package lay a hand-carved angel, delicate and detailed. She eyed Charles, but he shook his head and nodded to-ward Andrew.

"You carved this?" Livy asked, gaping.

He grinned.

"Yourself?" She eyed the exquisite detail again. "I'm impressed. No, amazed. It's beautiful." She pressed the tiny carving to her chest. "Thank you, I'll cherish it."

"You're an angel, Livy. It seemed right."

"I love it. It's my very own Christmas treasure." She looked toward Helen who smiled with understanding.

While they thanked each other for the gifts, Grace appeared at the doorway with a tray of hot chocolate and a plate of Christmas desserts. Livy longed to speak with Andrew, but the family's excitement continued without a break. She knew her talk would wait until Christmas Day.

Chapter 10

Christ Church radiated with candle glow, garland, and wreaths. Following the service, Helen sent Andrew to tell the Dailys what time they should arrive for Christmas dinner. Livy cringed inwardly, wondering how Agatha would react when she learned of her new relationship with Andrew. She hoped to spare the young woman embarrassment.

As they left the building, Roger approached her and murmured in her ear. "Andrew told me the news. I am happy for you, Livy. You deserve a fine man like Andrew."

Embarrassed, she mumbled her thanks, but when she stepped outside, she filled with relief. If Roger knew, then Agatha would be forewarned.

As the bays trotted along the street, snowflakes drifted from the sky like downy feathers. Arriving home, Andrew beckoned Livy to remain in the sleigh. "Mother, Father, I thought I'd take Livy for a short ride."

Charles patted Andrew's arm with a sly grin. "Let me send out a buffalo robe for you."

Helen didn't hide her pleasure. "I'll take Davy

inside. We have many more stereopticon cards to view, don't we?"

When he agreed and followed Helen into the house, Livy was grateful. In a moment, the stable boy rushed out with a heavy lap robe, and Andrew took the reins, guiding the horses onto the roadway.

Gliding through the fresh snow, Andrew drew a nervous breath. He gathered the straps in one hand and wrapped his free hand around Livy's. His heart swelled at their nearness. When they reached the river, he turned the bays along the shore until they approached a small grove of trees that blocked the wind, and he reined the horses to a standstill. He marveled at the hazy golden sun making diamonds on the falling snow. Wrapping his arm around Livy, he nestled closer to her side, and she cuddled nearer.

"Could we talk?" His heart thundered in his ears. "I hoped we might be ready to—"

"I wanted to talk with you last evening, but the time never seemed right."

Praying her words were what he longed to hear, he waited, suspended until he could no longer tolerate the silence. "And what do you have to tell me, Livy?"

"I do love you, Andrew."

"Oh, Livy, you've made me the happiest man on earth. Then, you'll marry me?" He captured her face against his palm.

"Yes."

"Soon?" he asked, awed by her radiant face.

"Soon."

He drew her into the fold of his arms, and Livy

embraced him fully. He lowered his mouth to hers, and she yielded to his kiss. Though the cold wind blew past the sleigh, Andrew's body warmed and ignited with love for the cherished woman in his arms. When they withdrew, he faltered, seeing the look of concern on Livy's face.

"We're not free of problems though, Andrew. I know my life will be lonely when you're away at the logging camp, winter after winter. And though I don't know exactly, I'd imagine a lumberjack doesn't make a large income. So I've thought about it and decided I'd move here soon and teach music. I enjoy it very much, so it'll be no problem. By the time we're married, I'll make—"

He couldn't halt the laughter that rose in his throat, and when it escaped, Livy's face blanched, then she glowered. "I don't think you should laugh at me, Andrew. I'm being sincere in my—"

His heart soared at her willingness to share the family responsibilities. "I'm not laughing at you, dearest, dearest Livy. I'm not a lumberjack."

She gaped at his statement.

"I own the logging company, my love. You'll be a wealthy woman one day, I'm certain. But please, teach music if you'd enjoy it. I'll never ask you to give up something you love. I'm not that proud."

She covered her face. "I'm mortified. I didn't know."

"Don't be embarrassed. I thank God for your generosity. And Livy, this will be my last full winter at the camp. Now, with three years experience, I'll hire a competent manager, and most of the cold winter nights, I'll be at your side. I love you, Livy."

Livy's face shone with a radiance, he'd never seen before. "We can marry in June," Andrew said. "Would you like that?"

"I'd *love* that." She pulled her warm hand from the furry muff and caressed his icy cheek.

"Then let's hurry home," he said. "Our announcement will be another gift to my parents. 'Olivia Schuler has consented to give me her hand in marriage.'"

With Livy nestled to his side, Andrew cracked the whip, moving the bays back to the roadway and hurrying home to share the news.

Epilogue

O n a warm Tuesday evening in early June, the bridal party gathered inside Christ Church. As the organ's rich tones filled the sanctuary, the bridesmaids and groomsmen marched with measured steps down the aisle.

To Livy's great joy, Ruth's recuperation was amazing, and today, in the place of Livy's mother, Ruth followed the attendants on Andrew's arm. Livy caught her breath at his striking appearance in an elegant morning coat and sky blue cravat.

With her arm linked to John's, Livy waited. Her wedding dress, an exquisite Paris gown of ivory tulle and lace with its fitted bodice, was a gift from Helen and Charles. Behind a fashionable bustle, the skirt draped to an extensive train.

On her dark curls, Livy wore a lace veil belonging to Helen. Earlier as she dressed, Livy had stared in the glass, amazed at the extraordinary woman who peered back at her.

On John's arm, his loving smile echoed her own happiness. As the organ swelled and pealed the bride's processional, she took her first step toward the altar. John pressed her hand covered with a lace glove, and Livy's heart lifted with a joy she knew they both felt.

In her left arm, she carried a lovely bouquet of lilies, Stephanotis, and orange blossoms, a gift from Andrew. Inside the bouquet, she had attached the tiny carved angel, the keepsake Andrew had given her at Christmas. As she made her way passed family and friends, the flower's sweet fragrance surrounded her.

On a Sunday before the wedding, Andrew had surprised her with a wedding gift—a lovely teardrop diamond pendant that today hung around her neck on a gold chain. She'd never known such luxury or such love.

When they reached the altar, John presented her to Andrew, then joined Ruth in the front pew. With Andrew's hand on hers, the pastor's words filled her heart with assurance. *"Charity suffereth long, and is kind; charity envieth not; charity vaunteth not itself, is not puffed up, Doth not behave itself unseemly, seeketh not her own, is not easily provoked, thinketh no evil; Rejoiceth not in iniquity, but rejoiceth in the truth; Beareth all things, believeth all things, hopeth all things, endureth all things.*

"Charity never faileth."

Andrew riveted to the pastor's words. *"When I was a child, I spake as a child, I understood as a child, I thought as a child: but when I became a man, I put away childish things."* He recalled his past foolish behavior and the foolish notion that Livy was plain and demure.

Today, her dark hair, crowned by the fragile veil, highlighted her delicacy. She was a woman of beauty, spirit, and deep affection. She completed his life with joy and love.

The pastor's voice rose, "And now abideth faith, hope, charity, these three." Andrew sought Livy's face, and at that moment, the Word of God wrapped them in complete oneness. "But the greatest of these is charity." Looking into each other's eyes, Andrew desired no other treasure in his life, only their vows of steadfast and undying love.

GAIL GAYMER MARTIN

Gail is native to the Detroit, Michigan area. A retired high school teacher of English and speech and, later, a guidance counselor, Gail presently is on the adjunct teaching staff in the English curriculum at Detroit College of Business. Though she has written most of her life, Gail began to write professionally in 1995. Besides her novels, she writes parenting articles, Sunday school materials, and is the author of six worship resource books. She is also a contributing editor of *The Christian Communicator*.

Angels
in the
Snow

Colleen L. Reece

When I consider thy heavens, the work of thy fingers,
the moon and the stars, which thou hast ordained;
What is man, that thou art mindful of him?
and the son of man, that thou visitest him?
For thou hast made him a little lower than the angels,
and hast crowned him with glory and honour.
PSALM 8:3–5

Prologue

. . .a bird of the air shall carry the voice,
and that which hath wings shall tell the matter.
ECCLESIASTES 10:20

Wyoming Territory in the late 1880s

N o one knew where it started.
Some said the mysterious stranger who rode into Jubilee and quickly passed on through brought the news. Others believed it came from the East, passed person-to-person over the shining, silver Union Pacific Railroad tracks from Cheyenne to Rock Springs that turned blood-red in the sweltering sun, then traveled northwest to the Teton Valley by stagecoach. The more fanciful maintained hundreds of golden-leafed cottonwoods and aspens avidly whispered the news to one another each time the autumn wind blew.

No one knew where it started, but young and old agreed: It was one of the most important messages the town had received since learning of the Little Bighorn

Massacre in 1876. Before nightfall, every Jubilee inhabitant, except those sleeping in the cemetery next to the town's only church, had heard the news: Matthew Coulter was coming home.

Matt Coulter: unsurpassed in western Wyoming at riding, roping, shooting.

Matt Coulter: driven from Jubilee in disgrace seven years earlier.

Matt Coulter: bright-haired cowboy with a smile like an angel.

The young man had not been smiling that long-ago day. Blue hatred flashed from his eyes at his accuser, Jedediah Talbot, before Matt fixed his piercing gaze on the judge who had been imported for the trial. The wizened man pounded a gavel on a small table in the saloon-turned-courtroom, then gestured out the window to the towering Teton Mountains.

"See those shadows?" he barked. "Take a good look. If any man of you has the slightest shadow of doubt that Matthew Coulter rustled this man's cattle from the Lazy T, there will be no hanging." He slammed the gavel down again.

His charge had an effect. In spite of some fairly convincing evidence, the twelve men were either unable or unwilling to convict Matt. They returned a startling verdict, especially since the accused said nothing in his own defense except for the single quiet statement, "I never stole a head of cattle in my life."

"More than I can say for some in this room," Sheriff McVeigh, the grizzled, long-term keeper of the peace in Jubilee and Matt's best friend, called.

Guffaws and titters greeted his remark. They were quickly silenced by a third heavy thud of the gavel and a sheriff-directed glare from the judge.

An hour later, the jury shuffled in from a back room where they had been deliberating. "We ain't sure whether he's guilty or not," the foreman flatly stated. He carefully avoided looking at Matt. "Because of that, we ain't goin' to hang Matt Coulter." He scratched his head and sighed. "However, things bein' what they are, we'd like to suggest for him to mosey on."

"Since you haven't found him guilty, he can do as he pleases," the judge snapped. "Case dismissed." He lifted his creaking bones from his chair and strode from the room. A loudly-protesting Jed Talbot tailed him.

After a few awkward moments, Matt followed. The curious crowd surged through the swinging doors and watched him mount his magnificent black stallion, King. McVeigh laid a detaining hand on King's neck. "No need for you to leave, Matt," he said, loudly enough for all to hear. "Like the judge says, you can do as you please about following advice that don't hold water. I say, stay."

Coulter stared into the sheriff's eyes. A muscle twitched in his set jaw. His lips thinned to a seam. "Thanks, but I don't stay where I'm not wanted." He swept the crowd a contemptuous glance and touched his heels to King's flanks. Head high, shoulders as stiff as if he had a rifle strapped to his spine beneath his buckskin jacket, Matt slowly urged King down the dusty street. He didn't look back, not even when a girl's clear voice called, "I believe in you, Matthew Coulter. Go with God. Prove your innocence. Then come home to. . ."

The ringing affirmation of faith broke in mid-sentence. A few bystanders later insisted Matt checked King for the space of a heartbeat before urging him into a dead run. Others said, "No such thing." In any event, the poignancy of the moment stilled the jeers common to someone being run out of town. The crowd watched until King and the man with whom many had shared grub and campfires, melted into the lengthening afternoon shadows cast by the frowning Tetons.

No one spoke then or later of two hidden factors everyone, except perhaps the judge, knew played a part in the jurors' decision, good men though they were.

First, fifty-year-old Jed Talbot, owner of the Lazy T cattle ranch in the foothills, was the most hated man in Wyoming Territory. On the rare occasions he appeared on the dusty or snow-clogged streets of Jubilee, inhabitants wisely kept out of his way. The raging demon born and nurtured by Jed's years of hard drinking would hold full, triumphant sway until satisfied.

The stern discipline Jed normally exercised over himself, and always over the cowhands who hired on with him—most of whom quit and rode away in a few weeks or months—vanished like August snow with Jed's first drink. Jubilee knew from past experience once the rancher "gave his devil a run," Talbot would sober up and return to what most folks derisively called the "Tipsy T."

The second reason was Jed's seventeen-year-old daughter, Lass, noble and truthful as her given name, Alicia. Lass was admired and respected even more than her father was despised. Milk-and-water maidens pleased their mamas with pretended horror at Lass Talbot's antics, but they secretly longed to be like the strong young woman who many believed actually ran the Lazy T.

Tales of her courage and daring provided fodder for campfire and town gossip, and Lass Talbot's fame spread through the often harsh, unforgiving land. It increased a hundred, nay, a thousandfold, after the trial. Let those who would, prate of vanished heroines. When the courageous girl publicly challenged her father's iron authority and pledged unswerving loyalty to her friend Matt Coulter, she became dearer to Jubilee than Joan of Arc or Helen of Troy.

Young and not-so-young cowboys, ranchers, even merchants, rode miles out of their way to catch sight of Lass on her favorite horse, Diogenes. No hairpins could keep her thick, wildly flying braid beneath a hat. It gleamed in the sun and matched to a tint the chestnut stallion's glossy coat. Her superb figure bent forward when she called into his ear—a picture to linger long in the beholder's mind.

Yet two obstacles blocked the dozens of would-be suitors longing to camp on the girl's doorstep and win her hand. Both appeared insurmountable.

Chapter 1

*But they that wait upon the L*ORD
shall renew their strength; they shall mount up
with wings as eagles; they shall run, and not be weary;
and they shall walk, and not faint.
ISAIAH 40:31

Two obstacles blocked those who yearned to win Lass Talbot. Both loomed higher than Grand Teton, the 13,770-foot monarch of the mountain range that reared above the valley and Jubilee. Dried leaves and rolling tumbleweeds whispered Jed's threat to run off any man foolhardy enough to come courting his daughter. True and exaggerated stories told of those who dared the Lazy T owner's wrath, only to find themselves staring into Talbot's surly face and the business end of a rifle barrel. Such tales effectively dampened most of the intrepid swains' ardor. One by one, they reluctantly gave up their pursuit of Lass. While they might continue to admire her from afar, common sense prevailed; so most settled for other girls with less fire but with more reasonable fathers.

A few bold enough to persist readily admitted Jed wasn't the only problem.

"How come you ain't interested in any of us cow-pokes?" a new hand asked Lass after being smilingly turned down when he offered to saddle her chestnut stallion. "We ain't a bad lot. Well, no worse than most." He grinned and shoved his disreputable sombrero far-ther back on his curly head. "We'd shore admire to ride with you," he said in a droll voice. "S'posin' of course we could keep up with Di-Di—what's his name again?"

Lass threw her head back. A rare trill of laughter rang out in the sunny air. She stroked her horse's beau-tifully curried mane. "His name is Diogenes (*Di-ah-jen-knees*) and you're absolutely right." A bewitching dimple showed in her left cheek. "You can't keep up with him. Only one horse ever could." A shadow crossed her face.

A familiar pang went through her.

An icy voice cut into the conversation. "What's car-rying on out here?"

Lass caught sight of her glowering father marching toward the corral. Her heart sank, knowing all too well what lay ahead. How little he resembled the father she had adored, the broad-shouldered hero of her little-girl days! Lass couldn't remember seeing her father smile in the eight years since they laid gentle Alice Talbot to rest in the cottonwood grove she loved. On that long-ago afternoon, Jed's twinkling blue eyes dulled to slate; his laughing mouth became a seam that held in all but the harshest words.

Undeniable evidence of years of dissipation marred

his once-handsome countenance. Broad bands of white streaked Jed's chestnut hair. He appeared at least ten years older than his actual age. He seldom shaved and held his bristly chin higher every day. Now he strode toward Lass and the friendly cowboy like some avenging Nemesis. "Get off my ranch," he ordered the cowboy.

Dull red stained the young rider's face. "Why? I didn't do anything."

"I'll not have the likes of you hanging around my daughter. Pick up your pay and go, before I lose my temper and throw you off." Talbot turned his glare toward Lass. "Either go riding—alone—or get in the house. I've told you before to stay away from the hands." He spun on his heel and headed back toward the sprawling log ranch house that had once been not just a house, but a warm and welcoming home.

The discharged cowboy took a step forward, muttering under his breath. Fire leaped to his eyes. "He ain't got no call to talk to you that way," he protested.

"He's my father." Lass managed a smile of thanks. She could see from his reaction her soft words changed his anger to sympathy, so she finished saddling Diogenes and rode away. From a rise beyond the ranch, she watched still another in the long line of hands driven off the Lazy T disappear into the bunkhouse, then come out carrying rifle and bedroll. A little later, he mounted the horse on which he had ridden in looking for a job less than a month before.

No real regret filled Lass, but the memory of his innocent complaint, *How come you ain't interested in any of us cowpokes*, pricked like a burr under a saddle blanket.

To escape her thoughts, she impulsively leaned forward and called in Diogenes' ear. He responded with a magnificent leap forward. The rush of air created by his long strides stung and reddened the girl's smooth cheeks and brought tears to her eyes.

Although she allowed Diogenes to run until the ranchhouse was lost behind a low hill, Lass could not outrun her churning thoughts. "Whoa, boy!" The chestnut changed from gallop to canter, slowed to a trot, and in answer to his rider's pressure with knees and reins, halted well back from the edge of a rise that afforded a splendid view of the valley and mountains. Lass dismounted and tossed the reins to the ground so her horse would stand, as trained. He was barely winded and soon began munching a patch of grass while Lass seated herself on a sun-warmed rock and stared at the world around her.

Why must the cowboy's innocent question buzz in her brain like a pesky fly? Was fear of her father's anger the real reason she couldn't get interested in one of the boys or men eager to win her approval, or was she simply using him for an excuse? It wasn't the first time she had pondered the questions. "It probably won't be the last, either," she told Diogenes, her only confidant except for God. Lass sighed and wrinkled her forehead, then grinned. When she was a small girl and told secrets to her first pony, she had looked around to make sure no one heard. People would surely laugh at a girl who talked to horses. Now it didn't faze her. Diogenes was a better companion than most folks she knew.

"It's because you understand," she praised him. He whinnied in response.

Lass flung herself flat on her back and gazed into the inverted blue bowl above her. Her keen, range-trained eyes discovered a tiny speck. She watched it grow until it became recognizable: a graceful eagle, making wagon-wheel circles in the sky. Love for God and the land filled her and temporarily blotted out the persistent questions she knew needed answering.

At last she sat up, took a cross-legged position, and settled down for a heart-to-heart talk with her horse. The dimple in her left cheek came and went as she remembered her father saying, "You talk *to* horses, *with* other people. You can't carry on a conversation with something that has no way of responding."

Lass had indignantly replied, "Diogenes responds, just not in words." She didn't add that a toss of her horse's fine head, a low nicker, or a gentle nudge with his nose said volumes. So did the way he surveyed her with intelligent brown eyes when she spoke.

How come you ain't interested in any of us cowpokes?

Lass broke off a bit of sage, crushed it so its pungent scent filled her nostrils and addressed the nagging questions she knew would not go away until she did.

"I always hated those namby-pamby storybook girls who fluttered and flirted and waited for a knight to come riding up on a white horse," she told Diogenes. A mischievous grin tilted her lips upwards. "If I'd lived then, I could have outridden any of them, especially if I'd had you."

Diogenes inched nearer and snorted. Lass took it for agreement. She absently patted his smooth neck and stared unseeingly across the cattle-dotted grazing lands to the sloping foothills. "I don't know how much horses remember, but you should know by now where your name came from. I've told you often enough!" She sternly eyed him. "In case you've forgotten, Diogenes was a Greek philosopher. According to legend, he walked the streets with a lantern. When people asked why, Diogenes supposedly said, 'I am searching the world, looking for an honest man.' "

Lass thrilled to the story, as she had done a hundred times. "No chivalrous dandy in a tin suit for me," she told her horse. "Someday, God and father willing, I may find a truly honest man."

You thought you had, her rebellious heart reminded. *Where are they now? The black stallion King and the man whose honor you upheld before the whole town? In all this time, why didn't Matthew at least write. . . .*

A few tears seeped from behind her eyelids. Lass forced them back and proudly lifted her head to again face the sky. The eagle had returned, soaring above the earth and its problems and heartache. A favorite scripture came to mind; Isaiah 40:31. Lass softly quoted, ". . .they that wait upon the LORD shall renew their strength; they shall mount up with wings as eagles; they shall run, and not be weary; and they shall walk, and not faint." A great longing to be free as the noble bird above her possessed the troubled girl. Would she ever be free, to live and to love?

Unable to bear the exquisite pain of too long a silence, too many uncertainties, Lass slowly slid into the saddle and turned toward home. Again she urged Diogenes into a run. Again, the wind whipped her face. This time it dried her tears. Yet even as before, it could not silence the mocking voice that had haunted her since she was seventeen years old and watched the only man she ever truly loved and trusted ride away from Jubilee—and out of her life.

Late November brought more than snow to Jubilee and the Tetons. Rumors about Matt Coulter continued, increasing in intensity, but with no visible results.

"Just who is this Matt Coulter, anyway?" a pale-faced newcomer demanded of the local storekeeper. "How come everyone's talking about him?"

The succinct answer, "If you were Jedediah Talbot, I reckon you'd know," whetted the stranger's curiosity to razor sharpness, but the storekeeper's level-eyed stare and clamped lips warned the conversation was over. Not so the buzz and meaningful glances between Jubilee inhabitants whenever Matt Coulter's name came up—which it did constantly. The question, "What will Talbot do?" inevitably followed. Shrugged shoulders, raised eyebrows, and the significant shake of heads were the only responses. Talk hadn't run so rampant since the serious Indian fighting in Wyoming Territory stopped in the summer of 1876, bringing welcome peace to the settlers.

Sheriff Matthew McVeigh, weathered from his long years of keeping the peace in the frontier town, only grunted at the inquisitive newcomer who attempted to pry information out of him. "Sonny," he told the indignant young man, "around here it's healthy to keep your nose out of other folks' business unless you want to risk getting it cut off."

One snowy afternoon in early December, rumor became certainty. The stagecoach rolled into town behind a team of exhausted horses. A lone passenger stepped down.

"He doesn't look like much," the newcomer complained after a quick glance at the arrival.

"What were you expecting? Billy the Kid?" someone taunted, but no one laughed. Matt Coulter was a far cry from the ruined man who had left Jubilee seven years earlier. He still had the same glorious golden hair, forget-me-not blue eyes, and angelic face—if one overlooked the lines time had etched into a once—carefree expression. Lithe, thirty years old, and "powerful as a mountain lion and twice as dangerous," someone whispered.

Matt gave one lightning-fast look at Jubilee's straggling main street, then looked neither right nor left, but headed straight for the sheriff's office.

By nightfall, everyone for miles around knew Matt Coulter was back, wearing a U.S. Marshal's badge and a grim expression. It struck fear into the hearts of all those who had ever been involved in questionable activities. Maybe Matt hadn't come back for Talbot, after all. Maybe he was tracking someone else. Certain secret, shady deals were hastily canceled. With a U.S. Marshal in town, it was a good time to lie low.

Chapter 2

But the LORD said unto Samuel,
Look not on his countenance, or on the height of
his stature. . .for the LORD seeth not as man seeth;
for man looketh on the outward appearance,
but the LORD looketh on the heart.
1 SAMUEL 16:7

M att Coulter, a U.S. Marshal. Incredible. Questions followed, asked over drinks in the Sagebrush Saloon and teacups in the homes. Tongues wagged as if tied in the middle and loose at both ends. When had Matt become a lawman? Why? Where? Most important, why had Coulter really come back? Mutters of, "Glad I ain't in Talbot's shoes," raced like wildfire. So did anticipation. Would Talbot finally get what he deserved?

Sheriff McVeigh heard the talk along with everyone else in Jubilee. He glared and pulled down the corners of his mouth until he looked liked a prowling cat that had swallowed a sour mouse. "Good thing it ain't summer.

Folks around here would have sunburned tongues from flapping them in the breeze."

Old memories die hard, especially when they concern possible injustice. So it was with Jubilee. Jury members shook in their shoes and gave serious thought to packing up in the dead of night and moving their families elsewhere. They grew until the foreman of the jury came out of the general store and nearly plowed into Matt Coulter.

Matt's smile didn't reach his steady blue eyes, but his quiet, "How have you been?" went a long way toward setting folks' minds at ease. So did the fact that he offered his hand to the man who had pronounced sentence on him.

"I never felt so downright skunky as when I shook Coulter's hand," the foreman later confessed to his cronies at the Sagebrush Saloon. "I mumbled somethin' about I wished things could have been different." He took a swig of beer and wiped foam from his mouth.

"What did Coulter say?" someone prodded. An impatient growl rose from the crowd of listeners. "Hurry it up, will you?"

The foreman set his mug down on the age-scarred bar. The solid thud rang loudly in the silent saloon. "I'll be jinxed if he didn't up and say, 'Seven years is a long time. You did what you felt you had to do. No hard feelings.' Then he shook my paw 'til it near broke my fingers." He flexed those callused members, and an awkward grin spread over his face. "Didn't have the gumption to ask how come Matt came back if he felt that way." The foreman sent a significant glance at the others. "Reckon none of us has to."

"Mighty tough on Lass," someone commented. "She and Coulter were always good friends." A murmur of sympathy set restless feet shuffling. "Wonder if she knows Matt's back?"

"I sure ain't going to be the one to tell her," someone said.

"*I* sure ain't going to be the one to tell her daddy," another voice chimed in. "I'd just as lief stay on top of the ground for a while, not under it."

A murmur of agreement swept through the gathered crowd. A bold young cowboy burst into an exaggerated rendition of, "Oh, bury me not, on the lone prairie." He hung onto the last note until a burst of laughter drowned out his plaintive song, then grinned a devil-may-care grin and finished his drink.

"Pipe down, you lunkheads," the bartender ordered. "Jed Talbot's nothing to laugh about." His reminder sobered the rowdy crowd as nothing else could have. Every man present knew the bartender spoke the truth.

"Someone's gotta tell Jed," the foreman stated after a short silence. He grimaced. "When I was knee high to a bumblebee my mama used to tell me a story that reminds me of us. It was about a bunch of mice, and—"

"You had a mama?" jeered the singer. Mock awe settled over his now innocent-looking face. "All this time I thought they found you 'neath a cactus."

The foreman shot him a look that would have shriveled a less daring cowboy. "You want to hear the story, or don't you?"

"Shore. Me and the boys always did want to hear a

story about a bunch of mice." The cowboy smirked and rolled his mischief-filled eyes.

The foreman ignored the sarcasm. "As I was sayin' before Big Mouth here interrupted, the mice had a bad problem. The family cat. Somethin' had to be done before he ate up any more of the mice's relatives. Those left came up with a bright idea: hang a bell on the cat's neck, and he couldn't creep up on 'em."

"Pretty smart," the interested bartender put in.

A smug smile crept over the foreman's face. "Not as smart as they thought. There was still a mighty important question. *Who would bell the cat?*"

A moment of letting the story sink in passed before the singing cowboy stood. "I ain't no mouse. I also ain't belling any cats." He sent a significant look around the circle of watching cowhands. "And I still ain't telling Jed Talbot who stepped down from the stagecoach." He jammed his worn Stetson down on his head and strode out of the deathly silent Sagebrush Saloon.

Because of the town's general agreement with the cowboy's sentiments, several days passed before news of Matt Coulter's return reached the Talbots. Sheriff McVeigh, Jubilee's unanimous choice of messenger to the Lazy T, had suddenly decided to take a long-delayed vacation.

"Now?" Matt demanded. "How come?" Suspicion leaped to his mind like an Indian to the bare back of a wild mustang. His eyebrows drew together in a forbidding line, and he cocked his head and slitted his eyes at his friend.

"Why not?" Pat McVeigh grinned. Every line in his unshaven face showed how much he was enjoying the interchange. He always had loved verbally sparring with Matt. "I've been putting off going to Denver to visit my dear old mother for many a day." His sorrowful tone didn't match the twinkle in his eyes.

"Your dear old mother is in better health than you are, you old fraud," Matt snapped. "Who's going to keep the peace in Jubilee while you're gone?"

The sheriff tilted his worn swivel chair back until Matt thought he'd go head over teakettle backwards. The chair gave a loud squawk of protest. "I reckon a properly authorized U.S. Marshal ought to be able to hold the town together for a couple of days. No more than a week, or maybe two, at the most." He cocked a shaggy eyebrow. "Wouldn't you say so?"

"In a pig's eye, if you mean this U.S. Marshal," Matt rudely told him. "What would Jed Talbot say?" Yet even as he protested, a live coal of excitement ignited and set a fire raging inside him. What better way to show Jubilee Matt Coulter was not the man he had been seven years earlier? Not the careless rider who gave much thought to his wild, free life on the range and little to what lay beyond his mortal years? Was this the purpose for which he had felt called back to Jubilee?

Bang! McVeigh's chair came forward with a crash of its front legs. His eyes gleamed. "Talbot doesn't run this office. I do. Always have, always will, unless I get voted out, which ain't likely. No one else wants the job, not even Talbot."

The words, "He will rage," slipped from Matt's lips

of their own volition.

A banner of triumph waved in the sheriff's face. "Let him." His sunbaked hand reached across the battered desk to the young man he had loved since childhood. "Well? Is it a deal?" He faked a hollow cough. "I do need a vacation."

Matt hesitated the same amount of time it took for a tiny vein in his tanned forehead to pulse a single time. His own hand shot out. "For better or worse."

McVeigh's grip threatened to paralyze Matt's strong fingers. After a moment, the sheriff released them and dryly commented, "Better or worse. Hmm. Seems to me I've heard those words before. In church, maybe, with a pretty girl walking down the aisle, wearing a white dress, and. . ."

Matt lost the rest of the sentence. A vision of a strong, seventeen-year-old girl who wished him God-speed an eternity before danced in his mind. That girl had laughed up at him, teased, and cajoled him. Lass Talbot: a good comrade—and so much more! He had fallen in love with her when she still wore pigtails and was far too young to think of love and marriage.

"What's she like now?" he abruptly asked.

The sheriff didn't pretend to misunderstand. He stroked his stubbled chin and quietly said, "She ain't married or promised."

"I know. Otherwise, I wouldn't have come back." The meaningful look that passed between them showed the rare friendship they had always shared. "I suppose it's because of Jed." Matt held his breath, fearing the answer yet needing to ask the question that had haunted him ever since he rode away.

"Naw." The sheriff leaned forward and propped his massive forearms on his desk, threatening to topple the stack of papers next to them. "What I mean is, she's twenty-four years old. Her own boss. Or she could be if she left the Tipsy T." Admiration flooded his weather-beaten face. "Folks say Lass just about runs the ranch single-handed. Jed's drinking has been getting worse." Concern clouded the sheriff's countenance. "Used to be, he held it down to coming into town a few times a year and rampaging around. Now I hear he's also drinking at home."

"Why does she stay?" Matt burst out. Feelings he thought he had conquered swelled into his throat, bitter as gall. "A girl like that."

The sheriff ran his hand over his grizzled face again. It rasped like a buzz saw and set Matt's teeth on edge. "I asked her once." He leaned back in his chair again, hands clasped behind his head. "Never will forget her answer."

"Well?" The question cracked like a rifle in the hands of an expert marksman.

A poignant light stole into eyes that had seen it all: Indian fights and settlers; births; death by sickness, violence, and old age; peace and prosperity; trouble and lawlessness. "Lass said when she figured she couldn't bear things for even one more day, she remembered the meaning of her father's name. She told me surely a man who carries a name that means what Jedediah means cannot forever withstand his daughter's storming heaven on his behalf."

McVeigh pulled out a red handkerchief large enough to flag down a speeding train a mile away and vigorously blew his nose.

"So what *does* Jedediah mean?" Matt demanded.

"*Beloved of Jehovah.* Can you beat it?" The sheriff blew again. "Jed Talbot, running around with a moniker like that!"

Matt's heart pounded. If he hadn't already loved Lass, this new revelation of a heart bigger than the Territory of Wyoming would have done the trick. Yet why was he surprised? Her faith and belief in a loving God after Alice Talbot died had strengthened all around her, except her father. In Matt's years away from Jubilee, memories of gentle Alice lent understanding of what Jed had suffered. Suppose he, Matthew Coulter, were married to Lass. His heart jumped at the thought. Wouldn't he also turn bitter if she died? Yes. Hadn't he done the same thing when unfairly accused and driven from Jubilee seven years before?

Chapter 3

*. . .he that loveth not his brother whom he hath seen,
how can he love God whom he hath not seen?*
1 JOHN 4:20

Jubilee had reeled with shock when Matt Coulter stepped down from the stagecoach that dutifully carried passengers to Rock Springs and beyond. Before they fully recovered, a strangely altered Sheriff McVeigh climbed aboard the outgoing stagecoach early one frosty morning. Curious onlookers found themselves in danger of having their jaws permanently dislocated from shock, for the sheriff grinned and called, "Take good care of my town while I'm gone, Marshal. Don't take any guff. You hear?" His stentorian voice echoed over the sparsely populated street like heavy thunder in a rock-walled canyon.

Hear? Matt's ears burned. He felt heat surge into his face. Anyone within a mile radius couldn't help hearing! A gleem in the sheriff's keen eyes spoke more plainly than words. For reasons of his own, which Matt could pretty well figure out, the sheriff meant the inhabitants of Jubilee to know who was in charge.

The stagecoach driver cracked his whip over the backs of his team. "Giddap!" His horses responded. Wheels groaned and began to roll. Ten minutes later, coach and horses dwindled to moving, black specks in the distance.

"Where's the sheriff off to?" the owner of the general store asked. "Must be trouble somewhere for the sheriff to head out so early." He wrapped his coat closer around his body and blew on his bare hands. "Cold, too."

A cowboy disagreed. "If there was trouble, the sheriff'd hightail it out of here on his horse, not that creaking stagecoach. Besides, he was all duded up."

The storekeeper looked worried. "Leaving like this isn't like Pat McVeigh." He turned to Matt for an explanation he was obviously unwilling to ask.

The new acting sheriff tore his gaze from the road leading out of town and looked into a sea of inquiring faces. "He's gone to Denver to visit his mother."

Astonishment rippled through the crowd and swelled when Matt added as casually as he could, "I'm filling in for him while he's gone."

"Well, I swan!" The storekeeper scratched his head. "If that don't beat all!"

Laughter bubbled up inside Matt and spilled into the quiet morning. "Well, boys? Think you can put up with me for a few days? A week? Two at the most?"

The little group exchanged glances before the storekeeper grinned and said, "Looks like we don't have much choice. McVeigh told you not to take any guff. He'll skin us alive if we try and make trouble while he's gone."

"That's for certain!" A grinning rancher cocked his head to one side and spat a stream of tobacco juice into the street, then warily eyed the acting sheriff.

"You ain't going to run me in for spitting in the street, are you?"

"Not this time," Matt retorted. "Just watch yourself."

A round of laughter greeted his sally and the small crowd dispersed. As they walked away, the rancher's voice floated back to Matt, "Talbot's going to have seventeen kinds of fits when he finds out what's going on here in Jubilee."

Matt silently agreed. He sighed and wrinkled his forehead. The last thing he wanted right now was a confrontation with Jed Talbot, yet how could he avoid it? He turned on his boot heel and ambled back toward the sheriff's office and jail, puzzling over the position McVeigh had put him in by leaving. If there were only a way to avoid further trouble! He sighed again. "I'm afraid there will be a lot more 'worse' to this job than 'better,' " he muttered.

Matt reached his destination and lifted a hand to open the sturdy door. He halted. Froze with his hand in mid-air. What if he—

"No." He shook his head. "It would never work!" Matt gave the door such a hard push that it slammed open and banged against the wall from the force of his attack. The action catapulted him into the room. He righted himself and closed the door behind him, feeling foolish and thankful the two cells beyond the open inner door sat bare and empty of occupants. Doubts about his harebrained idea gathered like thunderclouds preparing to assault the earth. Still, he couldn't quite banish or forsake the idea that had come to him. Bold, daring, a long chance.

Matt sat down in the sheriff's chair, folded his hands, and bowed his head. Should he follow through on the idea that had sprung full-blown into his churning brain? Common sense shouted, "No." The cold, hard reality was: if the plan failed, everything at stake would be lost. Probably forever.

Yet in spite of the terrible odds against success, the instinct Matt had learned to respect and follow in order to survive long, hard years tantalized him with the thought: *Suppose the plan works? It would solve everything. Forever.*

Head still bowed, Matt Coulter forced his dilemma from his mind. The quiet morning offered time and privacy to remember, to recall things he often shoved aside in the interest of more urgent problems. He closed his eyes, forced himself to relax, and let the past sweep into the silent room.

❦

"I believe in you, Matthew Coulter. Go with God. Prove your innocence. Then come home to. . ."

Lass Talbot's voice broke before she finished the sentence. Was the missing word "me," Matt asked himself a thousand times as he drifted down the broad and easy tumbleweed trail that led so many cowboys to perdition. Pangs of regret mingled with hatred and bitterness. He railed against the God who allowed blameless men to be punished. Prove himself innocent? He could not. Would not. Doing so meant inflicting pain greater than the loss to Jubilee of a single cowboy, a range rider who had dared dream of happiness beyond his reach.

A year passed. Two. Three. Matt wandered the length and breadth of the West, from the Panhandle of Texas to the Dakotas and Canadian Border. His riding, roping, shooting skills meant no lack of jobs. He and his black stallion, King, won prize money at rodeos. Time dulled his anger against the jury who had neither condemned nor exonerated him, but his hatred of Jed Talbot and love for Lass burned brighter with each passing day.

Four years. Five. Riding on when the restlessness within him became too strong to resist. Whooping it up with the best—nay, the worst—of his companions, with a single exception. He steered clear of women, especially those who worked in saloons. Several times, it meant riding away when a jealous swain resented the attention girls paid the indifferent cowboy. Lass Talbot might never know of his loyalty, but he would.

The sixth year of exile brought change. A mean steer Matt and King were chasing on a Texas ranch suddenly reversed directions and charged. Powerful horns plunged deep into the stallion's side. King fell, carrying Matt to the sun-baked earth. Matt tried to spring clear, but one foot lay trapped beneath his dying horse. With a terrible roar, the steer went for Matt. By the time help came, Matthew Coulter lay bleeding and broken.

Kind ranch hands and a grave-faced doctor cared for him, but they held out little hope. "If he weren't such a magnificent specimen, I'd give him no chance at all." Doc shook his graying head. "Little enough chance, even though he is."

In the midst of pain and delirium, a powerful hand gripped Matt's right hand. "Don't give up," a man's deep voice ordered. "God will see you through."

Matt tried to tell the speaker God had abandoned him long ago. The words became an unintelligible croak. Matt was too weary to try again. The voice called again. The grip on the injured man's hand increased in intensity; a frail lifeline to cling to in the ebb and flow of agony that left Matt exhausted. Time became indistinct in that raging river. During one lucid moment, Matt wondered: Did the stranger stay beside him night and day? Each time the pain receded, he felt strength flowing into his body from his unknown companion. It gave him endurance to face the next wave of pain.

A week or an eternity later, Matt opened his eyes and wonderingly looked around. His mind cleared and he examined the room in which he lay. Whitewashed log walls. The smell of medicine. Sunlight half-heartedly poking through clear glass between calico curtains. A merry fire blazed in the open fireplace.

He languidly turned his head toward his right hand. It lay limp on a brightly covered patchwork quilt. It also felt strangely naked. No longer was it clasped in another's. Matt raised his gaze from the bed and surveyed the tall figure hunched in a hand-hewn rocker. The twin to Matt's quilt covered the unknown, sleeping man. Silver hair topped a deeply lined face, bearing evidence that its owner had kept constant vigil for a long, long time.

Matt's body involuntarily twitched. The man opened his eyes. For a moment, Matt thought he would drown in the steady gray gaze. He started to ask who the man was, why he had stayed with him, but the stranger forestalled him.

"I am Pastor Andrew," the deep voice Matt knew so well quietly said. "I am so glad you are better! God is good."

Matt could only stare. He had seen a thousand glorious sunrises and thrilled to each, but never had he seen such radiance in a human face. He swallowed hard and weakly forced out a few words, "Why do you care?"

"My Lord loves His children. So do I." He laid a hand over Matt's lips to still further speech. "When you are better, we will speak of many things."

It was the beginning of friendship—and much more. Matt learned that Pastor Andrew's wife had died a few years earlier, leaving him alone. He had insisted Matt be brought to his home after the accident. During the long convalescence that followed, Matt discovered another with the faith and trust he had only found in Lass and her mother. Pastor Andrew led Matt to Christ step by step, more by what he was than what he preached. Weeks later, Matt brokenly said, "I reckon it's time for me to ask Jesus to be my Trailmate. What do I do?"

Joy shone on the old pastor's face. "You know the way, Matt. Confess your sins. Ask Jesus to forgive you and invite Jesus to live in your heart."

"Is that all? It doesn't seem like enough." Doubt filled Matt's heart.

The steady, gray gaze grew concerned. Matt felt

Pastor Andrew could see into his very soul. "Jesus cannot live in a heart that carries hatred and bitterness."

Matt felt as if he'd been hit by an avalanche. "You mean. . ." He choked and couldn't go on. Six years of raw emotion boiled up inside him.

Pastor Andrew reached for his worn Bible. "1 John 4:20 asks, 'how can a man love God whom he hasn't seen if he doesn't love his brother whom he has seen.' Matthew, you have to love God more than you hate Jedediah Talbot."

A geyser of anger exploded. "That rotten skunk cheated me once. Now he's going to do it again?" Matt jerked open the door and started out.

Pastor Andrew's quiet voice stopped him on the threshold. "Only if you let him." He paused, then spoke words the troubled cowboy knew he would never forget. "You had no choice before. This time, you do."

Chapter 4

Be not forgetful to entertain strangers:
for thereby some have entertained angels unawares.
HEBREWS 13:2

Lass Talbot stood at her bedroom window and watched the softly falling snow with blurred eyes. How quickly and beautifully it camouflaged the leafless cottonwoods and aspens, wrapping their naked branches in a blanket of warm white! She took a deep breath then slowly released it. If only she could be wrapped in warmth, protected and sheltered against storms far worse than those that swept down from the north and gripped Jubilee in their wintry clutch.

Lass sadly turned from the window. She wrinkled her forehead in silent protest against the sound of her father's voice raging in the sitting room of the log ranchhouse. Jed's voice grated on, desecrating the holy hush just outside her window. Lass caught her lower lip between her teeth. The contrast between the landscape's purity and her father's profanity sent a blizzard of pain straight to her hurting heart. Until today, even in his worst moments, Jed had never before sworn inside their home. Was this the end? Could she continue as she had from day to day, passionately hoping and praying for her father's redemption? "Please, God, give me strength and guidance," she prayed. "I need You so."

Hot tears scorched the inside of her eyelids, but Lass refused to let them fall. Her father despised any sign of weakness in himself or others. Once he had been compassionate, understanding. The Lazy T had been a joyous place, ruled by Alice Talbot's rod of love. After she died, Jed had hardened. Now Lass sometimes felt her father's heart had turned to pure granite. He paid grudging respect only to those as strong as he.

She glanced back out her window, desperately seeking peace from the gentle, falling snow. "That's why Father hates Matt Coulter so much," she whispered. "Matthew is strong." She traced the outline of a snow angel on the frosty glass.

It's why you love him. You always have. You always will, an inner voice said.

The troubled girl's heartbeat quickened. She felt blood rush to her head. "I?"

Yes, you, the little voice accused.

"That is absurd! We were childhood friends, nothing more."

Oh, yeah? her heart mocked. *Then why did you call after him that day, begging him to come back to you?*

Lass covered her ears, trying to still the taunting voice. Too honest to attempt to deceive herself longer, she faced the suspicion she had refused to face a hundred times before. "Lord, it's foolish," she brokenly said. "It's been seven years." She thought of the heartache that had plagued her all that time. "Seven years grieving over a man who rode away without looking back."

A scripture sprang to mind. Lass had thrilled over it when her mother read it to her many times during their years together before Alice answered the final call.

"And Jacob loved Rachel; and said, I will serve thee seven years for Rachel thy younger daughter," Genesis 29:18.

Another well-loved verse followed, bringing fire to the girl's cheeks.

"And Jacob served seven years for Rachel; and they seemed unto him but a few days, for the love he had to her," Genesis 29:20.

Lass whirled from the window and threw herself onto the patchwork coverlet she had fashioned for her narrow bed. Could hearts break from pain? "At least Rachel knew Jacob loved her! I don't even have that, Lord. You know as well as I do, Matt Coulter hasn't seen fit to send a single word in all these long years!" She laughed bitterly. She had no need for caution. The thick, heavily-chinked log walls both held in and kept out voices, unless they were raised in anger like her father's.

"I'm no Rachel, to wait and wait and wait. What if seven more years pass, as they did for her?" She beat her fists into her pillow. "Lord, why must life be so hard? Sometimes it is so unbearable, I don't know how long I can hold on here."

Heavy footsteps and a loud thump on her door brought Lass to her feet, hands still clenched. "Who is it?"

"Your father. Come out this instant," Jed bellowed.

Lass hesitated. The last few months had taught her the wisdom of riding off on Diogenes or taking refuge in her room to escape her father's profane ravings. She knew from experience there was no reasoning with him when he drank. For years Jed had restricted his sprees to town, but lately he avoided going into town and did his drinking at home. Strong as Lass was, she could not withstand the change in his personality triggered by a bottle.

"Come out, I say!" The heavy door creaked on its hinges.

Lass considered climbing out the window and thought better of it. It would be no easier facing him later than now. She flung wide the door. "Yes?"

"Did you know he's come back?" Jed roared. He resembled an angry bull Lass had once seen charging a rodeo rider. The Lazy T foreman, Dusty, only remaining hand from before Alice Talbot died, stood a few feet behind Jed. He awkwardly twisted his work-stained hat and dug the toe of his worn boot into the braided rug at which he stared.

"*Who?*" It came out in a whisper. Only one person's return could bring such fury to her father's face. Lass tried to quell the voice shouting inside her, *He's here. Matthew Coulter has come back.* She must not betray by word or look the joy she felt leap into her veins with every beat of her tumultuous heart. Now was the time to dissemble, for her sake, Matt's, and her father's.

Jed frothed at the mouth and stared at her from red-rimmed eyes. "Matthew Coulter, that's who! That stinking cattle thief should have been hanged. Would have been if the jury'd had any gumption." A string of profanity followed.

Lass couldn't stand it any longer. "How dare you use such language to me, Father?" She planted her fists on her hips and whipped up scorn to still her trembling knees. "You would horsewhip any man who spoke so in my presence. Now you bring these vile words into our home! What would Mother think, knowing you have so little respect for your daughter—*and hers?*"

Jed's jaw dropped. His face paled.

Lass took quick advantage of his stunned silence. "I didn't know Matt Coulter returned. How could I?" she demanded. "I haven't been to town in ages." She looked at Dusty. "When did he come?"

"Coupla days ago," the obviously embarrassed foreman replied. He took a deep breath. "That ain't all."

Jed snapped out of his temporary shock and spun on one heel. "What?"

Dusty kept his gaze fixed over Jed's shoulder and on Lass. "Coulter's wearing a U.S. Marshal's badge and—"

"Get out!" Jed thundered. His right hand hovered above his hip where a gun belt hung low. His fingers changed to a claw, ready and waiting.

Lass had seen him angry and belligerent before, but never like this. *Dear God, don't let him shoot Dusty!* She pushed past her father and stood between the two men. "You'd better go," she told Dusty over her shoulder.

"Leave you here with him like this? Not in a hundred years!" The foreman caught her wrist and swung her aside. He stuck his face into the maddened man's countenance and shouted, "Jed Coulter, I've put up with a lot in the last eight years, but I ain't standing for this. You've no call to take your madness out on Lass!"

"I said for you to get out," Jed hissed. He touched his gun significantly.

"If I do, I'll tell the acting sheriff you pulled a gun on me and send him out to pack Lass off somewheres so she'll be safe from you," Dusty threatened.

One word appeared to penetrate the sodden brain. "*Acting* sheriff?"

"Yeah." Dusty paused, then grinned again. "McVeigh's taking a vacation."

Lass felt her mouth drop open. An icy chill sped up and down her spine. She gripped the foreman's sleeve. "Wh—who is taking his place?"

"Matt Coulter." Satisfaction oozed from every pore of the weatherbeaten face.

For a long, terrible moment Jed stood frozen to the floor. His face sagged. Lass felt he aged a good ten years in that moment. She started toward him from force of habit. He waved her off and reeled backwards until he reached his bedroom, which was next to hers. The heavy door couldn't quite deaden the rasp of a seldom-used lock after he slammed the door shut.

"Sorry you had to be in on that." Sweat beaded Dusty's kindly face when he turned to Lass. "I never saw a man so eaten up with hate." He mopped his forehead with an over-sized kerchief. "Do you want me to take you to town?" Hope showed in his eyes. "Or you could ride in on Diogenes and stay a spell with someone." He worried the rug again with his toe until it lay in a crumpled mess. "Just until Jed settles down. He always does."

The temptation to walk away and never return faded. "I'll stay," Lass replied.

"If you ain't an angel, then I never heard tell of anyone who is," her long-term friend burst out. "I'll just mosey over to the bunkhouse, get my bedroll, and come back for the night." He nodded at a couch. "Looks like a good place to bed down, just in case. I mean, it's a lot softer than my bunk."

Lass recognized his attempt to lighten the situation. She started to tell Dusty it wasn't necessary for him to stay and keep watch. Memories of the ugly scene they had just witnessed stopped her. "Thank you," she quietly said.

"No trouble at all." He grinned, put on his hat, and started for the front door. "You'll be all right while I'm gone, won't you?"

She held her breath and listened for sounds from her father's room. None came. "I'll be fine." She searched for a smile and tremulously put it on. "I'll go in my room and lock the door."

"Stay there," Dusty commanded. "It ain't smart to take chances when your daddy's letting his dark nature loose. Trust me, Lass. I know what he's like."

Lass fled to her room and locked the door, as much against the tears that threatened to gush because of the faithful foreman's caring for her, as against possible intrusion by her father. How good to know she had an earthly protector in place of the father who should have been her comfort and stronghold!

A few minutes later, Dusty tapped on her door. She opened it and assured him she was all right, then relocked the door. Curled into a ball of misery, she tried to concentrate on happier times. In a few weeks, it would be Christmas. Her spirits sank, as they had each Christmas since her mother died. The Talbot annual observance of Christmas for the past eight years had been a travesty.

"Lord, as far back as I can remember before Mother died, Christmas was such a time of wonder," Lass told her Friend, Jesus. She closed her eyes and let her mind wander on paths to the past, trails that led back to happier times when Jed Talbot laughed and joined wholeheartedly in celebrating the birth of Christ.

Were those days gone forever? Would life continue its sameness? No, she decided. Not with U.S. Marshal-Acting Sheriff Matt Coulter back in Jubilee.

Chapter 5

I will remember my covenant with thee
in the days of thy youth,
and I will establish unto thee an everlasting covenant.
EZEKIEL 16:60

In addition to a heart filled with love, gentle Alice brought to her marriage with Jedediah Talbot a rich dowry from doting parents who adored their only child. She also brought three traditions, begun in the mountains of Virginia by her great-grandfather and solemnly observed by all who came after.

First, no one in Alice's family ever opened presents on Christmas Eve. "It is a time to celebrate the birth of Jesus," Great-grandfather had announced to his bride generations earlier. "A time to read the Scriptures and ponder on what the world would be like if God had not loved his rebellious children enough to send His Only Son. A time to keep holy and fill the air with song and praises."

From babyhood, Great-grandfather's children knew

better than to ask for presents from the gaily decorated tree that adorned their home on Christmas Eve. They piped out carols of old from the time they could lisp, then grew up and taught their own small, round-eyed children the tradition, that it might not be lost to future generations.

The second tradition was less holy but equally important. Every year when snow lay in the yard on Christmas Eve afternoon, all who were young and young at heart bundled up, threw snowballs, and made snow angels. Great-grandfather's usually stern, bearded face filled with mischief as he lightly packed snowballs that broke apart in flight and showered his family. Smiling Great-grandmother wore a cloak and scarf of her own weaving. She taught the rosy-cheeked, excited children how to make snow angels. The family praised God with Christmas laughter and the simple joy of being together.

The question, "Will it snow?" hovered in the crisp air annually and repeated itself a hundred times following Thanksgiving. The weather seldom brought disappointment. Passing years engraved memories of "Christmas Eve snow" on hearts so deeply, they helped ensure the ritual would be observed long after Great-grandfather and Great-grandmother had passed on to their heavenly home.

While the first tradition fostered worship and the second family fun, the final tradition was the most cherished. It offered the opportunity for the youngest and the oldest alike to experience the real meaning of Christmas.

"Consider how it was when Jesus was born," Great-grandfather told his family. "The Wise Men brought rich gifts; the shepherds, only themselves. What we give is not so important. What counts is for us to give our best to Jesus."

"Will Jesus come get presents from under the tree?" the oldest child asked.

"No, my son. He takes His presents from our hearts." Great-grandfather smiled. "Jesus tells us in Matthew, Chapter 25, that any time we feed the hungry, take in strangers, give clothing to those in need, or visit the sick or those in prison, it is the same as if we were doing all those things for Him."

"He did?" the saucer-eyed boy asked.

"He did?" his equally impressed sisters and brothers echoed.

"Yes. Jesus also says those who do these things will inherit the kingdom he has prepared for us." Great-grandfather smiled again. "But we must do our good deeds secretly. Jesus tells us in Matthew 6:4, He will see those secret deeds and reward us openly."

He pointed out the window to the row of snow angels etched into the smooth white surface. "Those are snow angels. You can be 'secret angels,' by doing good and unselfishly giving to others of your time, your treasure, and your love."

From Great-grandfather's simple words, the final tradition sprang. Each family member sought ways to be "secret angels." They performed private, unexpected deeds of kindness to one another. Food baskets mysteriously appeared on needy families' doorsteps. Bits of money or treasured possessions quietly passed from person to person with no fanfare, no recognition expected.

If the recipients suspected the source of the gifts, they remained silent, unwilling to deprive the givers of hugging to their hearts the joy of true and selfless giving.

Over the years, those who delighted in being "secret angels," discovered something unusual. They remembered their often-sacrificial gifts long after the memories of the brightly wrapped "tree gifts" they joyously unwrapped on Christmas morn faded. This, too, they passed down to their children.

Alice Talbot was among those of the fourth generation who faithfully kept the three cherished traditions, even though Wyoming Territory lay miles and a lifetime away from her Virginia home. She inducted her adoring husband, and later, their only child, into her childhood customs. The Lazy T family continued Alice's heritage for sixteen happy Christmas seasons. Jedediah Talbot only laughed when a gaping Dusty once caught his rancher boss making angels in the snow with Lass and his beloved wife.

"Want to join us?" Jed called.

Dusty gulped. "Naw, not me. I-uh-gotta mend some harness." He strode away as fast as his bowlegged gait could carry his range-hardened frame, mumbling to himself while peals of laughter rang out behind him.

It was the last Christmas laughter rang out at the Lazy T. The following year, snow fell on the quiet mound where Alice Talbot had been laid to rest.

❧

Lass stirred from her reverie and shivered. A quick tug on her patchwork coverlet brought its welcome softness over her body. She snuggled into its familiar depths and gradually felt herself warm, at least on the outside. She still felt as icy and barren inside as the glaciers on Grand Teton. "If only Mother had lived," she murmured. Icicles of pain poked into her heart. After eight long, years she still hadn't recovered from the loss of her mother. Perhaps it wouldn't have been so hard if Father had been different, if he had turned to her seeking mutual comfort instead of blaming God for his wife's death.

From her prone position, Lass could see out the top of her window. Dusk had settled, but enough light still touched the earth to show it was still snowing. It had been much the same on the day eight years before when Jed announced, "If you want to stick up a tree for Christmas, put it in your own room." He paused. The misery in his face caused Lass to take an involuntary step toward him. His outflung hand held her off. Bitterness replaced the grief in his face.

"We'll not be indulging in all that angel foolishness, either." His words fell like hailstones, bruising his daughter's soul. "No need, now that Alice is gone."

The echo of his heavy steps as he crossed the living room and slammed out the front door resounded in the sixteen-year-old girl's heart. She wanted to cry out, to protest they must not break the precious family traditions. She could not.

She knew only too well that when her father spoke like that, she need not argue.

Now she slid down under her coverlet even farther. Her twenty-four-year-old heart protested as strongly and silently as it had done long ago and every Christmas since. After a moment, a tremulous smile softened her lips. She could only remember a few times when she refused to obey her father. That Christmas eight years ago was one of them. Even after her father's edict, Lass knew she could not and would not break the unbroken chain of family tradition. She would respect and continue as much of her Christmas heritage as possible without openly rebelling. Father might bar her from doing so outwardly. He had no control over what she silently and privately did. Besides, he would never know unless he one day returned to the faith of his ancestors and she could tell him.

Lass closed her eyes. Her smile spread, lifting her spirits by remembering the past and looking toward the present and future. Every Christmas Eve afternoon since her mother died, she had managed to slip away long enough to make a snow angel. It didn't matter how bad the weather was or that she must quickly obliterate every trace of her angel in the snow. Flinging herself on the snowy ground and moving her heavily-clad arms and legs up and down until she left an imprint brought a wealth of memories of her mother and better times. It also renewed hope that coming years might be different and better.

Lass followed her solitary rite by a private time on Christmas Eve. She quietly read aloud the story of the birth of Christ from the Gospel of Luke. She repeated her daily plea for her father to repent. She sang praises in a true, sweet voice. Lass had little fear of interruption, but performed her worship in the shelter of her own room. Even though Jed Talbot chose to absent himself from the Lazy T on both Christmas Eve and Christmas Day, there was always the chance he might return. Lass wanted no confrontations to mar Jesus' birthday.

Sometime between Christmas and New Year's Eve, a goodly sum of money appeared on her pillow. The first year this happened, Lass tried to thank her father for the impersonal gift. What she really wanted was for him to put his arms around her and hold her close, the way he used to do.

Jed gave her a stony stare and said nothing. Neither did he acknowledge the hand-sewn shirts and the socks she faithfully knitted and left in his room that year and in the years that followed. It became a tradition Lass secretly hated.

She again roused from her musings. Her unsteady fingers lighted a candle and placed it so it would shine on the time-worn sheets of paper she took from their hiding place in a box beneath her bed. Each page held only a short prayer. They all said substantially the same thing. The girl's heart swelled when she read words she wished with all her heart it had never been necessary to write.

Heavenly Father, perhaps someday I will again be able to openly observe the three priceless traditions. They must not be lost, especially the "secret angel" giving. I have no gold or frankincense or myrrh. Even if I possessed them, I wouldn't be allowed to bestow them. I do have a gift for my earthly father, something far greater than any of those the Wise Men brought: the gift of prayer. This I vow to give, not only at Christmas but every day of the year. Great-grandfather admonished his family to always give their best. This is my best, Father. May it be acceptable unto You.

Lass slowly folded the sheets and returned them to their hiding place. In a short time she would write another such message, unless God, Himself, intervened with a miracle to change her father. Goodness knew she had done everything she could, to no avail. It hadn't been easy not to reproach him, but for the most part, Lass had held her tongue, telling herself surely things must get better.

Now they had grown infinitely worse. It had been bad enough to be the target of range gossip, even though Lass knew most of it was kindly toward her. Today the unbelievable had entered the log ranchhouse: language so vile, it surely must be an affront to the God who had once been Head of the Talbot household.

A cry for help and release rose from Lass, an appeal first uttered by David. *"Lord, how long wilt Thou look on? Rescue my soul. . ."* Psalm 35:17.

Chapter 6

Then said I, Woe is me! for I am undone;
because I am a man of unclean lips. . . .
ISAIAH 6:5

hat would Mother think, knowing you have so
little respect for your and her daughter?
Throughout the endless night following
the showdown with Lass, her stinging indictment
resounded in her father's brain until he thought he
would go mad. After he buried Alice, he had painstak-
ingly built a wall of defense against pain, using bricks
of anger, bitterness, and drink. It effectively kept others out and his torment within, where no one could see.
Not even God. Especially not God. Had He not be-
trayed Jed by taking Alice? Agony gradually subsided
into numbness.

Now Jed's carefully constructed wall lay in shards
beneath his dusty boots. His numbness fled like shadows at noon. He had never felt such exquisite pain as
the flood of almost-forgotten feelings flowing from his

exposed heart—not even when Alice left him. His daughter's words had swept aside every pretense. For the space of a heartbeat, Jed had seen in her eyes the man he had become. Nay, the beast. A drunken sot who turned away from Lass when she most needed him, too concerned with his own feelings to consider hers.

Fully clothed, Jed lay in the clutches of the whiskey; yet inside his still body, a spark he hadn't known still existed began its work. It flickered, subsided, flickered again and caught like match to pine kindling, scorching upward until Jed wondered if he would die. He thought he had known the depths while drinking. They were nothing compared to the flame within Jed that continued to rage. Higher and higher, until he could stand it no longer. "Please, let me die," he screamed, unable to recognize his plea was but a whisper no one but the God he had despised could hear. "I cannot go on living this way."

Sleep from sheer exhaustion claimed him, interrupted by a herd of nightmares. Jed awoke at last, amazed that his mind felt clear. He wrinkled his nose at the heavy odor of sweat and whiskey that permeated the room. He rose from the bed where he had flung himself after locking the door the previous night and peered through the window. Jed normally found himself murky as the growing dawn after a drinking spree, crouched like a living thing outside the log house.

No sound came from his daughter's room. Jed shuddered. Would Lass ever forgive him? Could she, when she learned what he knew he must tell her? He longed for liquor to fortify him for the ordeal that lay ahead. No. If he once succumbed to temptation, there would be no turning back. There never was.

The dim reflection in the glass showed a haggard face that rightly belonged on a hundred year old. Or a dead man. Jed fell back. So that was what people saw when they looked at him! *He had brought it on himself.* He staggered to his bed, sank to its edge, and buried his face in his hands. "Alice, oh, Alice!"

An hour or a lifetime later, Jed couldn't be sure which, he stood and quietly began preparing for what he knew was the only way out. He changed into warm clothes, packed a few other things, and buckled on his gun belt. "I won't need much where I'm going," he muttered grimly.

Like a midnight prowler, Jed worked the noisy lock until it gave way. He inched his door open and waited to see if the noise had disturbed Lass. She must not know what he planned to do. Her door remained closed. Jed rejoiced. He stepped into the living room, grabbed his rifle, and stealthily crossed the room. A quick forage in the well-stocked pantry provided the scanty stores he wanted.

Lamplight from the bunkhouse sent a sickly yellow stream into the early morning air and fear into Jed's heart. If Dusty saw him, his game was up. Luck held until Jed finished saddling Duke, the most powerful horse on the Lazy T. He swung into the saddle. Another few minutes and he'd be gone. Snow had begun falling. By the time he was missed, not a ranch hand could track and find him.

Matt Coulter could.

Jed flinched. Now was not the time to think of Matt Coulter. A man fleeing for the reasons Jed had created needed to be clear-headed and "unstampedable."

"Hey, Boss, how come you're riding out so early? Lass ain't sick, is she?"

Jed froze. What rotten luck! He glanced toward Dusty, who was hurrying toward him from the bunkhouse. Even the faint light couldn't hide the concern in the foreman's face. "Lass is fine. Still asleep, far as I know." Did his voice appear as unnatural to Dusty as to himself? "Thought I'd check the line shack."

"What for and why now? A storm's brewing." Dusty sounded amazed. "No one's likely to use it in the dead of winter." He cast a suspicious look at Jed. "Besides, last time any of our boys were there it was fine and dandy."

Jed's nerves stretched to the breaking point and gave way. "Mind your own business, you old buzzard! If you say anything to Lass, you're fired." He ignored Dusty's inarticulate protest, spurred Duke, and turned to face the west.

"When will you be back?" the undaunted foreman yelled after him.

"Maybe never." Jed leaned forward and felt the sting of snow pellets on his face, pellets no colder than the possible implications of his answer.

Lass awakened earlier than usual, filled with foreboding and heaviness of spirit. In spite of her warm blankets and coverlet, she felt cold. More than the chill of winter had entered her heart. She hated to leave the security of her room. What would Father be like this morning? What would they say to one another? She had been too mentally fatigued the night before to even consider a new day.

At last she rose and made ready for whatever lay ahead. She paused to offer thanks to God for keeping her through the night, then earnestly prayed for strength to face the hours before her. Forcing a smile to her lips, she unlocked her door and stepped from her room. Lass strained to hear sounds from her father's room. Silence prevailed, and she gave a sigh of relief. She needn't start breakfast just yet, but would let her father sleep until their usual hour.

Freed from routine, she bundled up and stepped outside. Snow whirled to the ground in its maddest winter dance. Lass sank ankle deep in the soft stuff when she noticed Dusty standing by the corral and plodded over to join him.

"Morning, Dusty. Wonder if the snow's going to keep up?"

"More like keep down," he said sourly, although he touched his hat to her. "It's been doing this since dawn."

Astonished at his tone, Lass demanded, "What were you doing up so early?"

She smiled and added, "I thought with most of the hands off the ranch until time for spring roundup you'd be catching up on your sleep."

Dusty avoided her gaze. Not even a trace of his usual fond smile for her crossed his sober countenance. "Not today." He respectfully touched the brim of his hat again. "If you'll be excusing me, I have work to do."

He stalked off, leaving her to stare at his retreating back and wonder what on earth ailed him.

"Is anything wrong, Dusty?" Lass called.

He stopped abruptly and hesitated just a mite too long to be convincing, then he turned and gave her a grin that definitely looked pasted-on. "Now what could be wrong? Ain't it a beautiful winter day?" He rambled on, acting more evasive with every sentence. "Don't worry your pretty head over it."

"Over *what?*" she flashed back at him.

Chagrin erased traces of innocence, but Dusty again tried to throw her off the track of what obviously gnawed at him. "Don't mind me. I'm just mumbling."

Lass rushed to him as rapidly as boots sinking in the snow allowed. Her heart pounded with fear. She grabbed the foreman's coat lapels and hung on for dear life. "All right, Dusty, let's have it. Is something wrong with Father?" She knew by the look that crept into the foreman's face she had hit dead center.

"I—he—" Dusty's stammering fell on deaf ears. Lass turned and struggled back to the house. She didn't even wait to kick off her snowy boots but stumbled to Jed's bedroom door and beat on it with both fists. "Father?"

Not a sound came from within.

Lass beat again with one hand, turned the knob with the other. To her relief, the catch released. She pushed the heavy door inward and lunged through it. The room lay empty. Mussed sheets and blankets showed someone had slept in the bed. Some of the girl's fear lessened, but when she checked the room further, it rose again. Enough clothing was missing to raise an alarm. "Dusty?"

"I'm here, Lass." Nothing remained of the foreman's surliness. "You weren't supposed to know." He shuffled his snowy boots and looked down at them. "Your daddy said he'd fire me if I told you he rode out early this morning. Said he was going to the line shack." Wild horses couldn't have dragged out of him Jed Talbot's final words about maybe never coming back.

"The line shack? In this weather?" Lass stared disbelievingly. "Why?"

"He wouldn't say." Dusty heaved a sigh that sounded like it started in the toes of his boots and worked its way upwards. "I couldn't help wondering if it had something to do with his learning yesterday that Matt Coulter's now a U.S. Marshall and acting sheriff of Jubilee." His steady gaze never wavered.

Lass weakly sank to the edge of the mussed bed. Why must this new trouble come upon them when they already had plenty? "It must be pretty bad for him to ride out in the dead of winter," she brokenly said. The suffering Jed had put her through paled in comparison with the love beating strong in her heart now that her father could be in grave danger. "Was he drunk?"

"No!" Dusty yanked himself up to full height. "Far as I could tell, he hadn't been drinking at all this morning. Funny thing." He scratched his head. "There was something different about him. Even when he yelled at me, he seemed kinda like the Jed Talbot he was before your mama died. Beats me, but he did."

Her mind flew to the line shack she had often visited, but never in winter. Were there supplies to last her father if a blizzard trapped him? Neighbors who were just as experienced with the rugged terrain of western Wyoming in the dead of winter as Father had died trying to outride storms. Could he conquer and survive?

She sprang to her feet. "Why are we standing here? We need to go after him."

"We couldn't make it a mile from the ranch without getting lost. Don't worry. Your daddy's bound to be at the line shack by now. By the way, if you ain't had breakfast, I could go for a second one." Lass quickly prepared ham, eggs, and biscuits, more to please him than from hunger. She poked down some food because she must eat, while Dusty tried to cheer her with funny range stories.

Two hours later the snow stopped. A knock on the door sent Lass flying to see who had come.

Matt Coulter stood outside, leaner of jaw than when he left. Yet the blinding light in his eyes Lass remembered so well steadily shone. In the split second before she flung herself into his arms, Lass knew what her heart had been trying to tell her for seven long years. That poignant blue light was for her.

Chapter 7

Teach me thy way, O LORD,
and lead me in a plain path, because of mine enemies.
PSALM 27:11

L ass Talbot buried her face in Matt Coulter's sheepskin-lined coat. Her tears mingled with the snowflakes melting on the sturdy garment and cooled her burning cheeks. A moment later, powerful arms surrounded her. If only they would never let her go! For the first time in years Lass felt safe, protected against every storm that raged. She lifted her face to the one above her as naturally as a sunflower turning to the sun. Matt's winter-chilled lips curved into a smile of incredible sweetness, then found her own. Time, place, and the clump of Dusty's boots carrying him to the open ranchhouse door melted into unimportance. Nothing mattered except the fact Matthew Coulter had returned—to her.

"Well, now. If this ain't a sight for sore eyes!" The Lazy T foreman's drawl recalled Lass to the present.

She gasped and broke free from Matt's arms and the spell cast by his kiss. The single teasing kiss he had stolen when she was a girl belonged to long ago. This was a man's kiss. It paid homage to the woman Lass had become. Without a single word, Matt Coulter had claimed his mate and bound them together with eternal vows Lass knew nothing could ever break.

"Are you two going to stand out there all day?" Dusty complained. "You're letting a whole lot of cold air into this nice warm room."

Matt's eyes gleamed and a joyous laugh erupted. "So we are. Getting an unexpected greeting like this chased everything else out of my mind."

Lass felt her face heat. She hastily backed into the living room with Matt right behind her. What must he think of her, throwing herself at him that way? *I don't care,* her heart sang. *He came. He's here. He's mine. I've waited seven years. I'm not going to let anything take this or Matt, away from me. Ever.*

"I reckon you just put your brand on her," Dusty dryly observed. "Good for you, son, and welcome home." He held out a rough paw and shook Coulter's hand. "Never did believe you were mixed up in that cattle stealing business."

Lass saw the warning look that passed from Matt to Dusty, the hard grip of hands before Matt quietly said, "Thanks. I always knew where you stood." He slipped out of his wet coat and hung it on the outside doorknob, then closed the heavy door behind him. His body took on a certain stillness but his voice remained steady when he glanced around the room and casually asked, "Is Jed here? There are a few things I need to talk over with him."

Something in the set of his jaw shattered the veil of happiness enveloping Lass. She wordlessly stared at Matt. The U.S. Marshal's badge on his heavy shirt gleamed brightly. Lass couldn't tear her gaze away from the symbol of authority. So he hadn't come just to see her. Hopes for a rosy future dimmed. How could she have forgotten the trouble between Father and the man she loved most, next to God? Must she again become a wishbone, torn two ways?

And if you do? a mocking inner voice taunted. *What then?*

In the hush that followed Matt's question, Lass silently prayed for help. Part of her mind heard the scrape of Dusty's boot and his quick explanation of Jed Talbot's absence. The other remembered a verse learned at her mother's knee. *"Teach me thy way, O LORD, and lead me in a plain path, because of mine enemies." Psalm 27:11*

Lass fought against the unhappiness rising like floodwaters within her. If ever anyone needed to know the ways of the Lord and to find a plain path, she was that person! She closed her eyes, feeling she walked a narrow trail between yawning canyons of love and duty, each threatening to swallow her up if she faltered or stumbled on even one step of the path. Her determination to allow nothing to stand in the way or destroy her future happiness seemed childish; a cardboard sword defiantly held up in the face of insurmountable obstacles.

Matt Coulter's sharp, "He went out in this storm? Is he insane?" yanked Lass out of her miserable reflections and back into the present.

"Lass wanted to go after him, but I told her it would be worse than insane," Dusty said. A wrinkle grew between his eyebrows. Lass could tell he was trying to keep up a cheerful expression for her sake, for he added, "I'm pretty sure Jed had more than enough time to make the line shack before the worst of the storm. He wasn't drinking, and he was riding Duke. Biggest and best horse on the Lazy T, far as I'm concerned." He smiled at Lass but his eyes remained anxious.

She made a little sound of protest and Matt turned to her. "Dusty's right," he thoughtfully said. "It won't do your father any good for us to go hightailing after him and get caught halfway between here and the line shack." He pointed out the window. "The snow's thickening, and it was hard enough going when I rode out from town. All we can do for now is to wait and take for granted all is well."

"Jed Talbot's mighty good at looking out for himself," Dusty put in. "What I mean is, he knows the country and the weather signs. Chances are, he's long since at the shack, all holed up by himself and aiming to stay there until he's able to head for home. The temperature's dropping, which means the snow will freeze hard enough for folks to travel a lot easier if they have to."

What the men said certainly made sense, but the prospect of sitting around doing nothing sickened Lass. On the other hand, she felt relieved the inevitable showdown between Matt Coulter and her father was temporarily postponed. Who knew what would happen between them? Memories of her father's rage and whitened face from the night before when he learned Matt was not only back, but an official of the law on two counts, danced in the girl's mind. So did the inscrutable looks between Matt and Dusty.

"What do you know that you aren't telling me?" she demanded of them.

"Wha–at?" Dusty's eyes popped wide open. "Lass Talbot, you're too suspicious for your own good!" His lips shut in a tight, unyielding line.

The foreman's accusation didn't fool her even a little bit but Lass subsided. Nothing she could do or say would convince Matt Coulter to tell her whatever secret he and Dusty shared unless or until he was good and ready. She had battled his stubbornness for years and learned it was like two rams butting heads. As for Dusty. . .she grimaced. If a long-standing secret lodged beneath his worn Stetson, she had little chance of learning what it was now. This morning's slip of the tongue would not be repeated, especially after the warning look she had intercepted while it sped from Matt's eyes to Dusty's.

"There's plenty of room in the bunkhouse if you want to stay over," Lass told Matt. "If you think Jubilee can get along without its acting sheriff overnight."

His eyes crinkled at the corners. "I can't imagine anyone dumb enough to step outside his own home in weather like this, let alone miss an acting sheriff."

Lass felt her heart turn somersaults. To hide her confusion, she quickly said, "I'll whip up supper when it's time. You and Dusty may as well eat with me."

"That's an invite I don't pass up," the foreman chortled. "I'm plumb tired of my own fixings, since Cookie lit out for greener pastures." He pulled the corners of his mouth down. "At that, I'd rather eat my own cooking than the messes the boys who stayed on for the winter cook. They should be thrown out to the prairie dogs." He smirked and every line in his leathery face deepened. "Except I'll bet no self-respecting varmint would touch the stuff!"

Lass couldn't help laughing in spite of her worries. "I promise you won't toss my cooking to the prairie dogs, Dusty. Mother started teaching me to cook as soon as my hands were big enough to hold a spoon." She blinked back the mist that accompanied a vision of herself: a happy, bright-haired child who loved to trot from kitchen to pantry to root cellar after her mother.

"I remember your apple pie." Matt looked longingly toward the kitchen. "I don't suppose you have apples on hand, do you?"

"Barrels of them! We—I stock up in the fall to be sure we will have enough."

Several hours later, Dusty shoved his chair back from the depleted store of vittles on the table and with obvious reluctance shook his head when offered a third piece of pie. "I just can't eat like I used to," he mourned.

Lass giggled and caught Matt's look of disbelief. She had lost track of how many times she had passed the venison roast, mashed potatoes and gravy, home-canned vegetables, hot biscuits, and three kinds of jelly. Matt hadn't been far behind Dusty when it came to packing it away. She furtively observed him when he blinked his eyes and glanced at the foreman's empty plate. He could use a little more meat on his bones.

He'd always been tough as whipcord, but the years had fine-tuned him down until he resembled a winter-starved mountain lion.

For a few moments, Lass was able to lay aside her concern for her father. She let the blanket of her love wrap itself around her heart and fill its emptiness. She needed no mirror to know her feelings shone in her telltale face. She didn't care and gloried in her love. Matthew Coulter deserved to see the change from childhood bud to love in full bloom, born the day he rode away and sheltered deep in a heart that for years refused to acknowledge it remained.

Shortly after supper, Dusty gave an incredibly fake yawn and excused himself, leaving Lass and Matt to sit close to one another in front of a blazing fire. Their love was too fresh and sweet to linger on the past. "We have the rest of our lives, sweetheart," Matt whispered into her chestnut hair. "I wonder what Jubilee will say when U.S. Marshall-Acting Sheriff Matthew Coulter takes a wife?"

Lass felt herself blush. "They'll shake their heads and say they knew it all along."

She mimicked a village gossip. " 'Land sakes, how else would it be, what with Lass Talbot boldly calling after a man being run out of town!' " She bit her lip. How could she have been so stupid as to bring up the past?

Some of her joy dimmed. Tacitly consenting to be Matt's wife placed her in the dreaded position of being unequally yoked. Lass pressed her fingers to her temples. She could not, would not, think about it now. For this brief time, she would revel in Matt's love. If tomorrow brought separation, at least she would have tonight—and remember its sweetness all the days of her life.

Matt stayed silent for a moment, then said, "Someday when we have more time, I'll tell you about a man I met while I was gone. He helped change my life. It's too long a story for now." He kissed the tip of her nose. "I will tell you one thing." A soft and reminiscent smile curved his lips. "When he learned I came from a town called Jubilee, he told me what it meant. Hundreds of years ago, every seventh year was a year of rest. Fields and vineyards were not to be planted or harvested. Every fifty years was a Year of Jubilee, a hallowed year of proclaiming liberty to all the inhabitants of the land."

He stroked her cheek with a strong hand. "I wandered more than six years. The seventh offered rest. Even though it isn't officially a Year of Jubilee, I can't help feeling it brought me liberty and freedom. You see, Lass. . ."

Matt didn't have a chance to finish. Dusty burst through the door without knocking. "There's the devil to pay," he panted. "Duke just limped in." He paused and gulped for breath. Lass wanted to scream but no sound came.

Matt's face turned bleak. "Well?" His question cracked like a whip.

Dusty's reply rang a death knell in the girl's heart. "Jed ain't with him."

Chapter 8

The fickle winds of public opinion had shifted mightily in the few weeks since Matthew Coulter returned from parts unknown. His quiet presence and lack of ill-will toward those who once suggested he leave town made a great and lasting impression on the inhabitants of Jubilee. Many of those who had condemned him the loudest now proclaimed even more loudly that they, "never had put much stock in Jed Talbot's tale of cattle being rustled from the Tipsy T."

The settlement's change of heart brought an even deeper resentment of Jed. Men growled to their cronies in the Sagebrush Saloon that the wrong person had been run out of town. Others whispered a tar-and-feather party might be in order. Yet because of Lass, not even the most bitter among them would even consider lifting a hand against the father they despised, but knew she loved.

Into this volatile atmosphere rode grim-faced Matthew Coulter and an equally disturbed Dusty on a cheerless morning. They blew into the Sagebrush Saloon like a norther from Canada and wasted no time stating why they'd come. "Lass Talbot needs our help," the acting sheriff said tersely. "Who's with us?"

Riders and townsfolk, alike, sent their chairs crashing to the floor. A call for help on behalf of the girl they revered brought them to their feet, to a man.

Matt Coulter dared to hope they'd actually help. He heard Dusty draw in a quick breath, then froze when the bartender called, "What's the trouble, Sheriff?"

"Her daddy rode out to the line shack early yesterday morning," Matt said heavily. "Last night Duke came back limping, wearing an empty saddle."

Jaws dropped in amazement. The air chilled. For seconds, or an eternity, no one spoke. Finally, the young cowboy who had been summarily dismissed from the Lazy T for the crime of talking with Lass earlier that month uttered a mirthless laugh. "So Jed Talbot needs himself a rescue party in the dead of winter." He shrugged and shoved his Stetson farther back on his head. "Reckon I'll pass." He dropped back into his chair and propped his worn boots up against the edge of the table.

Approval whispered through the crowd. "Where's

your Tipsy T riders?" someone called. "I hear tell there's still a few Jed ain't run off." Rude laughter greeted his sally and several more men parked themselves back on their chairs.

Matt started to speak, but Dusty beat him to it. Face purple as twilight over the Tetons, he bellowed, "No-good bunch of skunks up and refused to go."

"How come?" the man demanded. A growl of support rose from the crowd.

Matt saw Dusty clench his big hands. "Oh, they all had their reasons. One was plumb wore out and couldn't think of leaving the bunkhouse," he sneered. "Another said he was coming down with the 'creeping awfuls,' whatever that's supposed to be. That set off the rest of them. They all decided they were feeling mighty poorly." He paused. "None of the hands have been on the ranch long enough to appreciate and be loyal to Lass." His voice broke on the last word.

Matt thumped his fist on the nearest table. Liquor splashed from partly-filled glasses. Midnight silence fell over the room. "Look, boys. I've got as much or more reason to hate Jed Talbot than anyone here, but a mighty fine girl—no, woman—needs help. Far as I know, it's the first time she's ever asked for it." Matt caught a few shamefaced nods of agreement.

Encouraged, he continued, "She agreed to wait at the ranch to see if any of you would come." He let his gaze travel from face to face. "You all know Lass Talbot and how much she thinks of her daddy, whether he deserves it or not. You all know she will head for that line shack to find Jed even if she has to go alone, which she won't. She won't. Lass will have Dusty, me, and I'm hoping some of you."

Again he scanned the men's faces. His heart sank. Few of them still looked him in the eye. Those who did wore defiant expressions. Some of those gathered shuffled their feet. How could he reach them? He must! Three searchers in a Wyoming Territory winter had little hope of finding Jed Talbot.

Words from months earlier sprang to mind, altered to fit the occasion. Matt felt his heart pound. He lowered his voice, but it rang in every corner of the silent saloon. "As acting sheriff, I could order you to go. I won't." His level gaze shifted from man to man. "What it comes down to is this: You have to decide whether you love and respect Lass more than you hate her father. If so, you'll ride out with us. Not for Jed Talbot's sake. For hers."

Matt waited long enough for what he said to sink in. "Dusty and I'll give you fifteen minutes before heading back to the Lazy T. We'll be at the store if any of you come looking for us." He turned sharply on his boot heel and strode out with the foreman at his heels. Had his impassioned plea been of any use?

Heat from the store's potbellied stove warmed Matt's hands, but not his heart. From his vantage point, he could see out the window and across the street to the saloon. Dusty crowded close, silent for once. Five minutes passed. Ten. Twelve.

The saloon doors quivered and swung open. Dusty gripped Matt's arm with the force of eagle talons and hoarsely said, "Someone's coming out!" A man emerged from the saloon and hesitated just outside.

"Jury foreman from your trial," Dusty hissed. His cruel grip tightened.

Matt's icy heart leaped like an antelope in full flight. He stared at the motionless figure just outside the saloon doors. The jury foreman glanced toward the store. He took two slow steps in its direction, halted, and turned back toward the saloon, as if unsure of his next move.

"Come over here," Dusty pleaded in what sounded suspiciously like a prayer.

The uncertain man wheeled and glanced at the store once more. Then he scuttled off down the street as if pursued by a thousand howling demons.

Matt hadn't realized he was holding his breath until his lungs felt they would burst if they didn't get air. "Well, that's that. Let's ride."

"How can we tell Lass?" Dusty brokenly asked. "Not a man here will put aside his feelings long enough to help one of the finest women God ever made!" The heartbreaking question rode sidesaddle all the way to the Lazy T.

Dusty need not have been concerned over telling Lass. She knew it the moment the men rode in unaccompanied by anyone from town. "All of one accord, they began to make excuses," she told Matt and Dusty when they stepped inside. "I can't remember where I heard that saying, but it fits. Well, no use crying over what can't be helped. I'm ready to ride when you are."

"I'd like to mop up the earth with all of them," her foreman blurted out.

Lass put her hand on his arm. "Don't blame them

too much," she sadly said. "Father has created bad feeling with almost everyone in Jubilee. It's natural they aren't willing to risk their lives for his sake." She searched for a smile and glued it to the lips she knew would tremble with fear and anxiety if she permitted it. "I'm just glad I have you and Matt."

Dusty turned away, but not quickly enough to hide the wetness in his eyes. "We're wasting time chinning," he gruffly said. "We need to hit the trail. Not that there will be much to follow, what with the snow and all."

"Dusty's right," Matt agreed. "Lass, won't you reconsider and let us go without you? We'll do everything we can to find your father. I promise."

Lass shook her head. "Thanks, Matt. I couldn't bear the waiting."

His jaw set in the line she knew so well. "All right, then. It's boots and saddles for all of us." He broke into the semblance of a smile that curled inside the girl's heart like a bird with its head beneath its wing to shut out storms.

Lass lost track of time long before they reached the vicinity of the line shack. Sometimes she felt they had been riding for days, endless time periods fighting the elements. Despite her frantic prayers, the weather worsened. The trek changed and intensified with every hour. Although searching for Jed remained important, the blasting wind soon challenged the riders to a battle for their own survival. Lass had been in tough places during her lifetime on the range, but none had ever threatened her life and that of her companions so violently as this

December day. Speech between them was impossible. Lass turned to her Father and Friend for help. Her tired brain refused to form the plea of her heart, but she knew One heard and understood. He always had. He always would.

Light snow swirled around her. It stung her face with icy slaps but kept her from sinking into apathy. At times she wondered why they were there, what they were doing out in the storm. Oh, yes. They were seeking that which was lost. The words triggered off another of the beloved Bible stories learned in the long ago days before Mother died and Father withdrew from her and the world. Lass could almost hear her mother's voice reading the beautiful words of the story, even above the howl and whine of the storm.

"How think ye? If a man have an hundred sheep, and one of them be gone astray, doth he not leave the ninety and nine, and goeth into the mountains, and seeketh that which is gone astray?"

In the midst of the storm, Lass again became a child. A child who pelted her mother with questions. "Were the mountains tall and rocky, like the Tetons? Were there deep canyons and rushing streams? Was the shepherd afraid to go? Did he wonder if something would hurt the ninety and nine he had to leave?"

"We don't know exactly what it was like in the country where the shepherd lived," her mother had replied. "I'm sure it was not easy. The shepherd may have been in danger and very frightened. He would, of course, have made sure the ninety and nine were safe before leaving them."

Lass had wanted to know other things in order to understand the story. "How did the shepherd know one of his sheep went astray? Did he count all the sheep in his flock every day? He had so many! Why was the lost one so important?"

"Remember what Jesus said when He began the story," Alice reminded. "He said, 'For the Son of man is come to save that which was lost.' That's why God sent His only Son. He doesn't want anyone in the whole world to ever be lost."

"Mother, if I were a lost sheep, would you and Father come find me?"

"Oh, yes!" Alice Talbot's radiant smile shone down through the years and set her daughter's heart aglow. "We love you too much to let you stay lost. So does God. Alicia, my darling, always remember this one thing: If you had been the only person who ever lived, or who ever would live, God would still have sent Jesus so someday you can live in heaven with Him. He loves you that much."

Lass squared her shoulders and rode on, comforted by the thought not three, but four, searched for the soul who went astray—in life, as well as in the storm.

Chapter 9

How think ye?
If a man have an hundred sheep,
and one of them be gone astray, doth he not. . .
seeketh that which is gone astray?
And if so be that he find it verily
I say unto you, he rejoiceth more of that sheep,
than of the ninety and nine which went not astray.
MATTHEW 18:12-13

J ust when Lass Talbot knew she could go no farther, a muffled shout from Dusty roused her to full
consciousness. "We're there. Thank God!"

Lass lifted heavy eyelids and started at the snow-
shrouded line shack, faintly visible through the thick
stand of trees surrounding it. Fear clogged her throat,
real and heavy as the drifts that nearly obliterated the
rude shack. Would Father be inside? If not, she knew
he was doomed. A man without a horse or shelter in
this kind of weather had no hope.

The white downpour lessened for a moment. She

blinked and stared harder. Was that—yes! A thin curl of smoke rose from the chimney of the line shack. Relief poured into her, so strong it left her weak and slumped in the saddle. She turned toward Matt to share her joy. The set of his jaw silenced the words crowding into her throat and demanding release. New fear sprang full blown. For a craven moment, Lass longed to cry out; to demand they turn back into the storm and away from the shelter they had struggled so hard to attain.

Don't be a fool, part of her mind chided. *Turning back means certain death for all of you. Warmth and safety lie inside those storm-beaten walls.*

So does the possibility of tragedy, whispered another part of her mind. Lass shuddered. What might happen in this lonely place between the two men she loved? If Father had been drinking—and it seemed inconceivable he had not—the simple sight of Matt Coulter would be more than enough to send him into a rage. Once it happened, there would be no stopping whatever retribution Jed Talbot might take against the sworn enemy he felt had gone scot-free.

"I must go in first," Lass told herself. "I'll stand between Father and Matt. Neither will be able to get to the other as long as I remain between them." Her lips twisted. Was the moment she had dreaded so long racing toward her with the speed of a cyclone? The time when she must choose between Father and Matt? *Please, God, not now,* she prayed. *Not here in this isolated shack with only me and a weary Dusty to intervene.* The very thought made her shiver.

"I'll take care of the horses," Dusty volunteered.

"Come, Lass." Matt held out his hand, gaze steady but unreadable.

She slid from the saddle and clumped through the snow to the door of the line shack. Now was no time to falter. The next few minutes would irrevocably determine her future, her father's, and Matt Coulter's.

Lass pounded on the door, vaguely aware of the tang of woodsmoke and wet clothing. "Father, are you here? It's Lass." She pushed the weathered door open and stepped across the threshold into a dim and strangely silent room. A sullen fire in the open fireplace provided the only light. Lass blinked until her eyes adjusted to the gloom. A huddled form lay on one of the rude bunks built to house riders caught far from home. "Father?" she repeated.

A soft moan sent her flying to the bunk. An unshaven face burning with fever looked up from the tangled blankets. Lass found no recognition in her father's eyes. She lightly shook his shoulder. "Father," she pleaded in a voice so filled with love it should have brought Jedediah Talbot back from the grave. It didn't. He pulled away from her touch and writhed in delirium.

A strong hand gently pushed her aside. "Let me, Lass. He doesn't know you."

She numbly stepped away, but came fully alive when Matt muttered something unintelligible even to her keen ears. "What is it? Is he drunk?" She sniffed the air for betraying fumes of whiskey but found none. "Matt, *what is it?*"

He ignored her except to say shortly, "He's sick, not drunk. Find a candle or lamp and get it lighted so I can examine him," he barked. "Build up that fire and heat water. Melt snow if there's no water inside. I have a hunch. . . ."

Lass didn't wait to hear what the hunch might be but flew to fetch a light.

Within minutes the line shack changed from forbidding to snug, a shelter against the storm for both searchers and the lost sheep.

It didn't take Matt long to discover the source of Jed's fever. While water heated, light from the lamp Lass held high revealed Jed's right shirt sleeve had been ripped away to form a crude bandage for a head wound. Lass gasped when Matt removed the badly stained piece of cloth. Once the compressing bandage was taken away, fresh blood leaked from a deep and angry-looking cut on the side of Jed's forehead. Dull red streaks splayed from it, an indication infection had already begun its deadly work.

"This appears to be the culprit," Matt said. He frowned. "I can't think why Jed didn't wash it out with whiskey. He had to be conscious after it happened or he couldn't have torn off his shirt's sleeve and put on the bandage. Or built a fire."

"I know why," Dusty—who had come in from caring for the horses—triumphantly told him. "Far as I can tell, there ain't a speck of whiskey in this shack and hasn't been since who knows when."

Lass whirled to fact the grinning foreman. "You mean. . ." Her voice died.

Dusty scratched his head and looked puzzled. "I don't exactly know what I do mean! It's just surprising that anyone, 'specially Jed Talbot, would ride out with a blizzard coming on and no whiskey in his saddlebags."

"How do you know there wasn't?" Lass demanded. Hope for something she could not explain or identify fluttered fragile wings and beat against reason.

"We had to unsaddle Duke, didn't we?" Dusty shot back. Lass caught his quick glance toward Matt. "We didn't say anything because, uh, you know what your daddy's like. Besides, we figured since we didn't find whiskey in the saddlebags, Jed probably had a bottle stashed in his shirt."

"Forget all that for now," Matt commanded in a stand and deliver voice. "We've got a fight on our hands. Jed needs a doctor. There's no way under heaven for us to get him one. That means each of has to do our dead level best to save him. This cut needs stitching. Can you do it, Lass? Dusty, what about you?"

Lass stared in horror and shook her head. Dusty gulped and looked sick. "I never did, but if it means saving Jed's life, I'll try. Can't you do it, Matt?"

The question hovered in stillness broken only by the now unconscious man's raspy breathing. Matt turned and gazed deep into the eyes of the girl he loved. The poignant blue light she knew and loved slowly came into his eyes. "Lass, my darling, after all that's gone before, can you trust me? Enough to put your father's life in my hands? And God's?"

The last two words didn't register. So it had come. The wishbone moment she prayed would never happen and had always known was inevitable. Memories from the past ran through her head like crown fire among summer-dried pines. So did her choices. If she refused to trust Matt, her father might die. Doing so would also mean the death of Matt's love. On the other hand, if he harbored revenge, what a perfect place to get it! Her father was so sick with fever he might well die no matter what choice she made. No one would ever be able to prove whether fever or a bungled attempt to care for him took his life.

Lass searched Matt's face for the slightest hint of triumph. She found nothing but concern, compassion, and love in the eyes of the man she cherished. So be it. Father's life lay in her choice. Right or wrong, she must follow the instincts and feelings of her heart; they had served her well all the days of her life. Lass pulled herself to full height and spoke in a clear, ringing voice. "I trust you."

Dusty made a choking sound and mumbled something about heating more water, but Matt opened his arms. Lass flew inside. Again she felt the hard beating of his heart beneath her cheek and felt she had come home. After an all too short, precious time, Matt gently put her away. "There will be time for us later. Your father needs us now." He strode across the room, rolling up his sleeves as he went. Five minutes later, he returned to the bunk, the skin of his hands shriveled from soaking in hot water. With incredible gentleness, he began the task necessary to save Jed's life.

The following hours came and went in a meaningless blur. Dusty packed in great stacks of wood and kept the fire blazing. Lass prepared simple food and prayed.

Matt sat by Jed's bunk, alert to every restless move. For three days and nights, they watched and waited for the fever to run its course and subside. When it did not, Matt told his companions, "We can try packing him in snow. There's the danger of pneumonia, but. . ."

Lass licked fear-parched lips. "Go ahead. The threat's no worse than this."

The drastic measure paid off. After the snow bath, Dusty and Matt rubbed Jed's body until his skin glowed, then wrapped him in hot blankets. The next morning, he opened glazed eyes—and looked straight into his sworn enemy's face! With a wild cry, he raised himself up, then went limp and fell back.

"Are we going to lose him now, after all our hard work?" Lass cried.

"Not if I can help it!" Matt said grimly. "Please God, let this only be a setback. I was a fool to let him see me before I could explain I didn't come back to get him!"

"You didn't!" Dusty exclaimed.

Lass froze. Enlightenment penetrated the dim recesses of her mind. "You just said *Please God.*" Words that had made no impression at the time swept in and brushed the cobwebs from her weary brain. "I remember. The day you stitched Father's head, you asked if I could trust you. You said, 'Enough to put your father's life in my hands? *And God's.* Matthew Coulter, are you a Christian?" She caught at his sleeve. "Have you forgiven my father?"

"I am. I have. I started to tell you the night Duke came in without Jed. There's been no opportunity since." He lifted her hand from his arm and sighed. "Again, this is no time to discuss it. Buck up, Lass. Your father still needs us."

All that day and night, the three faithful friends hovered like ministering angels over the man who had wronged them. "More like angels in the snow," Dusty succinctly said when the bad weather continued. Their efforts were rewarded. The following day Jed again opened his eyes. This time a slight stirring of his body warned the others. Matt immediately stepped to the far side of the line shack. Jed wouldn't be able to see him from the bunk.

"Lass?" her father whispered. "Dusty." He shook his head as if to clear it.

"Don't try to talk," the foreman warned, after Lass nodded. She suspected Dusty knew she couldn't have spoken if an avalanche threatened the line shack!

A faint trace of the smile his daughter once knew and loved crossed Jed Talbot's haggard face. "Who's the boss around here, anyway?" he asked.

"Lass and me," Dusty promptly told him. "Get some shut-eye. You can talk when you're stronger."

Jed moved his head from side to side. "I can't rest until I talk. Just in case. . ." His voice trailed off, and he stared at the ceiling with anguished eyes.

Chapter 10

And it shall come to pass, that before they call,
I will answer; and while they are yet speaking, I will hear.
ISAIAH 65:24

L ass clasped the hand plucking at the blankets.
"Speak quickly, if you must."

Jed's words fell like pebbles in a pond, sending waves of shock. "The night you showed me what I'd become, I prayed God would let me die."

Lass gasped, but her father relentlessly continued. "I knew I couldn't go on as I'd done since Alice died, one of the living dead. I could no longer stand the man I'd become. I believe that recognition was God's last warning."

Lass blinked. *Her father*, mentioning God other than in bitterness and blame? Matt appeared to have turned to stone. Dusty coughed and shifted position.

Jed didn't seem to notice. "I left my whiskey at the Lazy T. If I couldn't survive without it, I'd at least die sober." A mirthless grin brightened his stern face.

"Fate—no, God—had other plans. Duke and I made it to within a half-mile of the shack before he stepped on a rotten, snow-covered log. It broke. He fell. So did I. Something smashed against my head, and everything went black."

Jed licked dry lips. "Dusty, get me some water, will you?" His faithful foreman nodded and obeyed. The injured man drank it and continued. "I came to, wondering where I was and what had happened to my horse."

"Duke made it back," Dusty put in. "A little lame, but he will be all right."

"Good. Anyway, I don't remember much after that. I know I ripped a sleeve from my shirt and wrapped my head to stop the bleeding. I remember stumbling into the shack and reaching the bunk before blacking out. I woke up cold, got a fire going, then hit the bunk again. After that, nothing." Jed's face shadowed and he half-turned from Lass. "That's the easy part."

She tightened her grip on his hand. Her nerves twanged. She sent a warning glance toward the corner where Matt hunkered down out of her father's sight.

"Why don't you wait?" she whispered to Jed. "You don't have to go on now."

"I've waited too long as it is," he said harshly. "I suspect Dusty knows but is too loyal to say so. Maybe for Alice's sake." Jed turned back to his daughter.

"Matt Coulter never rustled a single Lazy T steer. I framed him. You were all I had left after Alice died, Lass. I couldn't stand the idea of anyone taking you away from me." A dull flush suffused his worn face. "I never worried until Matt came along. Then I saw in your eyes the same expression Alice used to wear."

Lass felt her face flame. She gave an inarticulate cry and started to pull away.

Jed refused to let her go. "Hear me out. Please." His eyes reminded the girl of a child pleading for love and forgiveness. "I don't have any excuse, except I was so bitter at God for taking Alice, I went loco." He lay quietly for a moment.

A change stole over his features. His eyes grew bright. His voice strengthened. "If I make it back to the Lazy T, I want you to send for Matt Coulter and Sheriff McVeigh. If I don't get out of here, it's up to you and Dusty. I don't expect Matt or the town to forgive me, but Jubilee needs to know the truth. God and I had it out the night I learned Matt had come back wearing a U.S. Marshall's badge and could put me away if he spoke up. Jail couldn't be worse than the prison of my own making I've lived in for years."

A wistful note crept into Jed's voice. "Lass, if no one—even you—ever forgives me, I think maybe God will. I wish I could be sure." Color flooded his stubbled face. "I want you to know it's not just because I'm scared and ashamed to face Him and Alice. If I'm going to cash in, I'd like it to be knowing Matt Coulter understands I tried to square things."

The sudden grating of heavy boots on the hard floor sounded loud in the small room. A tall figure stepped to the edge of the bunk. Backlighted by flames in the fireplace and the dull, yellow glow from a lamp on the rude table, Matt Coulter cast an ominous, looming shadow. Lass held her breath and waited.

Jed tilted his head back and looked at the dark form above him. "*You!*" He raised himself to a sitting position. "You were here all the time?"

"Yes." The affirmation left no room for compromise.

Jed's eyes burned from the shadows with a look Lass felt must scorch anyone in its path. "You helped Dusty and Lass care for me." Not a question, but a statement. "Were you the one who patched my head?"

"I was."

Why must Matt sound colder than the highest peak on Grand Teton? Lass wondered. Had her ears deceived her into thinking he'd proclaimed himself a Christian and had forgiven her father? The wonderful hope that sprang to life with Matt's declaration struggled to survive then chilled. So did the joy that surged through her when her father unburdened himself of his long-held wrong, recognizing there was little hope of forgiveness unless by God.

Jed fell back against the pillow. "In the name of all that's holy, *why?*"

Matt stepped aside until fire and lamplight shone directly on Jed. "A man called Pastor Andrew brought me back from the dead. When I was ready to ask Jesus to be my Trailmate, he told me I couldn't do it with hate in my heart."

Jed gasped, but the steady voice went on. "Pastor Andrew said I had to *love God more than I hated you*. That I had no choice when you cheated me of my good name, but you couldn't cheat me out of my salvation unless I let you."

"You had a choice the first time!" Jed muttered.

"You knew I railroaded you. Why did you say nothing except that you were innocent? It's stuck in my craw ever since. Couldn't you prove I was lying?"

Matt didn't answer.

Not so Dusty. "He did it for Lass, you long-legged donkey," the foreman blazed. "Begging your pardon, Boss, but I've had a lot of time to figure. The way I see it, Matt reckoned it was better to take the blame and ride out than show you up as a mean, ornery skunk. He couldn't stand having Lass lose her daddy less than a year after her mama was took."

Lass reeled from the truth. She stared at Dusty. At Jed. Finally, at Matt, who had kept the faith. Hot tears came. She turned from her father and blindly rushed into Matt's arms. "Why didn't you tell me? You could at least have written!"

She felt his arms twitch. "I did, Lass. The letters all came back."

All her anger and the hurt of thinking herself forgotten spilled out. "Father?"

His words sounded muffled. "Yes. I told myself it was for the best."

Matt's arm tightened over her shoulders, and he said to the man in the bunk, "Jedediah Talbot, you're a miserable sinner. So am I. There's one difference. It took a long time for me to admit it, but I did. God's forgiven me because of what His Son did a long time ago. You said you wished you could be sure God would forgive you. You confessed your sins before Him and before us, not knowing I was here." Laughter eased the tension in Matt's rich voice. "I'm glad you didn't know.

It makes it a lot easier for me to believe you mean it. That's what it's all about: being sorry; receiving forgiveness; riding new trails, with Him."

"You really believe God will forgive me?" Jed whispered. Lass wanted to weep at the uncertain hope in the question. How far Father had fallen from the joyous Christian man who was once head of the Talbot household!

"He already has, Jed." Matt's words rang with truth. "The Bible says so."

"Pastor Andrew showed me the promise in Isaiah where the Lord says He will answer before we call and that He hears us while we're still speaking."

Matt stopped. His voice dropped to little more than a whisper, yet sounded louder than a shout to Lass Talbot's heart when he said, "I also know God will forgive you *because I have*, and He's a lot more willing to pardon than I am."

Great tears coursed down Jed's leathery time-worn face. He made no effort to wipe them away. He had come to the line shack expecting to die. By the grace of God, he would leave a new man. He nodded and a few minutes later, his even breathing told Lass he had fallen into the sleep his body needed to heal.

Dusty cleared his throat and stepped to the window. "Storm's over."

Matt smiled down at the girl in his arms. The wonderful blue light Lass knew shone for her came back into his eyes. "In more ways than one."

Lass rested her tired head against his chest. "Yes. Oh, Matt. . ." She couldn't go on. For seven long years they had waited. Now their jubilee beckoned, more joyful than Christmas hymns. More fragrant than crushed hemlock branches. More golden than the ring Matt would soon place on her finger to make her his. More precious than the Christmas Eve snow angels they would make.

What "secret angel" gifts could she bestow this year? Anticipation sent a thrill through her. Dared she give her father the little store of Christmas letters that vowed to pray for him every day of the year?

Perhaps, even though it would break tradition by being given openly. Great-grandfather had told his family to always give their best. How little gold, frankincense, and myrrh meant compared with the gift of prayer!

"What are you thinking, my darling?" Matt whispered. The light in his eyes intensified until Lass felt she would drown in their blueness.

"About Christmas and the best gifts."

"What happened here today is all I need or want," he said quietly.

"And I."

Someday she would learn the full story of Matt's long years of searching. Someday he would know the pain she had felt when she believed he had deserted her. For now, it was enough to hold him close and silently thank God.

COLLEEN L. REECE

Colleen is a prolific writer with more than 100 books to her credit. In addition to writing, Colleen teaches and lectures in her home state of Washington. She loves to travel and, at the same time, do research for her inspirational historical romances. Twice voted "Favorite Author" in the annual **Heartsong Presents** readers' poll, Colleen has an army of fans that continues to grow, including younger readers who have enjoyed her "Juli Scott Super Sleuth" series for girls aged nine to fifteen and her contributions to the American Adventure series.

Christmas Cake

by Janet Spaeth

Dedication

For Megan and Nick, simply because I love you.

Chapter 1

E lizabeth smiled as she heard Joel's steps outside the door. He paused, and she mentally counted with him, *one, two, three, four,* as he stomped his feet on the wooden porch four times before turning the doorknob.

They'd only been married six months, and already she knew the rhythm of his daily life. He had to have a cup of steaming coffee first thing in the morning. When he ate, he started with the vegetables and worked around his plate, saving the meat for the last. And she could definitely count on those four stamps of his feet before entering the house.

It was a sign of his thoughtfulness. The early snow that covered their Nebraska homestead's yard was easily tracked into the house, and Joel conscientiously cleaned his feet as completely as possible before entering.

She looked up at him as he entered the room. His face was red from the cold, and he puffed on his hands as he rubbed them together briskly.

"Cold?" she asked unnecessarily.

"Yup." His monosyllabic answer was lightened by a

quick grin. "But it's November so we can't really expect different."

She smiled at him. The past six months with him were wonderful and joy-filled. The other women in town had told her eventually those four stamps of his feet, the coffee, the pattern of his dining, and the predictability of his ways would drive her insane, but she doubted it. Not when she was this deliriously happy.

"Cat got your tongue, Mrs. Evans?" His eyes twinkled as brightly blue as the clear plains sky as he studied her.

"No," she answered. "Just thinking that I am undoubtedly the luckiest woman on earth to have you as my husband."

The corners of his mouth turned up in a lopsided smile. "Luck?" he repeated. "Luck, my dear wife, had nothing to do with it. I saw you, I lost my heart to you immediately, and determined you were the woman I wanted to marry. So I did."

"Oh, you did?" She nodded, pretending to be seriously concerned. "And what about me?"

He stood towering over her, his hands on his hips. "Yes, what about you?"

What about her, indeed? In her memory she revisited their first meeting. She'd been leaving Sunday services at her grandfather's church in Omaha when another member introduced the young man accompanying him. "This is Joel Evans, the son of an old friend."

Her grandfather frowned slightly as the two young people's gazes met and locked, but his friend had reassured him, "Not to worry, Cal. Joel's just visiting from

Boston. He'll be here two more days, and that's it."

That evening both Joel and his elderly companion dined with Elizabeth and her grandfather, and by the end of the evening, both Elizabeth and Joel knew he would not be going back to Boston, not in three days, not ever.

They married six months later, after Grandfather was convinced their love was real and abiding, and that Joel had in his heart the same love of the Lord Elizabeth did. Within a month, they moved to the prairie farm so that Joel could try his luck at his dream: coaxing crops from the rich mid-western soil.

Grandfather had been loath to see her go, but despite his misgivings, they traveled on with his blessings.

It had worked out remarkably well. Soon after Elizabeth and Joel's departure, Grandfather met a charming widow only a few years younger than himself, and they just declared their own vows last month.

He was no longer alone in the big house on Locust Street, which relieved Elizabeth's mind, and if she were inclined to confess the truth about it, it also made him less fretful about his only relative living so far away.

She didn't worry about whether he was eating enough vegetables, and he didn't worry about whether she was safe from the winter winds. Instead, they committed their cares to the Lord and went on with their private earthly duties.

Elizabeth returned to the question at hand. "What about me?" she repeated. "I saw a man I knew I could love. A man I knew could love me. And after that, well, as they say, it all was history."

"You went after me with a vengeance," he agreed. "I had no choice but to give in." He sighed and let his shoulders slump. "I didn't have the strength to fight you."

"Oh, you pitiful thing!" She stood up and wrapped her arms around his frosty neck. "And I've been torturing you ever since."

They kissed, her lips warm against his still-cold mouth. This, Elizabeth knew, would never get tiresome, this age-old symbol of love. Their lips had barely parted when Joel clapped his hand to his pocket. "Lizzie! I almost forgot! A letter from my mother came today."

He pulled out a wrinkled envelope. The corner was torn, showing the distance it had traveled, but the elegant script of the senior Mrs. Evans was distinctive.

"What does she say?" Elizabeth asked, unconsciously smoothing down the front of her dress. Joel's mother made her nervous. It wasn't that she was indifferent or spiteful to Elizabeth—not at all—but rather that in her presence, Elizabeth felt tongue-tied and awkward. Mrs. Evans was so. . .so elegant. And Elizabeth was. . .not.

"She's coming for a visit!"

"A visit? Here?" Elizabeth looked around her and sank to the chair. "Here? She's coming here?"

"Yes!" Joel slapped the letter against his leg. "Yes! She's coming all the way to Nebraska! She's taking the train from Boston. We'll pick her up in Omaha and drive her out here."

"Here?"

"What's the matter, Lizzie?" His forehead wrinkled. "Is something wrong? Don't you want her to come here?"

"Oh, no, I mean, yes. No. Oh, Joel!"

His face clouded. "I thought you liked my mother."

"I do, Joel, I really do. And I am anxious to see her again."

He smiled at her. "That's better."

"When is she arriving?"

"She'll be here in a couple of weeks! She's coming for Christmas!"

This time Elizabeth didn't dare let herself say it, but she thought it: *Oh, no.*

The house was still basic. It was simple. What it actually was, Elizabeth finally admitted to herself, was unfinished. The floorboards were planks of rough-hewn pine, covered with inexpensive rag rugs. She'd counted herself fortunate to even have flooring; many of the women she'd met in town bemoaned the fact that they still had dirt floors.

She'd seen the Evans house in Boston. There weren't dirt floors there, and the floorboards were highly polished oak.

This house, this dear house, would seem like a hovel to his mother. And if she hated it, then perhaps Joel would see it through her eyes: the spaces between the planks, the knots in the rugs where Elizabeth had inexpertly tied the rags together, the cheapness of the thin yellow-edged drapes that had earlier seemed so cheerful.

Could he still be happy here? Elizabeth formulated the only prayer she could: *Please, God. Please.*

Dimly Joel's voice floated back in. ". . .And caroling and roasting chestnuts over the fire, and oh, my goodness, fruitcake."

"Fruitcake?" Elizabeth asked, feeling stupid.

"It's all the rage on the coast. Has been for a couple of years now. Aunt Susan makes a fruitcake that would. . ."

His voice faded back out, and Elizabeth let the feeling of dread settle in her chest. Caroling. Chestnuts. And now, fruitcake. Her beloved husband was going to hate Christmas out on the prairie. They couldn't go caroling, not when the houses were spread as far apart as they were.

And they couldn't do it alone, just the two of them. She'd need an extra bolstering of other female voices. Hers was, bluntly put, as pleasing as a saw on metal.

The nearest chestnut tree, as far as she knew, grew in the park near her aunt's house in Indiana.

And fruitcake? Now that didn't sound too bad.

Elizabeth sat up straight. Her husband was *not* going to regret staying in Nebraska with her. If he wanted fruitcake, then he would have fruitcake.

Just as soon as she found out what it was.

Chapter 2

A tiny swirl of cold crept under the quilt, and Elizabeth burrowed deeper.

Stamp, stamp, stamp, stamp.

Joel had already been out to feed the animals. She opened one eye and peeked out cautiously. Daylight flooded the room, telling her she'd clearly overslept. Dawn came late in winter.

She had no idea how long she'd slept, though. When they'd moved to the prairie, Joel said they were not bringing any clocks with them. "What's the purpose of knowing it's four-thirty-two in the afternoon?" he'd said. "In Omaha, that may mean something, but not to us. We won't need a clock to tell us the cows need to be milked. Their lowing will let us know. We won't need a clock to tell us when it's dinnertime. Our stomachs will tell us."

She threw the covers over her head. She should get up, but she was so tired. She'd stayed up most of the night worrying.

Something icy cold snaked down into the burrow she'd made and cupped her face. She sat up with a start. Joel stood beside the bed, grinning at her. He held out his hands to her. They were bright red.

"Lizzie, my dear, I do believe it's winter."

She leaped up and took his cold hands in hers. "Oh, Joel, are your hands going to be okay?" She held them to her face and rubbed them, trying to warm them. Panic bubbled up inside her. She'd never seen hands so brilliantly crimson. "You poor thing. They're probably frostbitten!"

His body shook a bit, and she looked up suspiciously. She hadn't been married to him nearly five months without learning something about her husband.

Sure enough, his eyes danced with hidden laughter.

She dropped his hands and glared at him. "Joel Evans, you tell me the truth this instant. What is going on?"

He crossed to the stove, which was burning cheerfully with new logs, and picked up the mittens she'd knit for him.

She'd knit them from thick wool, intended to keep his fingers safely warm while he was out on the cold Nebraska plains. She specifically had chosen a merry red that would, she hoped, be a cheerful note when the prairie winter seemed endless, as she knew it would.

But now they dripped onto the floor, vivid scarlet drops pooling on the raw wood planking. "I'm afraid your wool wasn't colorfast, Lizzie."

She'd been so anxious to show him what a good wife she was going to be that she'd failed to prewash the wool, or at least rinse the mittens out with saltwater before giving them to him. Her eyes filled with tears. She had let him down. "Oh, Joel, I'm so sorry!"

"No problem," he said, coming to her to give her a hug. "If my hands have to be another color, red is as fine a hue as there is. Besides, it'll wash off." He smiled at her. "So what do you have planned for today?"

"I thought I'd go through the wedding trunk your mother packed," she answered. "There were some Christmas decorations in there, I believe."

Joel frowned. "She didn't try to pass off that set of glass ornaments on you, did she? The ones that came all the way over from England on a packet ship and managed to arrive unscathed, not a single one broken?" From the way he said the words, the box of ornaments were clearly a family tradition, and the story of their arrival was near-legend.

"I don't think so," Elizabeth answered. "But I can't be sure until I go through the trunk again."

"Well," he said, grinning at her, "if you do find them, do me a favor."

"What?"

"Drop them. They're hideous."

❧

Elizabeth waited until Joel went back to the barn. He was worried that the increased cold might signal bad weather, and he wanted to make sure the animals were secure with food and dry hay.

She pulled the trunk out from the corner where it usually sat. Something tiny and dark scurried from the light, and she breathed a sigh of relief as it scuttled through the space under the front door, nearly flattening itself in the process.

It was probably a field mouse. By now she should be

used to them. The trick was, as Joel put it, to encourage them to live elsewhere when the house was the warmest place around in the dead of winter. She'd tried not to shudder as he talked about the mice. She'd nodded knowledgeably and agreed that they were an unavoidable nuisance, but inside she shivered with revulsion. Mice.

Fortunately no rodents had gotten into the trunk. Everything was still packed as nicely as it had been when Mrs. Evans ordered Joel to put it in the wagon.

Somehow it didn't surprise Elizabeth that his mother could pack this well. Even the table linen remained unwrinkled. Joel had built the house well, but keeping anything clean, let alone white, was a never-ending task. Dirt seemed to sift through even the tiniest crack in the door. Wisdom borne of experience living on the prairie told Elizabeth fancy white linen was silly.

Or was it? She shook out the linen tablecloth and studied it. It would look pretty on their table. The least she could do was make their home an inviting place. She laid the beautiful piece aside and investigated further.

She had gone through the trunk when they'd first arrived, being careful not to disarrange anything that Mrs. Evans had so meticulously packed. Elizabeth had glanced through the recipes and found them to require ingredients not available on the farm, and she'd cautiously retied the ribbon around them and placed them back in the trunk, thinking one day she would use them. That day had arrived.

At last she found what she was looking for. Mrs.

Evans had told her she'd placed them in there. Her fingers closed around the ribbon-bound packet. Even this, Mrs. Evans had prepared with her special touch. Ribbons!

And on the front of the bundle was, in Mrs. Evans' recognizable flowery script, "RECIPES."

Her hands trembled as she untied the packet. It had to be in there. It had to be. She began to pray in an undertone as she sorted through the recipes, "Please, God, let it be here. Creamed chicken on toast points. No, no, not it. I want this to be special for Joel, God, a Christmas that won't make him regret marrying me. Curried corn. How awful. Who would curry corn? Lord, please, oh, please let it be here. Here's apple bread. Close but I don't think that's it. Please, please, please. Fruitcake. Aunt Susan's fruitcake. Thank you, Lord!"

She sagged back in relief, the dear recipe in her hand. Here it was, the recipe that would make all the difference in the world to her. She scanned through it, her eyes widening at some of the ingredients, her head bobbing in agreement at others.

Such a recipe! She'd never seen anything like it before. Aunt Susan's spidery handwriting was clear and readable, though, so everything on it must be right. Candied orange rind? She shuddered. It sounded dreadful.

So this was fruitcake.

Joel banked the straw against the lower parts of the barn's interior walls. The wind whistled through incessantly, it seemed. He was using hay bales around the edge of the house. Here in the barn, where the planks didn't quite meet on the northeast side, he'd piled more bales, too.

Actually, with the animals generating heat, the barn was a fairly cozy place. A bit fragrant, perhaps, but warm.

He stroked the twin noses that poked through the slats of the stable walls. As soon as Joel had decided to stay on the prairie and try his hand at farming, he'd bought the two horses. He'd trained them himself, or, as he sometimes said laughingly, they'd trained him. They were like children to him. As inquisitive as children, at least.

"Come on, Day. You, too, Lily." The team followed the sound of his voice as they moved restlessly in their stalls and whinnied at him from the front where the gate was lower. "You need to get out and run a bit. Don't want you going soft on me."

The horses understood all of it, it seemed to him. He turned them into the corral and watched as they ran with the absolute joy of being outside.

He knew how they felt. He loved it there.

And he loved Elizabeth.

He didn't know anyone could be as blessed as he was at this very moment. He paused to thank the Lord for her and for all that she had brought into his life. She was such an unexpected gift.

Gift!

"Run all you want today, girls," he said to the horses. "Tomorrow we're going into town. We have some Christmas shopping to do."

What could he get her? He frowned as he kicked a clump of snow away from the corral's gate. He was not a creative man. But Christmas was Christmas, and it was almost there.

Whatever thinking he might have ahead of him, he'd better come up with something quickly.

❧

Their dinner seemed almost formal that night. Perhaps it was the embroidered linen she'd put on the plank table. Or perhaps it was the way that Elizabeth and Joel watched each other.

"You'd better give me that shirt tonight," Elizabeth said at last.

"What shirt?" Joel paused, his fork suspended midway between his plate and his mouth.

"The one you have on. Look how long the sleeves are! Why, they're almost to your knuckles!"

He glanced guiltily at his fingers and quickly popped the bite of meat into his mouth before hiding his hand under the table. He'd washed his hands before dinner— repeatedly. He'd even tried the strong lye mixture that he used in the barn, but the dye from the red mittens was stubborn. The last thing he wanted to tell her was that he hoped she liked red hands—because his were apparently going to be red for quite a while.

Chapter 3

Elizabeth tucked an extra blanket around the basket of eggs that were cradled on her lap. The air was still and crisp, with no hint of wind or storms, but on the prairie, it never hurt to take some extra precautions.

Besides, it was cold.

Apparently Joel thought so, too. He stopped and gazed at the front of the wagon, his mind clearly engaged on imagining something.

"You know," he said, "I saw some willow down by the creek. Come spring, I think I'll go down there and get some saplings. They might be flexible enough to build an arch over the front of the wagon. Then we could. . ."

He chattered on as he got into the wagon. With a light flick of the reins, Joel let Day and Lily know it was time to go.

Elizabeth only half listened to Joel. The gait of the horses on the frozen ground jostled the eggs, and she had to hold onto the basket tightly. Occasionally, though, her fingers strayed to her pocket where the precious recipe was safely nestled. What if she lost it? She should have made a copy of it, but there hadn't been time. She would just have to be extra careful with it.

How much the ingredients for the fruitcake would cost worried her dearly. Since the sunny days of August, she'd put aside some of her egg money in a credit at the store, planning to use it for Joel's Christmas gift. She hoped that she'd have enough accumulated to trade evenly.

". . .And that'll shelter us from the elements when we go into town. What do you think, Lizzie?"

Guiltily, she realized she had missed everything Joel had been talking about. Something about willow saplings, bending them, elements. . .

She took a wild stab at it. "It'll work quite nicely, I think."

He rewarded her with a smile. "You don't have a clue what I've been talking about, do you? What's up, Lizzie dear? Christmas secrets?"

Her fingers brushed the recipe. "Yes, Joel, Christmas secrets."

She loved this man so much, it seemed impossible for her heart to hold any more joy. All she wanted was to make him happy, to keep him smiling. And in return, she knew that he wanted the same for her.

It wasn't as easy as she'd dreamed it would be, though. In her adolescent reveries, she'd been the perfect wife, serving perfect meals. . .and knitting perfect mittens. Mittens that didn't bleed bright red dye over her husband's hard-working hands.

He wore his old leather gloves today, since yesterday's fiasco forced him to stop wearing the red woolen mittens. She hoped his hands stayed warm enough.

Maybe she could purchase some more yarn, and she could knit him some new mittens that wouldn't bleed on his skin. It was a good thought. She settled back and watched the dazzling winter sun create glitters of diamonds on the new snow.

Mr. Nichols, the owner of the general store, stood behind the counter patiently as she smoothed out the precious recipe.

"I'll need a pound of candied fruit peel, a pound packet of raisins, a small container of thick molasses, and a cone of brown sugar. I'll also need cinnamon, mace, nutmeg, and allspice."

"A tin of each?" Mr. Nichols asked, frowning slightly.

Elizabeth consulted the recipe. "I need no more than a teaspoon of each. Is it possible to get less than an entire tin?"

The shopkeeper rubbed his chin thoughtfully. "I think I can do that." He gathered the supplies and put them into the basket that had held her eggs. "Anything else?"

She looked at the recipe again. Eggs, flour, baking powder, salt, and lard she had. She shook her head. "I believe that'll be all."

"Good thing you brought in your eggs," he said. "Demand's high with Christmas coming, and not everybody's hens are laying as well as yours. Cold weather gets to them, I guess."

He licked the tip of his stubby pencil before he

began totaling the charges. When he gave her the sum, Elizabeth almost lost her breath. She hadn't expected it to be this much.

She looked longingly at the wool she'd laid aside. She didn't have enough money to buy all of the ingredients for the fruitcake and still afford the yarn for new mittens for Joel. Sadly she pushed the skein of yarn aside. It was a terrible muddy, brownish-gray color, ugly but serviceable. Joel needed mittens, but perhaps she could set the color in his red ones. That way he could have mittens and his fruitcake.

She'd seen the reminiscent glow in his eyes as he revisited his Christmases in Boston. If there was anything she could do to recreate even a part of those Christmases, she would do it.

"Have you had fruitcake before?" Mr. Nichols asked as he slid the now-filled basket to her.

"No, I haven't."

He rummaged under the counter and pulled out a tattered magazine. She recognized the name: *Godey's Ladies Book*. "Here," he said, thumbing through it, "there's an article about it. The missus showed it to me the other night."

Elizabeth scanned the page he showed her. According to the article, fruitcake was a favorite food of Queen Victoria's, and now it was considered a delicacy of fashionable people.

"You're the first person to come in and get the ingredients for it," Mr. Nichols said. "You're quite a style-setter, Mrs. Evans!"

" 'Is there any thing whereof it may be said, See,

this is new? it hath been already of old time, which was before us.' "

He gaped at her. "Excuse me?"

Elizabeth laughed. "It's from Ecclesiastes. This fruitcake that's all the rage in England and now the East Coast is actually an old recipe from my husband's family. What is old is new again."

A movement outside the store window caught her eye. Joel had stopped to talk to a few men, but he'd soon be in to pick her up. "Do me a favor, Mr. Nichols." She leaned across the counter and lowered her voice. "Do not say anything about this to my husband."

He nodded in understanding. "Prices a bit steep, is that it?"

"No, no, nothing like that." She paused and couldn't resist. "Well, except for that skein of wool. It shouldn't sell for a penny over forty cents, and you know it."

The door opened a crack, and she could hear Joel bidding one of his companions a Merry Christmas. "Don't tell him about this because it's a surprise. A Christmas secret."

Mr. Nichols straightened up and winked at her. "No problem, Mrs. Evans. No problem at all."

"Well," Joel said in a jovial voice behind her, "I probably should be worried that the shopkeeper is winking at my wife, but I'm hoping it means that she's getting a good price on her groceries."

Groceries! She'd totally forgotten about them.

"So what did you get?" Joel asked her, reaching for the basket and lifting one corner of the cloth she spread over the top.

Faster than she thought possible, she reached across and lightly slapped his hand. "Joel Evans, you know better than to go snooping this time of year."

Joel laughed and put his arm around her. "Let's go so we can get back home before dark."

As they left, Mr. Nichols called out, "Say, Joel, stop back by the next time you're in town. I've got some good liniment for those hands. I don't believe I've ever seen hands that chapped—and that red!"

❧

The little farmhouse, with its plank flooring and raw white walls, seemed especially cozy that night. The wind had finally picked up, blessedly after they'd gotten Day and Lily stabled, the cows fed, and the chickens settled with fresh grain.

The tips of Elizabeth's fingers still tingled from the cold ride home. In her anxiety to leave the store before Joel saw the ingredients for the fruitcake and figured out her surprise, she'd left her gloves on the counter.

Joel teased her about her vanity in not wanting to wear the extra pair that was on the floor of the wagon—big, rough cloth gloves so old that the fur lining was patchy with age—but she couldn't tell him the real reason.

She didn't dare let go of the recipe. It was enough that she'd lost her gloves. If she lost the recipe, too, she'd be devastated. Too much was riding on it, so she'd kept her hands in her pockets, her fingers curled protectively around the precious piece of paper.

She turned her chair to the fire and opened her Bible to her favorite passage.

"Read it aloud," Joel said from the other chair, which also faced the fire. He was nearly asleep.

She barely needed to follow the printed words as she began her favorite chapter from the Bible. " 'Though I speak with the tongues of men and angels. . . .' "

"1 Corinthians 13," said Joel, not opening his eyes. He continued with her drowsily, ending with, " 'And now abideth faith, hope, charity, these three; but the greatest of these is charity.' "

His head dropped to one side, and she studied his face. It was the face of a good, kind man, one whose love would indeed fail her not. She tucked the quilt closer around his shoulders and kissed his forehead.

When she counted her blessings in her evening prayer, she would include this night as one of them.

Chapter 4

D id I tell you I might not be back until after dark?" Joel asked, returning to the house for the fifth time since hitching Day and Lily to the wagon.

"Yes, you did, my sweet." Elizabeth turned him around and pushed him out the door. "Now go, or it'll be dark before you leave!"

She watched from the door as he walked to the wagon, put his foot on the sideboard, and then paused. She sighed as he returned to the house. "Joel, if you—"

Whatever she was going to say was silenced by his kiss. "There," he said when he drew back. "I knew I'd forgotten something. See you later tonight!"

This time she wrapped up in the thick shawl she kept by the door, and she accompanied him to the wagon. "Give Brother Jensen my warmest wishes for his recovery," she said as Joel slid onto the wagon's seat.

"Rotten luck for him, breaking his leg like this," Joel said, "although better now than during planting or harvest, I'd say."

"It will cheer him to see you, I know." She pulled the wagon robe tighter around his feet. "And I hope the cookies will be enjoyable for him. Don't eat them on the way."

Brother Jensen, the aging man who served as the pastor of their tiny congregation, had broken his leg in a fall from his barn loft. A widower, he had lain alone for thirty hours until someone stopped by and found him. The leg was slow in setting, and the church members were taking turns bringing him food and companionship.

Elizabeth was almost looking forward to Joel's absence. It gave her an entire day to work on the fruitcake. She tidied up the kitchen, made the bed, and swept the floors. Straightening the small house didn't take long. There were really only three tiny rooms: the kitchen, the living room, and the bedroom.

With a fresh apron tied around her waist, she set forth to make fruitcake. Joel had fed the chickens and gathered the eggs that morning. They were in a bowl on the table, with a note beside them. *Lizzie, where's the egg basket? Couldn't find it.* Elizabeth breathed a sigh of relief. If he'd gone looking for it, her secret would have been exposed.

The tins of flour, salt, and baking powder went next to the eggs. The tub of lard joined them. Then she reached into the far corner of the top shelf, where she'd hidden the ingredients she'd bought at the store. They were still tucked in the egg basket, where she was sure that Joel wouldn't bother to look.

As her hands closed around the woven handle,

something small and gray and very quick scampered out of the basket, leaped to the edge of the nearest chair, and jumped onto the floor. Without a second thought, Elizabeth grabbed the broom and chased it outside, where it vanished under the woodpile.

The field mice were getting worse. Every morning she had to chase them out of the house. She'd have Joel look into traps when he went into town next.

This is the prairie, she told herself. *I'm not the only creature out here. I have to expect that there will be mice and snakes and—*

She broke off the thought before she could go any further with it. She was alone in the house for several hours, and the last thing she needed to do was start thinking about what could scare her.

What she needed to do was make a fruitcake.

She took the basket down and set it on the table. A clean bowl, a baking pan, a spoon—she scurried around the small kitchen, gathering the utensils.

At last it was all ready for her to begin. She reached into her pocket and unfolded the recipe, although she didn't need it anymore; she had read it so many times, it was etched in her memory. She took the brightly checked cloth off her egg basket and nearly fainted.

The mouse had been busy. Every single packet had been gnawed into. The candied fruit peel had apparently not been to his liking, for he'd chewed into the package and then abandoned it after one piece. The raisins were a mess, and the brown sugar had teeth marks all around the cone. Even the tiny envelopes containing the spices had been torn into.

Elizabeth sank onto the floor and buried her face in her hands.

How was she going to make the fruitcake now? And how was she going to make this Christmas as good as the ones Joel had had before? She should have put the supplies in tins. She knew about the field mice, and she hadn't taken the appropriate precautions.

Everything was ruined. Everything.

Joel pulled into his pastor's farmyard and was greeted by the familiar figure of Brother Jensen at the door, waving to him.

The man hobbled out onto the hewn rock step and motioned to him with a rudimentary crutch. "Come on in, Joel! You didn't have to come all this way, although I'm mighty glad you did. It gets a bit lonesome out here, being stove up like this with my bum leg."

The inside of the pastor's house was tidy, but the fire was laid awkwardly and burned too cold. Brother Jensen apologized for it, explaining that, thanks to his broken leg, he couldn't bend over far enough to get it done correctly.

Joel realigned the logs so they were slightly angled, bark side down. "Where's the fatwood?" he asked, looking around the stove for the soft wooden sticks that would get the fire going.

"I'm out," Brother Jensen admitted. "I'm using what's at the bottom of the woodpile."

"And how are you doing that?" Joel asked suspiciously. "You shouldn't be digging around there with your leg."

Brother Jensen waved his objections away. "I didn't. Well, not much. Earlier this week Karl Lund stopped by and filled a pail full of kindling. It's nearly empty now."

"I'll fill it before I leave," Joel said, smiling with satisfaction as the logs caught and began to burn cheerfully.

Brother Jensen passed Joel a plate of the cookies Elizabeth had sent over. "Would you like one? Your wife certainly is a good cook."

Joel accepted one of the oatmeal cookies. "Elizabeth is a wonderful cook. There isn't anything in this world she can't make if she sets her mind to it."

"She brings my departed Abigail to mind. Now there was another fine woman. You're a fortunate man, Joel."

"Amen to that, Brother Jensen. She is a godsend of a wife, and I am truly blessed."

The two men visited about the price of wheat, the usefulness of the new threshing equipment that had arrived in Omaha, and the impending weather.

Brother Jensen grinned broadly when Joel told him his mother was coming. "We'll pray, then, whatever winter storms are ahead for us will hold off until the new year is settled in," the pastor said. "That'll give you time for a visit and time for her return."

"I appreciate your prayers," Joel responded, "although I'm not convinced God always listens to what we order up when we talk to Him."

The older man laughed. "Oh, He listens, all right. What's hard for us to accept is we might, just might, be asking for the wrong thing, and He's simply fixing things for us up there in heaven."

"So," Joel continued, smiling, "are you saying if we pray for calm weather and He delivers us a blizzard, there's a reason?"

Brother Jensen nodded. "We don't always see it right away, sometimes not for years, maybe not for centuries, but the Lord never puts down his Hand on this earth without good cause."

His voice was getting hoarse, and Joel realized the pastor needed some rest.

"I think I'd better get back," Joel said softly, rising to his feet. "Let me bring more wood in now. You're running low on logs."

"I'd appreciate it, Joel. You know what the Good Book says, 'Where no wood is, there the fire goeth out.'"

As he refilled the woodbox inside the pastor's house, Joel's thoughts turned to Elizabeth. The sun was starting to set, and he'd just make it home in time for dinner. What delightful meal would she make tonight?

Elizabeth sat in the middle of her kitchen, the precious contents of the egg basket now relegated to the garbage. Outside, the sun set in a vivid blaze over the prairie, pouring liquid purples and vibrant crimsons over the snow-whitened land. Only when the glorious display was gone, swathing the land in darkest night, did she realize that Joel soon would be home, and she had nothing ready for him.

Even as she thought it, she heard the sound of the wagon approaching. She hurriedly sliced some meat and bread. It was not much, but it would have to do today.

Stamp, stamp, stamp, stamp. Joel walked into the house.

And her heart overflowed with joy.

Chapter 5

I have to go into town," Joel said the next morning. "Again?" Elizabeth turned from the shirt she was mending, rose, and walked over to the window. The sky was a clear, promising blue. Not even one fluffy white cloud marred the scene.

He came up behind her and put his arms around her from the back. Together they stood, gazing at the prairie spread out before them, a vision of white snow and blue sky, all so startlingly clean and pure, it almost hurt to look at it.

"I doubt that it'll storm today," he said at last.

The prairie could, at any moment, turn menacing. They both knew that. A storm could blow in quickly, true, but she'd pack an emergency food bundle, and the buffalo robe would keep him warm and dry until the storm blew over.

"Anything I can pick up for you while I'm there?" he asked.

Her thoughts flew to the ingredients for the cake. She could hardly ask him to pick those up for her without arousing his suspicion. She turned to him and smiled winningly. "Can I go, too?"

"Uh, sure," he answered. "If you want to."

A flicker of something passed across his face as he said the words. Had she imagined it? It looked almost like—disappointment.

Her heart dropped like a stone. Didn't he want to be with her? Was he bored with her, with their small house on the plains, already? It had been his idea to live on the prairie. If he was tired of their life, if he wanted to be alone, she must be letting him down somehow.

She strengthened her resolve. She had to go with him to town. She had to make the fruitcake. It was a link with the home and the traditions he'd left behind for the flat Nebraska farmland.

Yes, the fruitcake. That would make him happy.

Joel was quieter than usual on the ride into town, but Elizabeth couldn't read his expression or his thoughts.

Every once in awhile he'd look at her and smile, and all her doubts would evaporate, no more substantial than the tiny puffs of snow kicked up by the horses' hooves as they followed the worn path through the snowy landscape. But for the most part, he kept whatever was going through his mind to himself. She would have given anything to know what he was thinking about so intently.

Fear, or maybe worry, washed over her, a feeling so overwhelming, she felt as if she were drowning in it. She had to do something to break into his thoughts.

"So what are you going to get in town?" Her words, unnaturally loud, rang through the still winter air like shots.

He glanced over at her and smiled almost guiltily. "Oh," he hedged, "something. Nothing."

"Well, is it something or is it nothing?" Her voice sounded more impatient than she had intended.

"It's neither. It's both."

She nodded. "Very well. Just as long as we're clear about it."

He laughed and let the reins drop onto his lap as he reached across the wagon seat and enclosed her in his arms. Day and Lily, used to the trip, plodded along methodically.

"You silly goose," he said as he held her closely. His lips were cold against her forehead. "Why do you think I'm going into town? It's not quite two weeks until Christmas."

How could she have been such a ninny? Of course he'd get her a present, just as she was making something for him: the fruitcake.

Curiosity caught hold of her. "What are you getting me?"

He shook his head. "Oh, no. You're not charming that secret out of me."

"Please?" she wheedled.

"No."

"Is it a hat?"

He shook his head.

"A new bowl."

"No."

"A necklace."

"No. You can quit asking. I won't tell."

"Oh, Joel." She sank back and pretended to pout.

"But you can tell me what *you* got *me*," he said as he picked up the reins and *tched* to the horses to go faster.

"I can't!" She tried to keep the panic out of her voice but was unsuccessful.

"Don't I even get to guess?" he teased.

"No. I mean, I'd rather you didn't."

He shrugged happily. "Then don't ask me any more questions about your present."

The remainder of the ride into town she spent half asleep, dreaming of Christmas secrets. The wagon rumbled to a stop, and she woke with a start. They were already in town, in front of Mr. Nichols' store.

"I'll be back pretty quick," Joel said. He glanced at the sky, and Elizabeth's gaze followed his. Along the horizon, thick white clouds were scudding towards them, the kind of clouds that carried snow, and lots of it.

"I'll hurry," she said.

They both stood beside the wagon uncertainly. "I'm going to Mr. Nichols' store," she said pointedly.

"Yes?" He grinned.

"If you, um, need to go in there, too. . ."

"Why would I need to go in there?"

It was indelicate, but there was no way around it. "For my. . .you know."

Her husband pretended surprise. "They sell you-knows in there? And all the time I thought they grew wild!"

She rolled her eyes. "My present, you lunatic. You said you were getting my present today."

"I am."

"But don't you need to go in there?"

"Not getting it there," he said, shoving his hands in his pockets and beginning to whistle.

"Where are you getting it, then?" she asked.

He lifted his shoulders and looked innocent, and at last she sighed and went inside the store, her curiosity still unresolved.

Mr. Nichols beamed at her as he hurried to her side. "Mr. Evans with you?" he asked after a surreptitious look around.

She shook her head. "He had some other errand."

"Then tell me—how did it turn out?" Mr. Nichols waited in anticipation.

Elizabeth twisted the ties of her bag in her fingers. "Not quite as I'd hoped," she said at last, her words so low that he had to lean forward to catch her answer.

He rubbed his hands together gleefully. "Even better! Then it exceeded your expectations?"

"Well," she hedged, "it didn't turn out at all the way I'd thought it would. It didn't. . .it didn't turn out at all, truth to tell."

He rubbed his chin. "Not at all? I've heard the texture of fruitcake is unusual. Perhaps that's the problem?"

She shook her head miserably. "I didn't get to make it at all. A mouse got into the supplies before I could."

"A mouse?" Mr. Nichols frowned. "Those miserable little creatures are certainly an annoyance. Everyone struggles with them invading their homes during the cold months of winter."

"I do the best I can," she said, looking down. "But there they are, no matter what I try."

"Well, I certainly wish replacing your ingredients

were something I could do without extra charge, but I'm sorry, Mrs. Evans, I can't."

"I know." Her voice was almost a whisper. "I brought eggs."

She handed the basket to him. "There aren't as many as last time," she said. "But I'm hoping. . ."

"I need eggs badly," he told her as he lifted the cover of the basket. "Everyone in town is busily baking for Christmas, and I can't keep up with the demand. Let me do some figuring."

As he pulled a sheet of paper from the counter and did some quick calculations, Elizabeth picked up the hank of yarn from the display. *What a horrid color.*

"Interested in the yarn, Mrs. Evans?" Mr. Nichols leaned in, as if to close the sale.

"Is this the only yarn you have?" She knew she shouldn't even be inquiring; she didn't have any way to pay for it. She almost sighed with relief when the shopkeeper shook his head.

"No, I'm sorry. That's all I have left. The colorful skeins went earlier, for Christmas knitting, I assume."

"Well, then," Elizabeth said, giving the yarn one final pat, "I'll stay with what I have."

"It looks to me like we're about even, Mrs. Evans. I can replace your ingredients in exchange for the eggs."

"I can't pay for it," she said, "and I won't buy on credit."

"I'd be glad to extend you a line of credit," he said. "You're a regular customer, and your chickens are reliable. You can pay me later."

She paused. Mittens would be nice, but she could

not bring herself to take something she had not paid for. "No," she said, "I can't, but thank you for your offer."

The sound of a cough behind them alerted them to the fact that Joel was there, too.

"Time to go?" she asked, gathering the ingredients Mr. Nichols hastily assembled.

He nodded. "Looks like we have a storm to out-run." His voice sounded cheerful, but she detected an undercurrent of worry.

Elizabeth gathered up the supplies, checked to see that they were nestled in the basket. This time all of the ingredients were in tins. They were her last hope for a good Christmas for her husband.

Then she went out to face the storm with him.

Chapter 6

The flakes swirled with increasing intensity as Joel and Elizabeth ventured across the prairie. Snow gathered in thick heaps and piles in the folds of the buffalo robe and quilts Elizabeth had tucked around them.

What had begun as an easy winter snowfall drastically increased in strength until it became a full-bore blizzard. The temperature dropped measurably, and although his legs and feet were warm enough under the covers, Joel had to drive with his elbows tucked tightly against his chest to hold the blankets in place as the wind increased. An icy finger of frozen air slipped its way in as a gust lifted the top quilt, and he shivered involuntarily.

Joel reached up to wipe away the icy whiteness from his eyebrows and eyelashes, and snow cascaded down his sleeve. He didn't dare take his eyes off the road to shake the melting snow from his arm. He had to move them forward.

"Hyah, Day! Hyah, Lily!" The team sensed the urgency in their mission and took off as if they were in a race, galloping in perfect harmony. All around them, the snow moved like a living thing, and the cold wrapped itself around him until his fingers became stiff.

The path of the well-worn road was becoming obscured as the wind-driven snow filled in the ruts, smoothing it out so it matched the rest of the endless prairie. The storm altered the landscape as the wind moved the snow into piles and drifts, making hills that hadn't been there before. Nothing looked the same as it had on the ride into town earlier that day.

It was perilously easy to get lost.

Joel tried to keep the landmark tree in his vision, the place that would tell him where he needed to turn to the east. If he could see it, they would make it safely; but the fury of the storm increased, and the horizon was disappearing into a blur. Suddenly, the tree vanished.

All around him, everything turned white. He could barely make out his own hands holding the reins.

Whiteout.

It was every traveler's worst fear on the prairie, this time when the wind took the snow, picked it up, and made it into a whirling cloud of white that took away a man's sense of direction and often drove him farther out onto the prairie.

There was nothing to do at a time like this but hold true to the course, trust in the horses. . .and have faith in the Lord. This was, Joel figured, as good a time as any to talk to God. And he did. *God, it seems like I come to You more when I'm needing You than when I'm thanking You, and for that I truly apologize. But I'm in a fix here, and if You feel that it's right to take me in this storm, do so, but save*

Lizzie. Save my love.

He would have given anything to be able to take her in his arms and hold her tiny form to him. The winds paused briefly, and in this pocket of quiet he realized she was speaking. He couldn't catch every word, but he made out enough to recognize what she said. She was reciting from her beloved Psalm 100: " 'Know ye that the Lord He is God. . . .' "

What an odd choice, he thought. *A psalm of praise, now?*

The reins pulled in his hands, and he realized Day and Lily were turning. He tried to straighten them out, but they resisted.

"Day! Lily!" The wind tore the words from his lips and tossed them away with the flying snow. The reins slipped from his frozen fingers and flapped free. He couldn't catch them and watched as they disappeared into the white cloud that surrounded them. He had no choice but to give the horses their head and let them take them home. . .if that was, in fact, where they were going.

"Joel?" Elizabeth's voice cut through the wind, and he turned to look at her. Her next words vanished into the wind's roar, but the question on her face was clear. *Will we be safe?*

He smiled at her with an assurance he didn't truly feel. It was one thing to place all your trust in God; it was another thing entirely to be sure that you and God were of the same mind.

How did he know they would be safe on earth— when, in fact, the Lord might be planning for them to be safe in heaven? It was a theological question his wind-chilled mind could not fathom, but something crept through his numbed thoughts with lightning precision: he wanted to live—with Elizabeth.

The full measure of his love for her almost overwhelmed him. He'd always known he loved her. It was something he'd never doubted, not from the first moment he saw her on the steps of her grandfather's church in Omaha. He'd known then that this woman had his heart.

He was not one to believe in love at first sight, not at all, but what happened to him was different. Not that he could explain it, not then, not now. He was a pragmatist. He wanted proof, something solid he could point to and say, "This is real. I can see it. I can touch it. I can prove it."

But one thing became progressively more obvious to him: love was the one thing that could never be explained as he would like.

He smiled as Elizabeth reached for his hand and squeezed it. Even through the snow-crusted mitten, he could feel the warmth of her touch. Maybe this was the physical proof he wanted. Love was real in Elizabeth.

The horses stopped. He hadn't even realized they had slowed. The cloud of white that had been their nemesis dissipated somewhat, and he shouted with joy as he saw what was in front of him. "Elizabeth, we're home! The horses brought us home!"

He swung out of the wagon, nearly toppling when his deadened hand didn't grasp the edge of the wagon.

They were home!

He clumsily wrapped the reins around his wrist and led the horses to the barn, recognizing as he did so the irony of that. Here they were, just yards from the barn door, and he was leading in the animals that had brought them there.

The door was wedged partially shut with snow, and he kicked it free. Day and Lily trotted inside, their breath turning translucent in the warm barn.

Joel helped Elizabeth down awkwardly; his hands might as well have been wooden stumps. He blew into his mittens, his breath warming his cold hands. Experimentally he flexed his fingers, grimacing as his fingertips stung. The painful tingle was a good sign; the feeling flowing back into his hands meant that there was no frostbite. "The barn is safe. We will stay here and wait out the storm."

She nodded, and he noted how tired she was. Joel checked her hands and feet and even the tips of her ears to make sure she hadn't suffered any frostbite. He took a pitchfork and freed a bale of hay, releasing the sweet-smelling dried grass into a fresh bed for her. but she shook her head. "No. I'll help you curry Day and Lily. Then, we all will sleep."

Working together, they had the horses brushed and fed and in their stalls quickly. They tended to the cows and chickens, then collapsed onto the fresh hay.

They rested in each other's arms and were silent until Joel broke the stillness. "You were saying Psalm 100 during the storm, weren't you?"

She nodded drowsily. "It seemed appropriate."

"Why, though? Why were you praising God

instead of pleading with Him?"

She glanced at him. "Is that what you were doing, pleading with Him?" She smiled. "I was, too. But through it all, I felt drawn to the Psalm. 'For the Lord is good; His mercy is everlasting; and His truth endureth to all generations.' No matter that there was a storm, Joel, the Lord *is* good."

He ran his hand over her hair, now tangled and matted with hay, and touched her cheek, wind-bitten and raw. He had never seen anyone as beautiful in his entire life.

The Lord was, indeed, good.

Chapter 7

S tomp, stomp, stomp, stomp.

The unmistakable sound of Joel's entrance to the house woke Elizabeth. She knew she had probably overslept again, but she had been bone-tired after the trip through the storm, almost as if she had pulled the wagon herself.

Joel grinned at her as she stumbled to the fire. "Good morning, sleepyhead." He planted a kiss squarely on her lips, laughing at her reaction to his icy cheeks against her face.

"Is it still snowing?" she asked, pulling back as a shower of snow cascaded down her neck.

He shook his head. "The storm blew itself out late last night. Don't you remember coming in here?"

"Only vaguely. Are the horses all right?"

"They're no worse for the wear. Actually, they seem rather proud of themselves, bringing home the mister and missus all by themselves."

Mister and missus. How she loved to hear that. "I hope you rewarded them well."

"Each of them got an extra apple this morning.

That made them very happy. In the horse world, an apple must be the equivalent of a gold medal. Day and Lily came as close to smiling as I've ever seen."

The image of the two horses smiling was too much for Elizabeth, and she was still laughing as she returned to the fire, now dressed warmly. Joel stood at the window, looking out across the snow-swept plain. Something was bothering him, she could tell.

"What's wrong?" she asked, coming up behind him and wrapping her arms around his waist.

"I'm worried about Brother Jensen," he said. "He can't get around too well with that broken leg of his. The temperature has dropped so low that it would be dangerous for him to be out there, alone in his house, without a fire."

"Is it very cold?" she asked, already knowing the answer.

He nodded, his eyes not moving from the landscape.

"Then why must you go?"

It was then that he turned to her. "Lizzie, Brother Jensen is a man of God; but even if he weren't, I couldn't rest with myself knowing I didn't try to ensure his safety."

" 'Insomuch as ye have done it unto one of the least of these My brethren, ye have done it unto Me,' " she quoted softly.

Elizabeth knew, then, that he had to go. She'd worry, she'd fret, she'd stew. But she would let him go on his journey because he was on God's errand. She had to trust in that.

Besides, a little voice in her head reminded her, *he'll be gone long enough for you to make the fruitcake.* She smiled up at him. "Give Brother Jensen my best, won't you, please?"

The thought of finally getting the fruitcake baked was almost heady. She wrapped Joel in two scarves, the old red mittens, and a thick fur-lined hat; packed three pairs of extra socks and a spare sweater; and bundled the wagon seat beside him with quilts, blankets, and the ever-present buffalo robe.

As he was set to leave, she added a heated brick, wrapped in layers of cotton flannel, to the floor of the wagon near his feet.

She handed him a basket. "I'm sorry I don't have something fancier for Brother Jensen, but here are the leavings of lunch and some nice new bread. I included a jar of raspberries for color. They might be tasty on the bread."

"He'll appreciate anything you send, Lizzie."

She kissed him and urged him into the wagon. "You'd better hurry along now."

Joel looked at her curiously. "You know, Elizabeth Evans, you seem mighty anxious to get me gone. What's going on?"

She widened her eyes innocently. "Why, nothing. The winter days are short, and I don't want you riding at night."

Joel didn't seem entirely satisfied by her answer, but he picked up the reins, and Day and Lily instantly became alert. "I will try to be back before dark, but if I'm not, put a light in the window to guide me through the prairie night."

"If you are late, my husband, I shall put a light in

every window and all along the edge of the house and the barn, to bring you back safely." Her words were barely above a whisper.

With a click of his tongue to encourage the horses, he set off. Elizabeth watched him go until he faded to only a speck on the endless white horizon. At last a spasm of shivering sent her inside.

She took her ingredients down, congratulating herself on having had the foresight to place them in a metal container. They were, indeed, safe and fresh. Within minutes she had the table covered with the accoutrements of baking. One by one, she laid the ingredients out next to the bowls, the spoons, and the pan.

Then she tore into the bedroom and from the trunk where she had carefully hidden it, she took a piece of paper—the recipe.

The recipe seemed straightforward enough. It seemed a bit overladen with the flour and molasses, but Mr. Nichols had said that fruitcake was heavier than the usual cakes she was used to.

She creamed the lard and eggs to a frothy pale yellow, and then scraped the brown sugar cone until she had the correct measure. In went the sugar, the flour, the baking powder, the spices, and the salt, and she stirred and stirred until she was convinced her arm would drop clean off her body. The mixture was so dreadfully thick.

She consulted the recipe anew and checked her additions. Yes, it was right. Apparently, it was supposed to be this unyielding.

The recipe called for alternately adding molasses

and the candied fruit. The molasses gave the batter some liquid, but it was still terribly thick.

Elizabeth frowned and studied the recipe again. She had done everything correctly. Perhaps it was one of those miracles of cooking that she had never understood. She sighed and put it in the oven and sat down to wait.

Elizabeth had never been a good waiter. She alternately sat and fussed around the tiny kitchen, popping up and down like an impatient sparrow. The cake had to bake for at least two hours, possibly three, and she'd drive herself insane if she didn't take care of her edginess.

Finally she took her Bible and settled before the fire. She knew exactly what she needed to read. The glorious opening lines of Psalm 9 had the power to ease her soul: *"I will praise Thee, O Lord, with my whole heart. . . ."*

They reminded her of her grandfather. He had read opening verses of it in her wedding service.

She missed him, but he had been so happy at his own wedding that she couldn't begrudge him spending Christmas with his new wife and her family in Lincoln. Besides, there was the very real fact that this house would be stretched to hold the three of them when Joel's mother came. Adding two more people would tax it beyond its limits.

Perhaps after Christmas they could ride into Omaha and visit her grandfather and his new wife. She'd suggest it to Joel.

The most heavenly aroma reached her nose, and she was drawn into the kitchen. She couldn't resist a peek in the oven. Taking a mitt from the table, she opened the black metal door. Heat blasted her face, and she blinked reflexively before leaning closer. She didn't like what she saw. It smelled wonderful, but it looked awful. It was flat with a sudden depression in the exact center.

No cake she'd ever made had turned out like that. What could be wrong with it? Was it underdone? Overdone? Or—and she shuddered a bit at the thought—was it perfect as it was? For the first time since they moved to the claim, Elizabeth regretted not having a clock. She'd never had to bake anything this long, and she'd certainly never had to bake anything like this.

She gave it an experimental poke. The edges were springy, no, spongy. The depression in the middle was gooey and clung to her fingertip. The hot batter burned and she stuck her finger in her mouth.

It tasted good, a bit strongly flavored, but perhaps it would mellow after baking.

Elizabeth shoved it back into the oven. She'd leave it in there a bit longer, at least until the center set, and then she'd take it out.

Her stomach clutched with anxiety. Joel's whole Christmas was riding on this fruitcake—and so was hers. She couldn't focus on anything, not even her Bible now. She flitted around the house, straightening neat pillows on the bed, wiping off spotless shelves, adjusting a perfectly aligned painting on the wall.

The house had never been tidier.

She couldn't stand it any longer. She opened the oven door and pulled out the pan. It was still soft in the center, completely undone, but the edges were becoming harder.

Maybe she was so worried, she'd temporarily lost her ability to determine how long two hours were. She put the cake back in the oven and threw her coat on. She might as well check on her chickens while she waited.

The barn was warm, although it was warmer when the horses were there. The cows mooed a greeting, and she freshened their hay.

Her chickens clucked in anticipation of the grain she spread out for them, and she chided them as they eagerly pecked at the hem of her dress in their zeal to get at the food. "Patience, patience," she scolded, realizing the irony of the words as she said them. She was certainly no one to lecture a chicken about patience.

There was not enough to do to fill up the empty minutes while she waited for the fruitcake to bake. At last she pulled a chair up beside the oven and waited.

Time after time she checked, and time after time the results were the same. The edges were getting harder and harder, and the middle seemed content to stay uncooked.

When she looked out the window and realized sunset was falling over the plains, she knew she couldn't wait any longer. Joel would be home soon, and he certainly couldn't find the cake there. . .not yet, anyway.

She took the cake out, amazed at its weight, and put it on the sideboard to cool. It looked even worse in the lamplight. Muddy in color, pebbled in texture, it was a dreadful sight.

Another problem presented itself quickly. The aroma of the cake permeated every corner of the tiny house. She stirred up some spice cookies and put them in to bake. They'd be warm when Joel got home, and they'd disguise the smell of the fruitcake.

When the cookies were in the oven baking, she tackled the fruitcake. It had hardened even more in cooling, and now she could not get it out of the pan. The usual gentle pat on the bottom of the pan didn't work. A butter knife around the inner edges of the pan didn't work. A whack on the edge of the table didn't work.

In desperation she took the sharpest knife she had and tried to cut it out of the pan. With a loud clunk, the cake fell out onto the table.

It was, indeed, a heavy cake. She picked it up. The cake kept its form, even out of the pan, and except for the still-soft middle, the cake was as hard as a brick.

Perhaps it was supposed to be crusty on the outside, and inside it would be moist and delicious. She stood at the table, the knife poised over the cake.

If she tested the cake carefully, perhaps a judicious sampling from the bottom, she could for once and for all satisfy herself that the cake was all right.

Elizabeth tried a cautious cut across the bottom with the knife, holding her breath.

The knife blade bent.

She pressed harder.

The blade bent more.

She put her weight into the cut.

The knife threatened to snap. It was then she knew her worst fear had come true. The cake was as hard as the frozen prairie. Certainly this was not the fruitcake that was the rage on the East Coast. This fruitcake was totally inedible.

She opened the door and, with all her might, hurled the fruitcake across the open land, startling a flock of winter-roosting birds to flight.

With a somber heart, she returned to the fire to wait for Joel's return. And, as she had done so many nights in the past, she turned to her Bible once again.

This time the book opened to Proverbs and her eyes were drawn immediately to the verse that had always meant so much to her: *"Whoso findeth a wife findeth a good thing."*

The words seemed to mock her. "A good thing?" How could she be a good wife if she could not give him the Christmas that obviously meant so much to him?

"I should give up baking and become a stone-mason," she grumbled to herself. "I seem to have a real talent for that."

She loved Joel so much, her heart ached with the joy of it all. More than anything she wanted him to be happy and comfortable, and now she had failed him.

The clop of hoof beats and the creak of wagon wheels told her Joel was home. For the first time in their marriage, the sound made her cry.

Chapter 8

The sun was just peeking over the horizon as Joel put the last touches on the wagon. He and his mother would be riding quite a distance, and he knew how hard the seat of the buckboard could be. If they didn't get out frequently and stretch, they'd be numb from the waist down by the time they got to the house.

There was one stop he'd have to make on the way back, and he knew his mother wouldn't mind the delay.

"I'm going to stop by Brother Jensen's on the way back," he said, "and pick up the book he got us to give to Mother. It's a nice set of poems. She'll like that."

He had another reason for stopping there, one he couldn't share. He hoped Elizabeth would like his Christmas present.

She stood beside him, silently watching. She seemed almost sad, and he hadn't been able to get her to tell him why. She trailed after him like a shadow, not saying anything and yet full of unspoken questions. He almost jumped when she spoke at last. "Be careful."

"I will."

She didn't say more, and he paused before getting into the wagon. He turned to her. "Are you sure you don't want to go to Omaha with me?"

She shook her head. "No. Grandfather and his wife are away to spend Christmas with her family. And besides, I have to bake that lovely goose you brought back from Brother Jensen."

"Well, then." He stood and looked at her as if memorizing her face. She was so beautiful, his Elizabeth.

He wrapped her in his arms, and for the moment, time stood still. Together there was a power between them, much more than he had ever expected. This was love, but more than that, Elizabeth was his best friend. How did the Good Book say it? "This is my beloved, and this is my friend."

He tore himself away. "I have to go."

She nodded, and as he rode away, he heard her call, "Godspeed."

No clouds marred the clear blue of the sky. He couldn't have chosen a better day to travel, and even the horses seemed to anticipate the ride. They tossed their heads, their manes fluttering, as if to tell him, *Let's go*.

Joel arrived at Brother Jensen's house in good time. The pastor opened his door and limped to the steps, pausing to lean on his crutch.

"Brother Jensen, you shouldn't be out," Joel scolded as he leaped out of the wagon. He wouldn't unhitch the horses since his visit would be short.

"I heard a wagon coming," the pastor responded, "and my curiosity got the better of me. You heard that the book for your mother arrived?"

Joel nodded. "I can't thank you enough for suggesting it and then ordering it for me. I do appreciate it."

Brother Jensen beamed. "My pleasure. The book is charming, and I hope she'll spend many pleasant hours browsing through the poems."

The fire in the farmhouse burned brightly, and Joel noted that the woodbox held a considerable amount of split logs. He'd fill it to the top before he left.

"Lots of people have been by to visit," Brother Jensen said to Joel, "it being Christmas, you know. That woodbox has never been more than three-quarters empty. I know you're on an errand today, though, and don't have time to chat. You're picking up your mother, aren't you?"

"In Omaha," Joel agreed.

"I've got the book all ready for you." He handed Joel a small volume bound in rich green leather and edged with gilt.

"And the other—?" Joel prompted.

Brother Jensen winked conspiratorially. "The other? Now there's a gift that'll be appreciated. Everything's going to go just as planned, my son. Just as planned." He gave Joel a hearty pat on the back. "Now you'd better get on the road. You have a long drive ahead."

Joel left the house and climbed into the wagon. He paused long enough to wave at Brother Jensen, framed in the doorway, and then, with a click of his tongue, he was off to Omaha.

❧

Elizabeth had the entire day ahead of her. In this magnificent spread of hours, she somehow had to come up with a Christmas present for Joel.

Why hadn't she let herself take the wool for the mittens on credit? It would have been only a week or two before she'd have been able to pay it off.

"Because," she told herself out loud, "you are your grandfather's granddaughter." She smiled as she recalled his words, *There's no credit in credit.* She could almost recite the mini-sermon he gave on borrowing money. "A man should not take what he cannot pay for. It prevents him from being a foolish spender, and it keeps him from the poorhouse."

It was good advice, but for once, she wished she hadn't listened to it.

There was nothing to be done about it, though. The wool was still in the store, and she would purchase it with the next batch of eggs. Her husband would have his mittens, although not for Christmas.

She fed the chickens. They surrounded her with their usual anxious pecking and jostling. She loved her chickens. Her favorite part of tending them was reaching into the hay and withdrawing a newly laid egg, still warm from the hen's body.

They hadn't laid as many as usual, probably because of the cold weather, but she gathered what was there. "Now, my beauties, get to work. Remember, every egg you lay takes my Joel one step closer to new mittens." They didn't even look up from their feast. "Ungrateful creatures," Elizabeth said, laughing.

She returned to the house and did her morning tidying. A tiny brown field mouse scurried from behind the trunk as she moved it out to sweep behind it, and she chased the little creature outside.

The Lord must have had a reason for the mouse and the mosquito, Joel had said one August evening, *but why is truly one of His mysteries.* Elizabeth agreed. She'd never get used to either one of them.

The day sped by, filled with small tasks, and soon the time came to begin preparing dinner. The goose was truly beautiful. Elizabeth made the apple and raisin dressing that Joel liked, stuffed the goose, and put it in to bake. That, with the potatoes from the root cellar and the squash and the canned raspberries, would be their Christmas dinner.

If only the fruitcake had turned out!

It was too bad that the ingredients were so alien to the prairie. Now, if instead of candied fruit, there had been dried blackberries in the recipe. . .

"Neglect not the gift that is in thee." She could almost hear her grandfather's voice reciting the line from the Bible he used to remind her to be resourceful. She would improvise a dessert. She could do it; she did it all the time. But this one would be special.

A pinch of nutmeg and a heady dash of cinnamon were all that was left from her escapade with the fruit-cake, but these remnants were added to a sweet batter she stirred up quickly.

A grated apple, a handful of chopped nuts, a scoop of dried berries. . .all went into the mix. The spicy aroma soon joined the crisp scent of the goose baking.

Stamp, stamp, stamp, stamp. The sound heralded her husband's arrival. The door burst open, spilling Joel and his mother into the tiny house. The welcome sound of her husband's feet was sweeter to her than his next words: "What smells so good?"

"Is my son always this forgetful of his manners?" Mrs. Evans swept over to Elizabeth and enclosed her in a tight hug before releasing her and holding her at arms' distance. "Let me look at you! I must say, the prairie agrees with you. You are looking every bit as lovely as when I last saw you."

"And you, Mrs. Evans. Let me take your wraps while you tell me how your trip was." Elizabeth helped her mother-in-law take off her coat.

Mrs. Evans looked around her at the small house, and Elizabeth held her breath. If her mother-in-law found fault with it. . .

But instead, Mrs. Evans beamed. "This house is absolutely charming! It's cozy and warm and quite obviously filled with love!"

Elizabeth exhaled in relief.

Mrs. Evans sniffed in delight. "I must admit, I'm hungry. My son may be rude but he has excellent taste. Whatever you are cooking smells wonderful!"

"Brother Jensen gave us a wonderful goose, but I'm afraid it won't be ready for a while," Elizabeth apologized.

Mrs. Evans shook her head. "No, that's not what I mean. Something smells warm and spicy and inviting."

"It could be the cake, I suppose. It's about ready to come out now."

"I know you probably have everything planned out, but could we please have a piece of it now?" Mrs. Evans smiled at her.

"Listen to my mother beg, would you," Joel said

teasingly from the bedroom where he'd put his mother's belongings. "But she's right. It smells good, and I'm hungry."

Elizabeth laughed. "Well, that settles it, then."

She took the cake out of the oven and sliced it into servings. She watched anxiously as both her husband and his mother bit into it.

"This is delicious," Mrs. Evans said.

Joel grinned at her. "Don't I recognize some of our own raspberries and blackberries in it?"

Elizabeth nodded.

"So it's prairie fruitcake, then, isn't it?" Mrs. Evans's tinkling little laugh sounded like a hundred tiny bells ringing at once.

"Oh, don't you remember Aunt Susan's fruitcake?" Joel asked his mother, who smiled in return.

"Indeed. That was the first sign of the holiday season, when her fruitcake arrived at our door."

"When I think back on the Christmases of my childhood," Joel said, "I remember those fruitcakes."

"Weren't they something?" Mrs. Evans smiled at the memory.

"I think Lizzie's prairie fruitcake is better than Aunt Susan's," he proclaimed loyally.

Elizabeth felt her face grow warm. Was the terrible subject going to arise this early?

She pressed her hands to her heated face, and Mrs. Evans glanced at her.

"Elizabeth, are you all right? Look, Joel, she's flushed. Perhaps she has a fever." Mrs. Evans stood up and reached for Elizabeth's forehead.

"I'm all right. I just—I just have a confession to make. I wanted this Christmas to be special." She looked at her husband, who was watching her with concern. "It's Joel's first Christmas with me, his first Christmas on the prairie, and when he talked about his memories of Christmas, the fruitcake. . ."

"So you made this one?" her mother-in-law prompted.

"I made this one, but I wanted it to be like the ones Joel remembered." The tears began to flow as rapidly as her words. "So I bought the ingredients, and a mouse ate them, and then I bought more, but it turned out so awful that even the wild animals won't eat it. I threw it out yesterday, and I checked today: It's still there, with not even a tooth mark on it. Although," she finished, sniffling, "there are probably some broken teeth laying around it. It was like stone."

She blinked away her tears and realized that they were laughing at her. The man she loved and his mother were laughing at her! "It's not funny!" she protested. "It's all I have for Joel's Christmas present. I wanted to get him—"

Mrs. Evans hushed her. "There, there. We're laughing because we know what happened. You used Aunt Susan's recipe, didn't you?"

"Yes."

"Aunt Susan fancies herself quite a cook, my dear, but she is not. She's a sweet woman, but not in the kitchen. Her fruitcake is a tradition in our family, that's true, but we can—and do—live without it."

"Her fruitcake is like the Yule Log," Joel continued,

"except no self-respecting fire will touch it."

"Joel!" his mother chided, but she laughed.

"Well, it's true, Mother. It's harder than brick, more unbreakable than steel, and totally impervious to any natural forces known to man."

"I have a suggestion," Mrs. Evans said. "Let's make a new tradition here. It will be something good, something wonderful, something wise. We will call *it* Elizabeth's Christmas Cake."

"Do you know what Aunt Susan's fruitcake reminds me of?" Joel asked.

The two women shook their heads.

"It reminds me of the stone which the builders rejected. Remember?" He crossed the room and got the Bible from the table. "Here it is. Psalm 118:22: 'The stone which the builders refused is to become the head stone of the corner.' From an awful traditional recipe comes a wonderful new one. That is," he added, "if you will make this every year, Lizzie dear."

She was about to respond when something small and furry brushed her leg. She leaped up, ready to go for the broom, when Joel, to her astonishment, laughed.

"I see my Christmas present escaped."

He lifted up a tiny bundle of gray-striped fur. "This is your mouser. I know how much it bothers you when the field mice come to visit, and this fellow will keep them at bay. Won't you, Little Gray?"

Elizabeth took the kitten from him. It immediately began to purr, and Elizabeth lost her heart a second time.

"I hope you like him. Brother Jensen gave me the idea. He has a cat in his house, and it catches the mice for him. He told me the Larsens in town had a new litter of kittens, and that's what I was doing there the day we got caught in the blizzard—picking him out for you. They took it to Brother Jensen's house, and Mother and I picked it up today."

"So that's what all that intrigue was about!" Elizabeth exclaimed.

Joel laughed. "It was quite the plot."

"Well, I guess there's no reason to wait on giving you my present," Mrs. Evans said, "seeing as the kitten already brought it out to you."

Elizabeth noticed a trail of yarn from the kitten's paws all the way to the door of the bedroom. It was a beautiful blue wool, the color of Nebraska skies, the color of her husband's eyes.

She was speechless as Mrs. Evans rolled up the yarn and handed it to her. "Joel told me you had been looking at some yarn in the store but you hadn't bought any. I hope the color is all right."

"It's beautiful," Elizabeth managed to say.

Joel gave his mother the book Brother Jensen selected, and as they all chatted happily, Elizabeth took the goose out of the oven and placed it on the table.

Elizabeth noticed her mother-in-law touch the white linen tablecloth she'd sent in the wedding trunk. "I'm glad you're using this," Mrs. Evans said, almost shyly. "It was mine when I was first married."

"And you gave it to me?" Elizabeth asked in astonishment. She hugged her mother-in-law impulsively and was gratified when Mrs. Evans returned the embrace wholeheartedly.

"That tablecloth has seen many dinners served and eaten in love, and I'm glad it will continue to serve its purpose," Mrs. Evans said.

Joel grandly seated his mother and Elizabeth before taking his place at the table.

"The goose looks and smells divine," Mrs. Evans said. "God has certainly blessed this food already, but I believe we should give Him our thanks."

Elizabeth nodded. "Joel?"

She grasped the hands of her husband and his mother as they joined in the circle of prayer. She had never been happier, she realized, than she was at that moment. She'd been foolish to worry about recreating the traditions of Joel's youth.

The greatest tradition of Christmas was something that could not be roasted or knitted or baked. It was too big for any wrapping, except, perhaps, some swaddling clothes that enveloped the best gift of all.

Love transcended the unimportant boundaries of coast and prairie.

Joel began the grace. "For the gifts of Christmas—Your Son, Your love, and Your grace—we thank You. Your love is endless and magnificent, and what we feel for each other is only a portion of what You feel for us. May we be worthy of Your love, and may we love as You have taught us."

He paused and added, "Thank You for the circle of love we are enclosed in tonight, for bringing my mother safely to our hearthside, and I especially thank You for my dear Lizzie, who. . . Amen."

Elizabeth looked up in surprise and realized that

the kitten had gotten up on the table and was making off with a goose leg nearly twice his size.

Their first Christmas together, their first holiday memories.

She imagined them sitting side by side fifty years from this night, remembering the fruitcake that didn't work and the one that did. She could see Joel in her mind, his hair as white as the prairie snow, his smile still charming its way into her heart. She would love him forever. That was a tradition that would never change.

This Christmas *was* perfect.

The kitten jumped off the table with a thump, the goose leg grasped in its tiny teeth.

"Amen," Elizabeth said happily.

ELIZABETH'S CHRISTMAS CAKE
(Prairie Fruitcake)

Elizabeth didn't have all these ingredients at hand, but make the best of your modern grocery store and try this newer version. By the way, Elizabeth used dried raspberries and blackberries, but this is also good with any dried tart fruit, such as cranberries or cherries.

½ cup shortening
1 cup white sugar
1 cup brown sugar
2 eggs
1 ½ cup applesauce
1 ½ teaspoon baking soda
1 ½ teaspoon salt
1 teaspoon cinnamon
½ teaspoon cloves
½ teaspoon allspice
Generous dash of nutmeg
2 ½ cup sifted flour
½ cup water
½–1 cup chopped walnuts
¾–1 cup dried fruit
1 cup chocolate chips (optional)
Extra brown sugar for topping, about ½ cup

Grease and flour a 9″ x 13″ pan.

Cream together the first four ingredients. Mix in the applesauce. Add the baking soda, salt, and spices. Blend in the flour and then the water. Stir in the remaining ingredients. Sprinkle additional brown sugar on the top.

Bake at 350 degrees for 45 minutes, or until the cake tests done.

JANET SPAETH
Janet figures she has it all, living between the prairies of North Dakota and the north woods of Minnesota. She has been blessed with the "world's best family." From tallest to shortest, they are husband Kevin, daughter Megan, son Nick, and cat, Quicksilver. Janet is honored to write stories that reflect the happiness of love guided by God.

A Letter to Our Readers

Dear Readers:

In order that we might better contribute to your reading enjoyment, we would appreciate you taking a few minutes to respond to the following questions. When completed, please return to the following: Fiction Editor, Barbour Publishing, Inc., P.O. Box 719, Uhrichsville, OH 44683.

1. Did you enjoy reading *Christmas Threads?*
   ❑ Very much. I would like to see more books like this.
   ❑ Moderately—I would have enjoyed it more if _____
   _____
   _____

2. What influenced your decision to purchase this book?
   (Check those that apply.)
   ❑ Cover   ❑ Back cover copy   ❑ Title   ❑ Price
   ❑ Friends   ❑ Publicity   ❑ Other

3. Which story was your favorite?
   ❑ *Everlasting Light*   ❑ *Angels in the Snow*
   ❑ *Yuletide Treasures*   ❑ *Christmas Cake*

4. Please check your age range:
   ❑ Under 18   ❑ 18–24   ❑ 25–34
   ❑ 35–45   ❑ 46–55   ❑ Over 55

5. How many hours per week do you read? _____

Name _____

Occupation _____

Address _____

City _____ State _____ Zip _____